ECHOES FROM A DISTANT STAR

John McCool

Paperback/eBook/Dust Jacket Design:

Book Cover Zone

Interior Design and Typeset:

Sam Wright

Editing Services:

McCool Mythos Publishing

Paperback ISBN:

979-8-218-54667-0

"There are more stars in the universe than grains of sand on any beach, more stars than seconds have passed since Earth formed, more stars than words and sounds ever uttered by all the humans who ever lived."

Neil deGrasse Tyson

Never stop looking up.

Contents

Chapter One

Locilette jerked forward in his seat as his ship dropped through the large worm hole gate. His stomach began to churn in knots, and the entire cockpit began to spin around like a cyclone from the waters of Poseidon 2. A place he'd rather not think about in his present state. He hunched over, grabbing the trash can beside his seat, and vomited the little contents he had within his stomach. The sounds of his heaving echoed around the ship, but it didn't bother him. He always traveled alone for his work anyway, so he would save himself the embarrassment of his weak wormhole stomach from his colleagues.

He leaned back in his chair and wiped the side of his mouth on his black sleeve that ran the length of his arm. He closed his eyes for a moment to settle his body from the journey through worm space. Normally he would have taken medicine to mitigate the effects, but he had been in such a rush receiving this assignment that it didn't even occur to him to grab it before leaving his office. It was a mistake he now greatly regretted.

Locilette was a Ranger of the Fifth Degree from the Kronos System. The Order of the Rangers was a seemingly ancient organization that can trace its foundation to when the Arkaans first began to travel the stars. What once began as a mere police force for the farthest of colonies, the Rangers evolved into the first responders of any strange occurrences outside the jurisdiction of a star system. This led Locilette on more than his fair share of strange encounters over his ten years of service. Some he'd recall as interesting stories at house parties he and his wife would hold at their home on Kronos Prime, others he had to sign a seal of secrecy from the Order's Chief. Those were the stories that would keep any sane person awake at night.

Most of his calls weren't too bad, however. Most of his dispatches would come in the form of a missing ship that just veered too far off course, check the status of a down communication buoy, and even the occasional pursuit of a smuggler attempting to elude the clutches of a system's authorities. Whatever the case may have been, his job was to enter the deep dark of space for whatever the Order deemed appropriate. It was hard work. It was dangerous work. It was fulfilling work, and Locilette loved every single bit of it.

There was something about being the first responder on a situation call that thrilled him. He yearned for the adrenaline rush as he pieced events together to reach a verdict of what the best course of action should be. Being able to investigate on site, and quickly compile evidence into a coherent string of events was only part of his duties. His countless hours of training allowed him to be perceived to the citizenry as calm and collected on the outside, but inside, he was buzzing with anticipation. Every call allowed him to not only be himself, but be an arm of the law. An arm of the King himself, who sat upon the home world throne on Arkaa. The people of the

Arkaan Empire knew who the Rangers were, and had nothing but the utmost respect for them. Mostly.

There were those, however, who wished to remain shrouded from the ever watchful eye of the Rangers. Organized crime had been one of the most concerning thorns in the side of Chief Jorik during his lengthy tenure. No matter how many raids they conduct on illegal merchandise, weapons caches, and trafficking rings, there always seemed to be another to arise in its place. Locilette had the pleasure of busting a few cells of a terrorist organization that was probing one of the Enlil System's orbital cities for sabotage. Most of his career had been the take down of these cells, and each one he erased was a better feeling than the list of achievements that stretched out next to his name. His only reward was knowing that the people of the Enlil System can sleep easy knowing they won't have to wake up to another terrible explosion in a market square.

On some of his deployments, he would be sent to systems with little to no action at all. That would make the time away from home feel like the numbers clicking on the clock pass by at a snail's pace. Even though a quiet deployment is a safe deployment, he found himself almost begging the Pantheon for just a simple robbery, or even a missing person. *Anything* to break his ceaseless restlessness.

Locilette shook the vertigo from his head, and gave a thorough look at his ship's systems. The status of the Theseus displayed as a green silhouette on a large monitor to the left of the ship's flight stick. Numbers bounced back up as the ship began to regulate from the unstable environment that presents itself within a wormhole. A small section of the silhouette around the back engine area flashed momentarily before joining the rest of the ship's conditioning as a solid green line. He had noticed issues with that small section before, but never paid it much mind. It was more than likely a small glitch in his computer's structural detection that had degraded over time. This vessel had certainly seen better days, but Locilette knew she still had life in her, and could get the job done just as well as some of his fellow Rangers' newer ships.

He rotated his chair slightly to the right where a console was stationed just above eye level. He reached around behind it to flip on the large switch, bringing the monitor to buzz to life. A cursor flashed on screen momentarily, then a list of commands took over the screen's display. Locilette glanced out the front view port to see he had fully cleared the wormhole gate, allowing him free travel into open space.

The vast, endless darkness stretched out in front of him, broken only by the soft shining of stars millions of light years away. The light they gave off was ancient, but with proper wormhole traversal he could be at their current place in time within a matter of weeks. It was a momentous achievement in space travel that had only come to its modern form when he was still a child playing within the thick woods of Kronos Prime. Before such leaps in technology, space travel was done by bending space time, which was highly unstable, and before then it was done simply by sending a crew into cryo-sleep for a journey that on average lasted fifty to ninety years, depending on the distance. He slid his personal data assistant out of its holster on his belt and began to flip through the notes of his current call.

The Yanagi was a rather large cruiser that was registered to a security company operating out of the Artemis System on the opposite side of Arkaan space. The official statistics had it measured out to be around 700 feet long, accommodations for a crew of up to 1,100, and two massive swivel cannons lining the flat top. The history of the vessel was quite extensive. Locilette raised an eyebrow as its records began to scroll across the small screen of his PDA.

Yanagi had been under the command of the 7th Fleet stationed in the Caishen System, but was disbanded in favor of a more advanced vessel. It was built in none other than the Kronos Shipyard that sat in orbit of Kronos Prime's largest moon. Locilette smirked at the thought of two hometown boys meeting each other by happenstance way out here in the middle of nowhere space. He leaned back in his flight chair and brought the screen closer to his face. The vessel had been involved in several skirmishes with a Rebel cell on the outer banks of Arkaan space, and appeared to have been involved in repelling a tribe of Zorvathix laying claim seven years ago on Caishen 8. It was quite the impressive track record for a vessel gone offline.

He tapped his way down to find the latest information on the ship, scrolling up from the bottom of the small screen. The Yanagi was purchased by an unspecified group of merchants, and appeared to have converted the aged military vessel into a long distance freighter. It certainly wasn't anything out of the ordinary. Merchant guilds would often purchase decommissioned ships from the Arkaan Fleet or even planetary defense corvettes to fill their transport fleets with cheaper ships. Acquiring ships capable of deep space travel through auction was much more cost effective than commissioning newer freighters to be built.

Locilette sat his PDA on one of his monitors and reflected on the Yanagi's information. It wasn't normal for a freighter to travel alone in the void of space without some sort of escort. The only thing he could think of was it must have been tasked with a less than valuable haul. Perhaps it was rented to transport goods by some merchanteers from Caishen, or could it be used to move something else? Something that they would rather not have on the books.

He crossed his arms and swung the chair side to side for a moment before quickly jotting down his theories in his device. A large freighter on its own out here was an easy target for pirates who would happily overwhelm the vessel into surrendering and take it into their fold as a prize. Nothing concerned him more than the thought of gangs getting a hold of something potentially harmful that the ship could've been carrying. That was an unfortunate outcome that would only lead to bloodshed among the stars. He would hate to see what kind of threat they could pose if they could somehow reactivate those decommissioned guns.

He turned to the console to his right and cycled down to the drone command menu. Each tick down on the screen made a bright blue light dance across his face as the menu finally came into view. He tapped the select key on his keyboard, illuminating all three drone's statuses. Each one read they had full charges and were standing by in their pods nestled under the Theseus's wings. He selected each one and commanded them to recon the area for any signs of derelict vessels within their operational limits. With one final tap of select, the sounds of the drones launching echoed through the cockpit. A moment later, Locilette observed them flying off into the darkness though the view port, each one heading off in its own direction.

He swiveled in his chair to face the back side of the cockpit and pulled himself over to the radio set just behind his seat. It was an incredibly awkward place to install it, but the Ranger mechanics assured him that this was the only way it could be in a location with ample voltage to power it. So was the case with modern equipment being fitted on older vessels. A lot of the time the system just couldn't handle the power distribution of adding pieces that belonged in a much larger, more modern ship of the line. However, he being a Ranger, that meant charting courses to some of the most remote places in Arkaan space. That demanded a radio system that could transmit to farther distances at a faster speed. If calling in backup meant stepping over this large set of equipment, then that was just okay with him.

Locilette stood up tall and stretched as far as he could to the ceiling. He went through his whole stretching routine as his eyes beamed over the reports and upcoming training schedule on the large screen lining the wall. *Giviani B'varian, Horus 12, responding to a possible gang threat.* Giviani was a man he greatly admired, and one of the few recruits from his class that he'd care to keep up with since they graduated the academy so long ago. If there was one person standing under the fearless banner of the Arkaan Empire that could nip organized crime activity, it was him. He was a man with an astounding intellect and a soldier as fierce on the field of battle as any other. He was proud to consider him a friend and the godfather to his boys.

"Give 'em hell, buddy," Locilette whispered with a quick nod.

He fist bumped the screen before turning toward the main corridor entrance at the back of the ship's cockpit. The corridor stretched the entire length of his small sloop and was capped at the very back by the large metal door that led into the engine compartment. Four doors lined the metal wall, each having its own intended use, but Locilette used them for his own purposes. More times than not, he would be sailing the cosmos completely alone, so having a room dedicated for a non-existent crew seemed like a complete waste of space in his opinion.

The Theseus had the capacity to host a crew of 4-8, however, Locilette preferred to operate solitaire. When Rangers are dispatched to sectors within Arkaan territory, they are commonly assigned to a sloop or corvette-sized vessel with a crew of other Rangers. As they would enter their shared operational space, they would respond to calls via shuttle rockets. That wasn't something he was very keen on doing. Younger Rangers are required to yield to their assignment, but the more veteran Rangers of the Sixth Degree and lower had an option of purchasing their own ships to operate in. That's exactly what Locilette did.

The moment he received his commission for Fifth Degree, along with his substantial pay increase, he went about searching for his future responder. After several months of traveling to different spaceports around his native Kronos System, it greeted him like an old friend. The Theseus sat docked in the harbor of Kronos 5's orbital station with a large red *For Sale* digital sign sitting above the dock door. It was perfect, and exactly what he needed. Just as his mother-in-law warned him and his wife when they were searching for their first house, the perfect one always comes to you when you are about to throw in the towel; and so it did.

Sitting in the docking bay like a majestic lion, the Theseus awaited its new captain. Though officially listed as a sloop, the ship was about a quarter size smaller than the average modern sloop. This led to the idea that would set him on the course of solo adventuring among the stars. Instead of hiring an engineer, radio man, or cook, he would just learn it all himself. On his first few assignments, he would learn the ins and outs of the ship's repair manual, and even constructed a small crawl space within the engine compartment that would allow him to make necessary repairs that fit his way of doing things. This was not only incredibly beneficial to his finances due to the nonexistent labor cost of hiring a crew, but it did him good to stave off the boredom of life as a Ranger with no calls to respond to. He and the Theseus were now one, both taking care of each other's needs in the vast darkness of space completely alone.

He traced his fingers on the silver-colored metal wall as he knocked on the armory door in passing. He came to his bedroom door he always left wide open. He figured if there wasn't anyone to walk in on you changing, why even close it to begin with? He had the luxury of being completely naked in his own ship if he wanted to. Of course, he would never be so unprofessional on a deployment, but he enjoyed the thought of having such an option when most of his colleagues didn't.

His quarters were small, just big enough to fit his bed, desk, and his clothes, which hung neatly in a storage locker sitting along the wall. The light in the tiny quarters was dim, just the way he liked it. The lights dotted around his ship were ultra bright due to him installing new bulbs before he left on this current deployment. He liked the bright, white lights that could show any signs of dirt in the cracks of the flooring, but not in his private room. That was his sanctuary away from the day to day life of deployment. When he was in that room, he wasn't a Ranger anymore, but himself. This was the one place he allowed himself to just be Locilette, the man from Kronos Prime. A man with hobbies, dreams, and ambitions. A man who missed his family.

He sat on the edge of his bed and glanced over to the wall lining the foot of his bed. Spaced evenly every two feet hung a live photograph of his family. A memory forever captured within a five second window, endlessly playing in a loop. Each one brought him so much joy, but it came with a price. It made the pain of being away from home even more unbearable. He reached over and pulled one of the magnetized frames from the wall. He watched the loop of he and his wife spending a few weeks on the tropical world of Poseidon 3, which was one of their favorite getaways when the kids would stay at his wife's parent's home. He placed the frame onto the wall as it snapped from his hand to remagnetize to the chrome-like metal.

Locilette loved being a Ranger, but there was one thing in this vast, endless universe that he loved more. Something that kept him on his righteous path of the law, and gave him something to lead the change within the realm. Being a dad. The deployments of this job could be excruciating at times when it comes to being away from home. His usual cycle would be three weeks deployed and two weeks home. He loved so much time at once with his family, but whenever it was time for the cycle to begin, it felt like he would be leaving for an eternity.

Locilette knew how to count his blessings though. His two boys had a state of the art black wood designed house nestled on ten acres of beautiful land on Kronos Prime, the system capital of the Kronos Star System. His monthly salary was enough to allow his incredible wife to live her dream of being a stay at home mom and cater to the needs of their estate. He was so proud that he could give her what she had always dreamed of, even if raising two wild boys was ten times more difficult than his own line of work. He greatly appreciated her love and grace even when things become a little too much to handle sometimes. She was the perfect mother if there ever would be one.

Locilette was now coming to the end of his deployment cycle, and his anticipation to go home was building heavily within him over the past couple of days. This would more than likely be his final call before he headed back to the system Ranger headquarters to get debriefed before setting course to Kronos. However, something had been biting at him about this deployment that hadn't really affected him before. His boys were growing so fast that it seemed as if they had grown a foot taller since the last time he saw them. It began to dawn on him that these lengthy deployments, even though they were good money, left him missing some of the most important moments in his kids' early lives. This bothered him more than anything he could possibly imagine.

Being a Ranger was superseded only by his love and dedication to his family. There had been times on this cycle as he was drifting through the darkness of open space that he began to ponder on things. Is this actually worth it? Is the time spent away from his boys, his wife, and his home worth a childhood dream? He wasn't quite sure anymore. As far back as he could remember, he had always wanted to be a Ranger, and when he finally obtained that title, the rank of First Degree was all that dominated his thoughts. Being within the elite first degree Rangers was an honor that only a handful of great Arkaans could claim, with the King himself handing the title out personally. However, as the sands of time slowly dropped away, so increased his desire to just be home. Home with his family tucked away in their little piece of heaven away from the horrors of the universe.

He loved his career, he truly did, but damn it was hard to be away for so long. Maybe being a Ranger is just a stepping stone in his journey through life. Perhaps being a Ranger wasn't what he was always meant to be. He learned so much over the years, maybe it was time for him to hang it up and start a new venture that would allow him to be home every night with his wife and kids. *Yes*, he thought, *maybe it's time*. Like a light in the darkness of space it washed over him. When this deployment was finished, he would have a discussion with his family about the next step in their lives.

The faint sound of beeping eventually snapped him from his thoughts. He stood up quickly from his bed and peered around the door frame back into the cockpit. One of his consoles flashed a bright red, like a beacon in the dimly lit panel of instruments. He glanced back over his shoulder of the pictures of his family awaiting his return just as they did now on Kronos. They'll always be there for him no matter what. Always.

He trotted back behind his seat, making sure not to step on any of the bundles of wires that were laid about by the radio. He squinted his eyes to see drone 3 had detected something in the void and was standing by for further instructions. This had to be the Yanagi. Unless abandoned freighters were as common in this system as they were in his own home star, there was little doubt in his mind. As most of his vessel was pretty out of date, his drones were top of the line and had never let him down before. This had to be his assignment.

He rotated his chair to plop down with enough force to send the chair spinning back all the way to face the drone console. He reached up to the blinding strobe of the red light, and accepted the alert to cease it. He pulled the keyboard closer and clicked down on the situation report the drone had compiled on its discovery. A long stream of text materialized down the screen with bits and pieces of information that Locilette really had no interest in at this time. All he wanted to know was if he had scored his proverbial needle in a haystack, and to his delight, it was.

DRONE 3

The Theseus

Elapsed time: 15:04

Report: A stationary vessel detected 12 degrees starboard, 5 degrees high at a distance of 791 Units. Visual inspection discovered the vessel is registered as Yanagi. Registration number: 1A29471-B

Status: Immobile. Engines unused for an uncertain amount of time. Forward momentum is minimal. Scans through viewports return negative on life, however insufficient data leads to that being inconclusive.

Vessel potential derelict.

Return to pod?

[Y] or [N]

He clapped his hands together in celebration. The investment made into these new drones were already making an impact on his response time. With some of the previous models he'd worked with, it would take hours before he had heard even a peep from them. In a little under fifteen minutes, he was able to locate the Yanagi, as well as do brief observations that would take him an hour alone. He created a new case folder for the Yanagi on his computer and saved the drone's report to officially begin a formal investigation.

He leaned over to grab his PDA from its resting place on top of the ship's status monitor and plugged it into the drone command console. The screen on the PDA lit up with the green image of a battery connected to a wire flashing. Locilette sat it next to his keyboard and accepted the connection request that was now prompted on the monitor's screen. He leaned back into his flight chair and swiveled side to side as the green bar popped on screen. Slowly, the PDA established a connection to the ship that he could use remotely in case he would have to board the Yanagi.

His PDA was beyond archaic for work such as his. It seemed too often he found himself sitting in this chair waiting on fifteen-year-old technology to find a connection to a more updated ship system. Not too much more updated by other standards, but updated nonetheless. He fumbled with the loose arm on his chair, contemplating if in the event he did decide to spend a few more years with the Rangers, maybe it was time to invest a little bit into his on board and away mission communications. His ship was perfect for storing backup data from calls and investigations, but it didn't really matter if it took twenty minutes just to transfer a handful of crime scene pictures.

His mind began to drift. He began to wonder what kind of desserts his wife was making this evening. Was it some of her incredible truffles crafted from the local chocolatiers of Kronos Prime? Or could it be the dew drop pie she made for him on their first anniversary together? It was one of the most life-changing desserts he'd ever had the pleasure to eat, because it was far more than just that to him now. It was home.

The sweet aroma of the fruit baking in the oven filled his mind. He closed his eyes, and he was there. The rays of the early morning sun streaked across the wooden floor, like the many strokes from a painter's brush. Each beam of light led to the stove on the opposite side of the kitchen.

There she would be. Her sundress with her favorite lavender-colored apron tied snug around her waist. Flour covered her head to toe, but it never bothered her. Whenever she would catch him staring, a small smile would pass over the corner of her lips. She was perfect, and it was only the commotion of their boys that would force him to take his eyes off her. Something he would never take for granted ever again.

Upload complete. Communication established.

Locilette's eyes fluttered open not to the sight of his family, but the cold metal ceiling of the Theseus. His eye floated down to the screen before him that was flashing a

COMPLETE, which sent a stab of quick green light across the cockpit. He leaned his chair back forward and unplugged the PDA, turned off the monitor, and swiveled back to his flight controls in a single motion. He glanced over to the ship's status screen for one last check before gripping the flight stick and throttle.

His eyes lowered to his directional instruments and he carefully fired his adjustment boosters to correct his course. He slightly pulled the stick to the right and watched as the numbers slowly rose to 12. With a few nudges back on the stick, the ship slightly pitched upward 5 degrees, locking on to the Yanagi's position. Without taking his eyes off the viewport, he switched on his radar to his left, bringing the monitor to life. A small outline of the Theseus popped into the center as a bar whipped around it. Locilette glanced at it quickly to make sure nothing within a mile radius could interfere with his flight path. Satisfied, he grabbed the throttle and rocketed forward, leaving the wormhole gate behind.

The Yanagi awaited.

Chapter Two

The Theseus rocketed through the blackness of space. The sound of the engines pushing maximum impulse made a rhythmic tune that echoed around the cockpit. Locilette found himself in a bit of a trance as he focused on the low, waving sound. He caught himself involuntarily rocking as the orchestra of sounds washed him away on a peaceful wave of calm.

He liked the sound of Theseus's impulse engines. It was similar to the sound of a roaring fan that he had become used to using to help sleep that he had to install one in his quarters. Kronos Prime could bring some of the most scorching summers, so the ambient sounds of fans running was more than just a normal occurrence. It was like a little piece of home he could always take with him no matter where he was in the endless void of the galaxy.

Beyond some keepsakes from home, he actually installed a mount by his bed so he could easily snap in and out his old circle fan from home. His wife insisted that he just buy one that was for the ship only, but that wasn't the point. For him, it *was* home. If he used the same fan that would cool him and his wife on the warm summer nights, maybe the loneliness of being so far away would be blown away by the spinning blades. As silly as it sounded, it really did help him get a little sleep, which is something any Ranger operating on the edge territories could ask for.

The bright light from a nearby star shone through the port-side window, forcing Locilette to turn away. The Theseus's internal window shaders were so old and worn down that they could barely keep up with the penetrating light. Eventually with time, it would catch up to the point to block out most of it, but by the time that happened, he was already well past the star. He reached down under his flight chair and felt around until his fingers found the handle of his hook pole. He pulled it out and extended it as far as it would go to maximize his reach. He stretched above his various monitors that lined the left side of his control panels until the hook found its target. It connected with the pull tab of the window screen rolled up neatly above the thick glass of the view port.

Locilette pulled the screen down as far as he could maneuver around the monitors in front of the window, giving his eyes immediate relief. It was another ad hoc addition he had to make during his spare time, one he was relieved he took the time to do now. The intense white glow splashed across the floor underneath his feet, highlighting the dozens of cords and wires strung about in a chaotic web. It wasn't too often that light reached the floor, so seeing the unorganized mess sent an uneasy feeling through him. If the Chief were to inspect his vessel, he would surely catch an earful for representing the order in such an untidy response ship. A bit of housekeeping was way past due for his old bird.

From the corner of his vision, he took a moment to glance at the light of the star. It was beautiful. Bright streaks of radiance extended from the sides, like a crown of thorns topping the head of a fallen king.

Locilette broke from his mesmerizing trance as the realization of a golden opportunity was passing him by. He switched the ship's status screen on the monitor to the external portside observation camera fixed on the ship's hull. The side of the Theseus came on screen with the sight of the radiating light from the star reflecting off the ship's thick, metal armor. He swiveled in his chair and jumped up to pull the lever high on the wall above most of the instruments. A rumbling vibrated the floor, then the sound of buzzing, moving electronics came through the thick siding. His eyes darted to the screen as the siding opened to reveal the star panel array within.

The compartment door raised, sliding along the rounded top of the Theseus, making the entire vessel jolt as the locks engaged. The row of arrays slowly began to deploy as a long mechanical arm extended them outward, and into the perfect position to absorb the star's intense energy. A green battery icon popped on screen with a bar underneath to show the Theseus's current battery levels. A small thunderbolt flashed off to the side, indicating that the system was actively charging.

Locilette rarely let his ship's energy reserves fall below 65%. Every opportunity he had to charge up, he wouldn't let it escape him. During the early years of his career with the Rangers, he was assigned to a task force where the Captain would forgo charging his ship, leaving them in complete darkness for days on end. It was maddening to not only him, but his brothers in arms, as well. The ship's engine would be running fine, and life support was running to an extent, but the crew suffered immensely just to shave off a week on their travels. As long as there was enough power to fire the engines and the crew to breath, he didn't care.

The stinging cold air was something that he could still feel in his dreams. Right before power reductions would go into effect, the Captain would broadcast over the PA system around the entire ship boasting about the time saved on their journey. All the Rangers on that ship knew what that really meant. It meant suiting up in their thermals, cold meals, icy showers, and navigating the Frigate-sized vessel with nothing but the faint glow of emergency lights spaced out sporadically through the many corridors. It was a frozen hell, however, Locillete learned a very important lesson from that assignment: a ship without power was nothing more than an icy tomb.

A loud beep sounded off from the radar monitor. Excitedly, Locilette leaned forward to confirm and turn off the alarm. A blip began to flash dead ahead, not too far away. He peeled his eyes away from the monitor and to the viewport, but couldn't make out anything in the vast darkness. He adjusted his course slightly and pushed the throttle to the max to close the gap a little quicker. Every second that ticked by brought the small blip on screen closer and closer. The heading hadn't moved an inch, making Locilette come to the conclusion that whatever it was had been sitting still for quite a while.

He made a quick note of it in his PDA, then hopped up from his chair to push up the lever from the solar panels. The arm buzzed as it retracted the arrays back within the safety of its compartment, and the light beside the lever flashed from green to a solid red as the compartment door latched shut. With a quick glance at the camera feed to double check the door being secured, he switched the monitor back to the ship's status screen.

A glint of light flickered in the distance. Locilette pulled himself up, and leaned over his flight controls to get a better look through the forward viewport. This had to be it, he was sure of it. He turned the monitor of the radar up to face him. With a few clicks on the keyboard, the radar command menu prompted an identification ping. He tapped *confirm* on screen and looked out on the forward hull as the small comms dish rotated. A loud *ping* rang out from the console with a thin line appearing on the radar screen, rocketing away towards the dot. He watched as the line struck the dot, then bounced off for its return trip.

He crossed his arms and brought his thumb up to his lip to nibble on his nail as he watched the screen. His eyes would occasionally glance out the window, as if he could see the invisible ping returning. He took a seat back down in his flight chair and began to swivel slightly from side to side. The loud ringing of the ping echoed about the cockpit once more, making him jolt forward to the monitor as it processed the data. It was her. He found his needle in a haystack quicker than he would ever have dreamed.

The Yanagi sat there in idle space like a stick being carried by the waves. As the Theseus grew closer, Locilette could start to make out the shape of the vessel, including her noticeable stack of decommissioned cannons lining her top. He opened the case notes for the Yanagi on his PDA and noted the time of his discovery. Within a few moments, the ship was fully in his view. He pulled back on the throttle and then adjusted a few degrees port to line up with the derelict's side.

It was an impressive vessel. Its hull gleamed against the intense light from the nearby star that highlighted the ship's worn yellow paint. A long red stripe ran up the entire side, splitting it into two halves of equal yellow. The closer Locilette came, he could make out the dozens of windows dotting around the hull, making the paint appear to be full of black specks. Locilette strained his eyes to see if he could spot a sliver of light coming from within, but none appeared to show any at his current distance.

The two massive turrets came into view as Locilette pulled back on the flight stick to take a look at the side's top. The were both tilted horizontal to the ship's hull and turned to face her aft in accordance to Arkaan weapons laws. Every nonactive military vessel under the Arkaan banner was required to point each cannon towards their ship's aft because aiming it forward could be perceived as a threat, guns functional or not. Locilette found it to be quite useless in his line of work. Some of these modern ships could rotate their turrets 360 degrees in a matter of seconds, so why would it matter which way it was facing? Regardless of the circumstances, at least he knew he wouldn't have to write any potential crew members a citation for violations.

He had the Theseus make a long loop so he could get the entire ship within his view port. He cut the throttle and for the first time, he was able to see her name. *Yanagi 1A29471-B* was written on the side in large, white lettering. The flag of the Arkaan Empire was neatly painted underneath her name, proclaiming her allegiance to the King's realm.

Locilette took a moment to observe her. The ship wasn't moving and no lights seemed to be active on the hull, as was normal procedure for deep space traveling. He leaned back in his chair and floated his eyes over and over the long vessel. It was rather unlikely they were attacked by pirates for the simple reason the ship was still there. This would've fetched an incredible price if captured. The only logical reason for the ship's abandonment was a potential life support failure catching the crew unaware as they slept. However, with most vessels of this caliber, it was unlikely that every single one of the trained crew could let that go unnoticed. Even on his own ship, if there was so much as a dust ball floating in the air ducts, an alarm demands a system purge.

He spun around to flip on the radio, bringing it to life with a wail of white noise. He set it to scan all nearby frequencies, hoping to at least pick up some small radio chatter from crewmen in the engine room. The static bellowed from the ship's audio system, but that's all it was. Just the scratching sound of the radio waves filled the cockpit, making Locilette feel unsettled. At one point, he could've sworn he could hear someone talking on one frequency, but when it cycled back there was nothing. He shrugged as he relinquished the thought to over-analyzing.

He picked up the headset hanging off to the side on a hook and slid in on his head. He made sure to keep one ear muff off so he could still listen for any notifications from the various systems. He flipped the mic attachment down, adjusted the frequency, and held down the broadcast button on the wire hanging around his neck.

"Yanagi, this is Ranger Locilette of the Theseus. Please respond." Locilette spoke with a commanding tone. He waited for a few moments, but no response came. He reached behind the flight chair to switch the frequency to one commonly used by lower rank personnel. His hope was that a potential survivor, if any, may not have access to officer ranked communications channels.

He broadcasted again. "Yanagi, this is Ranger responder Theseus. You have been flagged as a potential derelict vessel. If you do not respond, you may be subject to boarding."

He relaxed and leaned back into his chair. He closed his eyes and listened to the air waves, hoping to get some attempt at a response from someone on the floating coffin that sat before him. The chair began to squeak in time to his absent-minded rocking with the rhythmic highs and lows of the radio tones. However, his hopes for a response from the crew began to die with every passing moment. He sat forward and looked over the Yanagi again. With a ship as large as this, there had to be someone that could've survived even a life support malfunction. There were pressure suits full of air tanks required on every vessel. It seemed strange to him that if this was the case, that at least one of the crew wouldn't act on it.

"Any survivors on board the vessel Yanagi," Locilette called out into the mic without taking his eyes off the ship, "if someone- if *anyone* is alive, please get to the nearest window and wave. If I can confirm you're still alive, I can get you the help you need."

Locilette slid off the headset and hung it back on the hook to the side. He pushed the throttle slightly to begin circling the derelict. His eyes stayed glued to each and every window he passed by, hoping he would see someone in need of help, but the only thing he could see was complete darkness. Not even an emergency light flashed in what he would've assumed was a major artery in a maze of corridors. He circled the ship a few more times before pulling away, stopping a short distance off the starboard side.

The last thing Locilette wanted to do was perform a boarding action. On derelict vessels like this, getting in wasn't the easiest thing to pull off. He could suit up into an external boarding suit to allow him to jump onto the hull of the Yanagi and find a service hatch. He hadn't actually attempted such a maneuver since Ranger school. He didn't like it then, and he certainly didn't like the idea of it now. However, he had a job to do, and if that was the only way to get inside that derelict, then so be it. It was the only way of forcefully inserting onto a ship without causing structural damage.

He rocked back into his chair for a few minutes to weigh his options. He could take the matter into his own hands and do a quick investigation, or he could simply send a drone back to the wormhole gate and await back up. That would take days though, maybe even weeks. It was time that Locilette didn't want to waste if he could hurry and be home with his family. Just a quick space walk and he can confirm the Yanagi is a derelict vessel, then call in a tow ship to bring her to the nearest shipyard.

He tapped a button on the drone console's keyboard to wake it from its screensaver. The three drones were listed as *Standing By* as they idly overlooked the massive freighter. The screen quickly changed to Drone One's command menu, which listed out the available orders its A.I. could handle. He programmed a custom order to search the Yanagi for any sign of access hatches he could crack open to get in, with a secondary objective to alert of any detection of life. With a few clicks to confirm, the drone fired its small thrusters to fulfill its mission.

He sprang to his feet and hopped over the radio system. He glided down the corridor until he reached the engine room in the back. He smashed the green button on the screen next to it, making it slide open. The engine hummed loudly as he entered, the smell of hot electronics hitting him as he crossed the threshold. He glanced over the various instruments to double check everything was still as it should be, then he slipped away to a small service closet tucked away behind some cleaning supplies and various crates he used for extra storage.

He slid the door open to reveal the external boarding suit dressed on a magnetized hanger against the wall. He looked at it with dissatisfaction. He *was* certified to use it, but the thought of putting his life on the line with a suit that he had never actually worn since purchasing it sent an unsettling feeling through him. Reluctantly, he pulled off the suit and grabbed the boots tucked back in the corner. He lifted the helmet off the egg shaped mount and tucked it under his arm. It felt weak. With little force, he was sure he could break the glass visor covering the entire front half of the helmet. He shook the thought out of his head. If it wasn't meant to be used for this purpose, then he wouldn't have it.

The humming of the idle engine faded as the door closed behind him. He stepped into his quarters and tossed the suit on his bedspread. He took one last look down at the helmet, but something was off. He wasn't afraid of anything. It's what made him such a willing and capable Ranger, but seeing his face reflected in the glass visor made his stomach churn. He flipped it around a few times to inspect it, however, everything appeared to be fine.

He carefully sat it down on his desk, making sure to point the glass towards the wall. He began to disrobe from his flight suit, but halted suddenly as an alert rang out from the cockpit. Without hesitation, he slid back on his shirt and rushed out to inspect the system. His eyes darted to the drone monitor as a red alert was blinking on the screen. With a quick jump over the cables of the radio, he confirmed the alert with a quick tap of a button.

Locilette wasn't quite sure he was reading the drone's report correctly. He was confused. He re-read it one more time just to confirm that his mind wasn't just playing tricks on him. After a quick scan of the hull's service hatches, the drone detected a light being activated near the hangar door. He knew he would've recalled seeing a light on that side of the ship, especially as it sat in mostly complete darkness.

He sat back down in the flight chair to unlock the throttle. He guided the Theseus under the large frigate to its other side that faced away from the beaming star. As he came flying by the retracted landing gear, he saw it. It glowed a bright gold against the blackness of space. It was a true beacon in the dark. It was one that Locilette would bet his life on wasn't there during his previous fly-bys. At least, he thought so.

The Theseus came to a stop a few yards away from the large hangar door. The cockpit now sat in mostly darkness as the vessel blocked out the star's light on the opposite side. He just sat there observing the light, puzzled by how it could be the slightest bit possible he missed it. No, he didn't miss it. That light was a signal, and he wasn't going to leave behind whomever it was that needed help.

He quickly fumbled the headset on his head. "Yanagi-Yanagi, this is the Ranger Responder Theseus. Please respond."

Nothing came back. "Yanagi administration or crew, this is the Ranger Responder Theseus standing by outside your hangar door. Please respond." He broadcasted again.

The sound of static filled the ear muffs in his headset. He stood up and stared at the hangar, crossing his arms. He couldn't help but imagine someone's last dying effort to seek help was flashing the hangar bay light to get his attention, and he missed it. He missed it because his mind was too focused on home. He wiped the burning sensation from his eyes as he realized that he was sweating profusely. He lifted his shirt up and wiped his face dry, then turned to the radio to switch it to a common frequency.

"Whoever is in there, please," he spoke softly into the mic. "I see the light. I see *your* light. I don't know what you have been through, but I promise I'm here to help. I can get you out. I can take you home. Please, you just have to give me a confirmation so I can initiate a rescue operation with the Rangers. Please."

Locilette slid the headset off and tossed it into his flight chair. He leaned forward on the flight console and studied the hangar intensely, hoping for any kind of sign. There was no way he could go home and face his wife with the thought of him leaving someone to die on a floating coffin in space. It could have been someone's mother or father trapped with their final moments being that of home. It could be a son or a daughter crying out for their parents with their final breaths. It was something he couldn't bear.

All he could think about was what if it was him? If he was trapped on a derelict vessel with no hope of escape, he would pray for someone to go the extra step and rescue him. Then his mind began to wander to his last moments as the life support systems failed. His boys bringing home their future wives for a big meal, his wife holding their grandchildren without him, the lifetime of memories he would be absent from was enough to break him. He was going over. Now.

He turned to head back to his quarters. He went to jump over the radio when something made him freeze. His head whipped around to the headset lying on its side against the backrest of the flight chair. He shook his head in frustration and bolted to his quarters. Just as he passed the large archway into the Theseus's corridor, he stopped again and turned quickly to face the cockpit.

He wasn't hearing things. The faint sound of static came from the ear muffs of his headset. With every ounce within him, he sprinted back to the headset, tripping on the radio system. He tumbled into his flight controls, sending one of the monitors crashing into the wall. He didn't care at the moment. It was something replaceable compared to the life of another person. Still on the floor, he fumbled the headset over his head and pulled the mic close to his mouth.

"Hello!" He called out into the mic, his eyes fixed on the hangar door. "Repeat last. Please, repeat your last transmission."

Locilette waited a few minutes waiting for a cry for help, but once again he was left alone with the silence of the radio waves. He finally made his way to his feet and slowly slid the headset off. He hooked it back on its holder then took a seat. Someone *was* in there; he just knew it. His intuition has never let him down before, so the only thing he had to go on was a mysterious light appearing, what he would assume was a potential radio broadcast, and his gut. It was time to go in.

He pushed the throttle forward just a tad, inching the Theseus closer to the hangar door. He estimated he was about twenty-five feet away when he pulled back, bringing his ship to a haunt. He swiveled to his drone console, but changed the program on the menu screen that dropped down a short list of ship features. His eyes floated down until he saw *Wired Impulse* appear on screen. He accepted it, then turned to look out the front view port. A small tube began to extend out from the nose of the Theseus. Locilette pressed confirm one more time, then a harpoon with a wire in tow fired from the tube and penetrated the Yanagi's hull.

He waited for the system to update the connection, then when the confirmation flashed across the screen, he scrolled down to command the impulse. The wire turned blue, illuminating the front of the ship all the way to the impact site of the harpoon. After a few seconds, the impulse ceased, the light with it. Suddenly, the hangar door popped open a small amount, but stopped short of enough space for the Theseus to squeeze through. Barrels, crates, and machinery all rocketed out into space with the sudden vacuum of the void. Locilette breathed a sigh of relief that no people were among it.

He retracted the harpoon and switched back to the drone control menu. He instructed Drone One, which was still standing by, to take a peek inside the hangar bay. The drone passed by the viewport and Locilette watched as it entered through the gap in the door. After a brief moment, the Drone sent back a command request. Without hesitation, Locilette commanded the drone to do a quick scan for life and the atmosphere in the Yanagi's interior.

His patience began to wear thin. As bad as he wanted to get over to investigate in person, he knew he had to follow the proper procedures or catch hell from his superiors. He shook his head as realized he hadn't logged the most recent events in his PDA yet. He unlocked it, then jotted down an abbreviated version including his intent on boarding. If he was forced to do a space walk, at least he didn't have to spend the time looking for a hatch. If he calculated right, he could easily shoot the gap in the hangar doors. Just as he finished typing on the small screen, the drone report came, making his eyes instantaneously shoot up to take in the information.

He studied every word that scrolled across. His eyes burned without the relief of blinking for several minutes, only getting their wish as the report concluded. Something didn't seem right. The report indicated there was no sign of recent life in the hangar, and the life support system appeared to be functioning, other than the air being sucked out of the hangar into the vacuum of space. That simply couldn't be. Someone had to have been in the hangar at one point to turn on that light.

Locilette was unsatisfied with that report. He would much rather do the leg work himself, anyway. He unplugged his headset from the radio set and plugged it into the side of the drone console. He scrolled down the list of commands to transmit the drone's audio to the

Theseus. A box with moving audio waves came on screen. He slid the headset on his head and placed both hands over the ear muffs to listen as closely as he could.

His eyes closed as he imagined the interior based on the sounds. A slight humming was the most prevalent noise coming through. An alarm began to sound after a few seconds that Locilette could only assume was to alert the crew that the hangar bay door was open. He strained to hear anything that was under the surface of the orchestra of normal ship noises, but nothing seemed to be catching his attention. He began to wonder if he truly was just hearing things.

Tapping. The faint sound of metal on metal echoed from off in the distance of the Yanagi's interior. The 360 degree audio made led him to the conclusion that it must have been coming from around 2 o'clock of the drone's current position, but of course there was no way to be entirely sure. He had been on a lot of ships in his career, and a noise like that was only made by either faulty machinery, or a careless crew member.

Locilette heard all that he needed to. He pulled off the headset and hooked it back on its home. He programmed a custom command for the drone to find a way to get the hangar door fully open so he could safely land the Theseus directly in her bay. The drone took a few moments to respond, but ultimately accepted the request. Locilette had his eyes bouncing back from the drone screen to the hangar door out of the viewport to keep up with the progress. He scanned the hulking ship over and over again through the glass in front of him, his nerves about making that jump gnawing at the back of his mind. Anything to avoid doing a space walk was good in his book.

Like a gift from the Pantheon, the gold light that had attracted his attention turned red, and the door began to slide open. Locilette couldn't contain his excitement as he jumped up from his flight chair with a clap of his hands and a small cheer. Now the real fun would begin. He updated his PDA with an enthusiastic tap of the small keyboard and sent a *hold* order to the now idling drone. He began to power off all non-essential systems to conserve power during his time on board. There was no telling how long his investigation would take on the derelict Yanagi.

Chapter Three

The door to the Theseus's armory slid open. It was a relatively compact room, but since it was only meant to accommodate a small team if needed, it didn't need to be bigger than that for the work that was expected of it. Whether it was a fully stocked war room on a capital ship or a converted supply closet, it didn't really matter in terms of size. As far as Locilette was concerned, if it could hold weapons and armor, it was considered an armory.

The bright white lights shone brightly over the racking lining the far wall across from the door where most of Locilette's gear hung. The left side held neatly-lined weapons that fit in each slot like a puzzle piece. He was never a big believer in wasting space, especially when space was as limited as it was on the Theseus. The right side of the racking held his two suits of armor; both with their mission ready capabilities depending on what trouble laid ahead. It was always a good idea to have a lighter armor ready to go for everyday patrols, but when things got a little out of control, the standard issue heavy armor was a Ranger's best bet out in the field. Each had a helmet sitting off to the side with various attachments already assembled.

Along the bottom half were his miscellaneous gadgets. Short range radar, night vision visors for his helmets, beacons, concussion grenades, and flashlights of many shapes and models were presented in a perfectly straight line. The only thing he didn't have, however, was a decent pair of boots. The last thing he always thought of before leaving on an assignment was his footwear. He always just figured boots wouldn't stop a magma bolt or shield his eyes from a flash burst. Even though he enjoyed the comfort of decent footwear, it was near the bottom of his list in terms of importance.

His attention was pulled to the back corner of the tiny armory. Taking up most of the side wall was a capsule built into the wall of the ship. Wires and power cables strung all around the brass-colored pod, which led to a small screen nestled in the center of it. This was what Locilette was really there for. He walked up to it and tapped the screen, bringing it to life. A bright neon green status popped on screen, letting him know that the unit was operational and prepped for duty.

He typed his personal identification number as well as his pass codes to the high-leveled clearance systems on the Theseus. The pod had three latches on the door keeping it secured. Starting near the top and working its way down, each one clicked, allowing the door to open. A prompt came on screen asking for a confirmation to initiate deployment. Locillette tapped the screen and took a few steps back as the screen began to beep loudly.

The front split open, revealing a tall, copper-like mechanical being within. Lights began to run up and down its body as it powered up from its long slumber. Its eyes flickered open and darted around rapidly before eventually coming to a stop, looking directly forward toward the wall on the opposite side of the room. Several audio testers buzzed from its mouth to calibrate the vocalization speakers system housed within.

It reached out to both sides of the pod, then stepped down onto the metal flooring, each foot clinked with each big step. It fully erected itself, towering over Locilette in the small armory. He didn't quite realize how big it actually was since this is the first time he had ever felt it necessary to deploy. It was a menacing-looking machine that made him feel a small sense of intimidation as it just stood there in silence. He was happy this beast of robotics was on his side. Its icy blue eyes blinked a few times before lowering its gaze to meet the man standing before him.

"Ranger Locilette, I am Brinks 89-01G Class B. I am a Secura-Droid programmed with the latest knowledge of defense and tactical-leveled military strategy. I am pleased to be assisting you on this mission. May I inquire about the nature of our task?" It spoke, its voice changing from several different pitches until it landed on a calming tone.

Locilette observed the massive bot. He was impressed. "Mind if I just call you Brinks?"

"Of course, sir. You may refer to me however you desire."

"Walk with me, Brinks," Locilette commanded, waving him out of the armory. "I'll fill you in on the bridge."

Locilette led the way out, listening to the clinking of Brink's heavy footsteps behind him. It felt a little strange hearing someone's footsteps, or even talking to anything at all out on assignment. It felt nice. He wondered why he never thought about activating the bot sooner to cure his loneliness way out in nowhere space. He stopped just as they crossed through the threshold of the cockpit.

"Alright, here's what-"

"You said it was a bridge." The Secura-Droid interrupted. "A command bridge is a center of command and control on large vessels. This appears to just be a cockpit for a shuttle."

Locilette was caught off guard for a moment. "Well, *I* call it a bridge, so a bridge it is, okay?

"As you wish, sir."

"Good, now to the mission at hand," he said, motioning to the viewport. "This is the Yanagi. It was called a possible derelict, but recent evidence has stirred me to reconsider that claim."

"What evidence would that be, sir?"

He nodded to the bright light shining through the window. "See that light? One of my drones detected it being activated after my initial investigation of the vessel's exterior. I believe it's a sign from someone trapped within."

"Is it in the realm of possibility that the light is motion activated and the drone mistakenly triggered it?"

"Well, I…" He hadn't thought of that. It was incredibly likely that it could've been the case, and he had potentially connected dots that weren't there. Now that he did think about it, the drone was flying pretty close to the ship's hull in search of a service hatch. As much as he didn't want to admit it, this was a likely scenario. "That's a great theory."

"Indeed. Is there any other evidence that would lead to the mislabeling of the Yanagi as being a derelict?" Brinks asked, taking a long look out the viewport, then back to the Ranger.

"Yes," he said, tapping the radio with his foot. "While trying to hail the Yanagi's crew, I heard a radio transmission come through while my headset was sitting on my chair. I didn't catch what it said, or who it could've been, but I'm sure I heard it come through."

The bot's piercing stare never broke from him as it analyzed the information. "Could the radio transmission you heard possibly have been a transmission from another vessel passing through the area?"

Locilette was starting to get the feeling that his Secura-Droid was beginning to question his integrity. He knew what he saw, and he knew what he heard. He didn't need some robot questioning his judgment out here in the field on an official assignment. There was someone on that ship, he could just feel it. That was something a machine could never understand.

"I know what I heard. This derelict response call is now a rescue operation."

"As you command it, sir."

Locilette nodded. "Alright, then. Let's suit up and equip ourselves for boarding."

The two made their way back to the armory. He was trying to mentally piece together his load out, but wasn't quite sure what exactly would be appropriate for an operation such as this. It had been so long since he had conducted a rescue operation that gear was the last thing on his mind. He would bring the essentials as he always did, but the way he saw it, weapons would only slow him down. If someone was in fact in trouble, the last thing he would want to do is sling a heavy rifle over his shoulder to carry someone out.

However, Locilette wasn't a fool. His experience had taught him that being prepared for anything the universe had to throw at you was the wisest thing someone in his profession could do. A Ranger without a translator couldn't communicate with the local dialects, a Ranger without a personal data assistant couldn't document an investigation, and a Ranger without a weapon couldn't enforce the rule of the King. Of course, every mission was different. A bit of every piece of equipment was better than completely not having it at all, even if it did add an extra 40 lbs of gear to haul around.

Locilette looked over his load out options one last time as he heard Brinks clink back by its pod. *Lighter was better for an investigation like this*, he decided. Just in case they needed to make a quick exit, he didn't want to be weighed down with a bulky suit of armor to go where the probability of life was slim at best. His eyes fell upon his custom-designed light armor that hung on the racks. The black helmet that accompanied it reflected the harshness of the ship's lights from the ceiling.

He unfolded the ebony one-piece combat suit and disrobed from his dirty flight suit that he now realized he had been wearing for three days. He stepped into each leg's hole then hoisted it up over each arm., zipping the opening in the middle all the way to the top, which formed a turtleneck around his throat. He made a series of quick movements and stretched to loosen up the form-fitting fabric. His combat suit wasn't the most comfortable thing he'd ever worn, but these things weren't designed with comfort in mind. It was a tool like anything else in the room.

Locilette pulled off the chest rig from the shelf and lifted it over his head. It slid down over his shoulders as his head and arms found their homes. He tightened the straps on the side, making the armored vest snug against his body. He kicked off his shoes and took a seat on the small bench that lined the wall next to the racking. He unlaced the field boots and slipped them high on his calves. As he tied them, he glanced up in time to catch a glimpse of Brinks staring.

"Your staring kind of gives me the creeps." He spoke directly.

Brinks turned his torso to look at a blank spot on the wall. "My apologies, sir. I did not mean to frighten you. Any such body language is purely unintentional."

"You didn't frighten me, just don't stare at me like that."

"Very well, sir," he said, still staring at the wall.

Locilette remembered why he never took the time to activate the Theseus's Secure-Droid before. They were creepy as hell, but more importantly, something about putting his life in the hands of a machine that mimicked a person just didn't sit too well with him. He was sure Brinks was going to be fine, but he had read reports that bots like this were prone to remote hacking if their firewall wasn't up to date. He shook that thought out of his head. He knew his over-precautious tendencies could get the better of him sometimes.

He stretched over to the bottom shelf of the racking to a black case tucked behind a few cases of ammunition. He sat it on his lap and unlatched the two clips on each side to slide the lid open. Two black devices sat snug within the cut-out protective fibers that resembled large footprints. Locilette pulled them out one by one, then sat them on the floor. He carefully placed his boots in the openings to form around them. The magnetized soles activated briefly as a test, then as soon as he was satisfied, he turned them back off.

"Alright, Brinks," he said, standing up to get the feel of his boots. "Do you have the latest weapons manual downloaded for the Plasma Arc Rifle?"

Brink's eyes turned a solid green as it ran a quick scan of its data banks. "Yes, sir, I believe I have the latest manual per the Theseus's last system update. May I ask which model it is?"

Locilette pulled it from the magnetized hanger and flipped it around a few times. His weaponry certainly wasn't state of the art, but it didn't have to be. As long as it could fire the latest Ranger standard rounds, he didn't see a reason to send an upgrade request. Even if it was outdated, the mere presence of a firearm was enough to dissuade anyone thinking about doing something reckless. After a few moments, he found the weapon's model and serial number stamped along the battery cartridge insert.

"Looks to be a PAR Mk 2," he announced.

"Ah, yes," Brinks spoke as he reeducated himself of the weapon's capabilities. "The Plasma Arc Rifle Mark Two was the standard issued rifle of the Rangers. However, according to my records, it was retired from service in exchange for the Mark Three two years ago. May I ask why you still arm yourself with an outdated weapon?"

"If it ain't broke, don't fix it."

Brink's head tilted to one side. "What is broken, sir?"

"I mean, if the weapon is still effective, then why go through the trouble of changing it?"

"I believe I see your point, however, if the Rangers expect you to be up to date on the latest technology and weaponry, then are you not responsible for adopting the changes?"

"I am, but sometimes it's okay to hold off a while on big updates like that," he said, clipping the pauldrons to his shoulder straps. "Speaking of which, is your firewall up to date?"

His eyes flashed green for a moment. "Indeed it is, sir. May I ask why you inquire about the status of my firewall?"

"I just want to be sure you aren't gonna get hacked or anything like that out there."

"The likelihood of my systems being infiltrated is highly unlikely," the bot said, raising one of its metallic fingers in the air. "However, I do admit the possibility is not completely zero percent."

Locilette shrugged. "My point exactly." He again picked up the PAR and tossed it at his bot. It waited to the last possible second, then its hands whipped up and snagged it from the air. It shouldered it in a combat stance and awaited for Locilette's approvals When none came, it stood up and slung it over its back where a magnetized holder kept it in place.

The battery cartridges for the PAR were kept in a large black crate in the corner to the side of the racking. Locilette pulled off one of the backpacks from the hanger and lifted the hinged lid. It was divided into four quadrants, each full to the brim with ammunition of various kinds. He unzipped the bigger compartment on his backpack and began stuffing a few dozen cartridges in, then tossed it to the bot. It caught the heavy bag with both hands, then slid its arms in to mount it on its back.

"Are we expecting danger, sir?" Brinks asked.

Locilette strapped a holster around his waist, and pulled off a Plasma Arc Pistol from the rack to examine it. "Well, no, but better safe than sorry. You carry the weaponry and I'll carry the tech and investigation equipment. That's why you're here, Brinks."

"As you wish, sir."

"One last thing," Locilette said, waving Brinks to the door. "Come with me real quick. I need to make a slight modification to you."

Locillette led the Secure-Droid to the engine room just a few doors down from the armory. The hulking bot stood in the doorway as he rummaged through some storage bins. He pulled out a small square piece of hide he had scored from a leisurely hunting trip on his last assignment, and took it to the small workbench. He sliced it into two equal-sized egg shapes, then nodded for the bot to come to him. Even with the humming of the engine, the clinking of its metal feet were quite noticeable.

"Sit down and stick your feet out," Locilette instructed.

Brinks did as ordered and lowered its massive copper body to the floor, extending both legs. Locilette pulled some super glue out of a drawer of the work bench and knelt down to get to work. He carefully squeezed a few squiggles of glue to the bottom of Brink's feet, then lined the hides as perfectly as he could get them. He pressed them firmly into place, then helped the bot up to its feet.

"There you go," Locilette said, slapping its metal shoulder. "Your own pair of shoes."

Brinks lifted one foot up to examine it, then placed it back down with not a single peep of metal on metal. "Thank you, sir. This is most generous."

"Don't worry about it. It's better to not announce ourselves from a mile away, even if this is just a rescue operation."

"Agreed."

Locilette nodded in approval at his handiwork, then motioned to the bot to follow him. He led them back to the cockpit, where he took a seat in the flight chair, then swiveled around to face the front viewport. On the monitor to his left, he fired up his guidance systems and programmed the trajectory he was hoping to go, but he worried about pulling off such a maneuver without proper guidance from an outside source.

Brinks leaned forward just a bit to examine the Yanagi from the window. "Do you plan on taking us into the hangar, sir?"

"Yes," he answered, grappling the flight stick and throttle. "It's going to be a little tricky, but I think the Theseus has enough clearance to just sneak in."

"Theoretically, yes. However, the room for error is quite slim, sir."

He sighed in annoyance. "I'm well aware of that, Brinks, thanks."

He took a deep breath to try and calm his nerves, but it did little to relieve him. It did give him peace of mind knowing that if he did take a few bumps on the way in, his ship was insured by the Ranger Organization. This was an official operation after all, and certainly wouldn't be the first time a ship got damaged during a boarding attempt. He just hated to be the one responsible for doing it.

Locilette unlocked the flight controls, and could feel the ship's movements within his hands. His eyes were glued on the hangar growing closer through the thick glass in front of him. He pushed the stick as far as he could to the right and nudged the throttle forward inch by inch. The Theseus slowly began to bank to the starboard side and glide along the periphery of the Yanagi until it was lined up with the opening. He could feel the sweat begin to drip down his face. His hands were clammy and hot as his grip on the stick tightened.

His fingers pushed the throttle forward, causing the ship to move at a snail's pace. Just as he was about to pass through the large hangar door, the guidance system began to sound an alarm. The siren wailed around the cockpit, making Lociette jump in his seat. The Theseus jerked to the side and bumped into the side of the open door. The sound of metal on metal pierced his ears, but the siren covered up most of the grinding sound. He steadied himself and corrected the ship back into the center. He tried to silence the alarm but couldn't focus enough to find the confirmation command.

"Brinks!" He called over the screeching wail of the siren. "Shut that thing off!"

"At once, sir."

Brinks quickly moved to the console. It tapped on the keyboard for a moment, but eventually relinquished to extending a cord from its chest and plugged it directly into the side of the console. The bot's eye glowed green, then a moment later, the cockpit returned to the humming of the Theseus's engine.

Locilette wiped his sleeve across his forehead, letting out a sharp sigh. "Thank you."

"No thanks is necessary, sir. I do as you command."

Again, Locilette gripped his flight controls and eased his way inside the Yanagi's hangar bay. Brinks examined the flight path, and shook its head as the ship slowly passed through.

"Please correct course 0.17 degrees port side, sir." Brinks advised.

Locilette reluctantly obeyed the bot's calculated trajectory. The ship turned slightly to the left. In no time, the entire front side of the Theseus was within the hangar, but Locilette didn't dare take a moment to look at his surroundings. His eyes glanced several times at the guidance system, which showed the smallest gap between his ship's hull and the hangar door. After just a few more agonizing seconds, he cut the throttle and allowed the Yanagi's magnetizing landing pads to pull the Theseus down for a safe landing. The ship touched down, jolting the two forward slightly, but Locilette was just relieved that it was over. Launching from the hangar bay was going to be a hell of a lot easier than landing.

He took a moment to observe the hangar from the front view port. Nothing; not a single soul was around. Shipping crates were tucked away neatly by the walls and a fork lift was plugged up to the chagrin outlet, as if to be used the following shift. From what he could observe, the Yanagi seemed to have been stuck in time, like it was awaiting the return of a caring crew that would never come. This made him incredibly uneasy.

Locilette did a quick scan of the hangar's interior just to double check the atmosphere, but everything came back clean. The Yanagi's life support systems appeared to be working perfectly, which just led to more questions. If the crew wasn't forced to abandon ship because of a system failure, then what could have happened? He made a quick note in his PDA of their successful boarding, then slid it into the pocket of his vest. He pulled himself out of the flight chair and nodded to Brinks in a motion to follow.

The two stood by the door of the Theseus. Locilette punched in his pass code, but hesitated to press *open*. He contemplated perhaps sending a couple of drones through the ship to recon first, but the thick thermal walls of a ship such as this would surely block the signal. He hated going into this essentially blind, but if someone needed his help, he was obliged to face anything head-on. However, his training was screaming at him to not enter an unknown vessel without proper back up. He was confident that Brinks could handle any sort of basic security needs, but his bot lacked the experience and skill of a Ranger.

He jogged back to the drone console and turned the monitor to face him. He selected the *messenger* command on the list. As far as he knew, there were no communication buoys out there, but he could get a drone back to the wormhole gate with a message. He quickly typed up a request for any Rangers in the area to converge on his location for a possible rescue operation, and uploaded all the notes he had taken thus far. He pressed *confirm* then *launch*. The drone popped out of the pod and zipped past the Theseus into open space from the open hangar door. He selected the drone that was still inside the hangar to ram the closing lever on the door console.

The floor began to rumble as the two massive doors slowly came together. Locilette took a look from a small window tucked away behind some monitors just to double check that the doors were actually sealed. With how things were going, it would be just his luck if the Pantheon decided to suck him out into space the moment he stepped out to die horribly alone. He shook that thought from his head and met the awaiting Brinks by the exit door.

"Prepared the Infil, sir." Brinks announced.

Locilette nodded as the bot drew the weapon attached to its back. The longer he stood there, the more the desire for home crept up on him. The alluring call of clean bed sheets and the whispering warm wind of Kronos Prime flashed in his mind. For just a small moment, he found himself feeling at peace. Even if he didn't retire from the Rangers, he was sure as hell using every single second of time off he had accumulated over his career. That day was about to come, but today was not that day.

He pushed the bright green light by the door and the metal plating buzzed as it detached from the Theseus. It unfolded down to the hangar floor with an abnormally loud *clink* when it made contact. A flight of steps extended from it with red guiding lights lining the way down.

It was quiet. A place such as this should be bustling with activity, no matter what time it was, but there wasn't a single peep other than the sound of the blowing air from the massive vent ducts crisscrossing overhead. Locilette leaned out of the ship's door and slowly looked around. Some debris and loose machinery littered the area from when he forced open the hangar door, but other than that, the area was just as pristine as he would imagine a hangar to be.

He took a few steps down, the eerie feeling hanging over him like a predator in the night made his hand hover close to his holster. This kind of quiet was unnatural. The only other time he could recall where the silence bothered him this bad was when he was a child on Kronos, and had to go to his elementary school at night for a disciplinary meeting with the principal. All he could remember was the few lights on that led down a locker-lined hallway into the deep dark of the other end. It was almost a scene that contradicted itself.

"Hello?" Locilette called out, his voice echoing in the large open space.

"I do not think anyone will return your hails, sir," Brinks said directly. "On account that this was labeled a derelict vessel."

"I already told you I'm confident someone is on this ship. We just need to find them, get them the help they need, and get the hell out of here."

"Of course, sir." it said, taking a few long strides away from the Theseus. "Hello!" His voice boomed from the amplified speakers, making Locilette wince for a moment.

They both stood in silence. Locilette closed his eyes and listened for any signs of a response. No surprise to him, nothing came. If anyone was able to just shout for help, he could've gotten them out a long time ago. However, something in the back of his mind just didn't sit right. If someone was able to turn on the hangar bay lights, why couldn't they use a radio? At the very least, they could've just met him in the hangar.

He pondered on that for an instant, his concentration breaking with Brinks turning to check on him. He glanced at the hangar door panel where his drone was still floating, awaiting its next order. He pulled out his PDA to ask his ship's computer to call the drone back to the pod. Then it hit him.

"The bridge!" He sighed.

Brinks cocked its head to the side. "I beg your pardon, sir?"

"The lights can be remotely activated at the bridge as well as all the other systems. If someone were to be in trouble, the first place they would most likely head was the command bridge. It would have communications, the ship's leadership staff, as well as emergency rations."

"A very logical theory, sir." Brinks said, running the calculations. "How would you like to proceed?"

Locilette observed their surroundings once more. There was a door far off on the left side of the hangar bay, and another mirrored it on the opposite side. He took a brief moment to weigh his options. The best place to start with any kind of rescue operation was to thoroughly comb the area for any sign of the missing persons involved. He figured even if they didn't find anybody, at the very least, they could pick up on any sort of small lead as to where the crew had disappeared to.

"Alright, here's the plan. We're going to split up. You head off that way," he commanded with a nod behind the bot. "And I'll take a look in the opposite direction."

"Very well, sir."

He pulled out his PDA from his vest and tapped it on his ship's nose. "Link up your internal communications to the Theseus so whatever you find can be recorded. Everything we do from here on out must be documented for our official investigation."

"Of course, sir." Brinks acknowledged, its eyes blinking green for a brief moment. "Connection established. I am ready to begin, sir."

With a slight nod, Locilette brought the PDA up to his mouth. "Ranger Locilette of the responder Theseus. Myself and my standard issued Secura-Droid are beginning the investigation of the presumed derelict vessel, Yanagi. The staff and crew of the vessel have disappeared without any sort of inclination as to their whereabouts, however, the previously documented hangar light leads me to believe that someone must still be on board. We will be conducting separate investigations of the nearby area around the hangar bay, and will report back in twenty minutes."

The PDA beeped as he released the record button. He locked it, then slid it back into its pocket on his vest. He gave Brinks another nod, then both turned to head in opposite directions.

Chapter Four

Brinks stood just on the other side of the door, which closed behind it just a moment earlier. It did a quick visual scan of what lay in front of it and adjusted its ocular receptors to see more clearly in the low light. A corridor stretched in front of it with a large door at the end. From what Brinks could identify, there was nothing beyond that worth of note. The soft paddings of Brink's feet were nearly inaudible as it made its way to the end of the hall.

Brinks began to record as it reached the door. Above the door frame was a sign that read *Brig,* each letter appearing to chip away from the unlit bulbs it was stationed in front of. It was rather unusual to have the ship's holding cells so close to the hangar in the event of a prisoner escape, but it certainly wasn't unheard of. However, there was one thing about the door that surprised even one such as Brinks: it was slightly ajar. A thin crack of light streamed through the slit in the opening. This was a clear break in protocol and was something Brinks knew it had to document. Under no circumstances should the door to a brig be left unlocked, let alone open.

It slid its metal fingers into the crack, then pushed the thick door open to the side. It was heavy. Even the extra power from Brink's mechanical arms struggled. It became clear that it was an electrical door that appeared to be offline. That would also explain why the *Brig* sign wasn't illuminating as it should've always been. Locations such as that must be clearly defined on every Arkaan vessel. Brinks flashed the manual for *Security and Transportation of Goods and Criminals* in front of its eyes just to double check. Brinks was correct, as expected.

A long room stretched ahead of the bot. Most of the lights appeared to be either nonoperational or perhaps there was a power issue to where the Yanagi wasn't producing enough for nonessential systems. If the ship was struggling to maintain a regulated power dispersion, there could have been a time where the life support system was put into jeopardy. It would certainly explain why the crew potentially left. However, Brinks wasn't a being of hypotheticals. Brinks made a quick note of that.

Five doors lined the right side of the room, each being designated a number which ascended the further away. The left side wall had a large window directly in plain view of the cells with reinforced metal wiring embedded within. Brinks calculated that this particular security measure was a bit redundant, but reasoned the idea behind it. The bot ran a few quick scenarios through its processor and the most likely one was it had to be left over from when the Yanagi was a security vessel. Criminals of war were 67% more likely to attempt an aggressive escape from captivity. With odds like that, even a bot could say *better safe than sorry.*

A light from a small desk lamp illuminated the interior of the room appearing to be the guard station. After a closer inspection, Brinks noticed paperwork thrown about the desks of the former officers. It could've been the untidied workspace of a couple of lazy security, or perhaps the officers on duty had to leave in a hurry, uncaring as to the important documents of bookings left behind. Brinks snapped a few photos through the window for Locilette's future viewings.

Brinks turned its attention to the cells lining nearly the entirety of the wall. It tried to look through one of the small rectangle windows but couldn't see anything in the thick darkness within. The bot's eyes clicked, then beamed a bright cone of light through the thick glass to get a better view. There was nothing of note within the first cell. As the bot made its way down, it stopped at each one, looking for a single ounce of a lead, but the only thing to report was a well maintained holding cell. Strange, compared to the rough shape of the guard's room.

The bot made it to the final cell that hugged the end of the wall. It did a quick routine peek inside, but stopped just as it was about to turn away. The light illuminated across the walls of the cell and revealed symbols that Brinks wasn't familiar with. The bot's eyes zoomed in on what appeared to be drawing with a piece of rock scraped against the white walls. It snapped a picture of it to the best of its ability and ran a quick search in its large database for frontier Arkaan occult symbolism.

Some of the orbital cities of planets far away from Arkaa produced strange religions to ease the souls of the citizens calling them home. When cross referencing the cell's symbols, Brinks discovered some of the strangest things that the living person chose to place their faith in. Some believed that a wandering space slug would bring their salvation before the end of the universe. Others were sworn to a pact of an extra-dimensional father-like figure that welcomes them home upon the day of their deaths. The list kept scrolling before the bot's eyes, the documented accounts of both active and inactive religions seemed to trail on to dates around the empire's founding.

One most interesting account told of a singular planet that worshiped the snow-capped peak of a tall mountain. Allegedly, trapped within an icy prison, one of the first colonists was said to have fought back an evil previously reigning god of the planet. He defeated the god in unarmed combat, something Brinks greatly doubted, then ascended to godhood himself. But in a final act of revenge, the former god pushed the ascended one into the icy depths below where he remains to this day. According to the prophecy written, the ascended one would once again rise from his icy tomb to lead the planet to salvation amongst the stars. Something that Brinks noted was that the planet wasn't named in any of its current information. It bookmarked it for research after the operation was complete.

The screen cleared from its vision, returning the bot to the darkness of the brig. The symbol was unique. It almost appeared to be an emblem of one of the many political parties that dotted the various star systems of Arkaan territory. It was a circle with a triangle on top. Within the triangle sat a perfectly centered cross and three vertical squiggles aligned inside the base circle. The symbols had no record that Brinks could find. Intrigued by this discovery, the bot tried to open the cell door, but wouldn't budge, as expected. Brinks moved its light around the tiny window to get the best view, but wasn't successful.

Brinks turned to the guard station. If there was a way to get into that cell, it had to be in there. Its large hand grasped the door latch, but it held firmly in place. When the power issues began, the guard station likely locked itself down to ensure the integrity of the contents within. The bot looked around the edge of the door, but it was clear that opening it by proper means was out of the question. This door was holding it back on an official Ranger investigation. According to the rules of policing frontiers act penned by our great lord and protector, the King of Arkaa, Brinks could use force if it was within reason to seize certain materials.

The bot de-magnetized the PAR on its back and placed the weapon's barrel a few inches from the door latch. Without a moment of hesitation, Brinks pulled the trigger, and a blast of blue plasma arced from the tip of the rifle. The brig flashed with a sudden burst of light followed by the clanging sound of the latch falling to the metal floor. Brinks nudged the door with its foot, allowing it to slowly swing open.

The only light within was a tiny desk lamp in the back of the room. Brinks's lights surveyed the entire office, and found it quite strange that this was the only entrance and exit to the station. It seemed like a strategic blunder to not leave an escape route for the security officers, but the bot wasn't there to correct the blatant failure in protocol. Papers were wildly thrown about the tiny office from what appeared to be a quick escape. Brinks's initial assessment appeared to be correct. A computer monitor was spun around to face the wall on the desk, but as the beams of light passed over it, it appeared to have a small hole in it.

Upon closer inspection, Brinks noticed the scorch marks. A weapon had been discharged at some point in time with the computer as the most likely target. The bot turned the monitor around, confirming that it was now completely useless. However, Brinks had another solution. It knelt down and extended a cable from its chest, plugging it into the front of the console. The computer's startup screen popped before Brinks's eyes with a yellow flash of the Yanagi's welcoming message for all staff.

The console booted up dreadfully slow. Even for one such as Brinks struggled to find the patience to sit as the minutes ticked on as the spinning disk of the loading screen continued on and on. Eventually, the screen flashed to a black menu screen with several folders spread throughout it in no particular order. The bot's eyes fell upon a fold named *Inmate Transfers*. With a blink and a click, hundreds of transfer requests filled the bot's view. Brinks read through all the information in a few seconds, but found nothing of note. Then came the most recent transfer. There was no name, no photo, and no prisoner identification number. Brinks was quite disappointed in the lack of adhering to the Arkaan transportation protocol on this ship. Locilette would certainly be hearing the complaints.

Brinks shut off the console and unplugged the cable to retract quickly back into its chest. It stood up and looked around the office for the cell door control panels and found it bolted down to the metal table that lined the length of the reinforced window. Each button corresponded with one of the cell doors, each labeled with the number assigned to it. One by one, Brinks pressed the buttons to cause the doors to pop open in a wide swing. After the final button was pushed, a loud buzz blared like an alarm. Brinks figured that it must have been a confirmation request to open the cell. The best assessment was that this cell was reserved for the worst offenders, so a confirmation was installed to ensure the officers were indeed meaning to open this particular one.

Brinks pressed the door release one more time to confirm the order. A loud click echoed through the brig, and the bot could see the door to cell 5 slowly creep open through the glass. Even from where Brinks stood, it was dark inside. For a cell reserved for the worst criminals, the lack of illumination within made the guard's jobs much more difficult to observe whoever was kept within. Brinks made a note of that.

The two beams of light came together to focus in on the interior of the cell. As Brinks stepped inside, it was clear that this cell wasn't quite like the rest. It was less orderly than the others. Used sheets and blankets still littered the metal bed, spilling over to the floor like someone just crawled out. A plate remained on the table with a half eaten meal still present, now rotting away from the weeks gone by. The toilet was stained to the point where not even a deep cleaning could hope to save it from the wretchedness it had seen over the many years of hardship. It was what the books of law that filled Brink's memory banks would call *unsanitary living conditions* and *cruel and unusual punishment.*

Brinks liberally snapped photos of the cell's interior to document the finds. Even if this had nothing to do with the crew's disappearance, at least it would show that the Yanagi's leadership had little respect for whoever was imprisoned within. The cone of light slowly inched its way up the walls until it hit the ceiling, revealing hundreds of smaller versions of the emblem carved into the metal above. Brinks did a quick sweep around and discovered the emblem wasn't contained just there, but it was everywhere. From the floor to the ceiling, from the bed frame to the fake window, each area had the peculiar symbolism adorning it.

The bot ran a calculation to determine the likelihood of a new religion spawning on a seasoned voyager, but the odds were slim. With a ship such as this coming and going with so many different passengers in such a short amount of time, the establishment of a form of worship could never hold. According to several texts of the psychology of Arakaans downloaded inside Brinks, religions are only formed after a small group of people are contained in an isolationist state for a long period of time. Unless this is an individual with the aspiration of bringing their other-worldly faith to distant worlds, the possibility of it being organic to the Yanagi was approximately 0.07%. Unlikely, but not completely.

Without warning, a loud slam came from behind. Brinks spun around to see the door to the cell had closed behind it. The bot placed both of its large hands on the door and leaned into the metal, but as expected, it didn't budge. It was unlikely the steady breeze from the ship's life support system was enough to blow that heavy door closed. The beams of light from its eyes scanned the surface of the door for any kind of hinge to forcibly cause the door to pop open, but that would be counter-intuitive for a room meant to keep people from escaping.

Through the tiny window, Brinks attempted to see if perhaps Locilette was in the brig hall, but there was nothing out of sorts. Brinks began to calculate the likelihood of the door's weight swinging it shut, but again it wasn't quite likely. The bot made a quick adjustment to its algorithm so that an event like this would never happen again. Before bringing up its decision making coding, something appeared to be a miss on first inspection. The door to the brig was closed. Brinks was absolutely certain that it left the door open when it stepped inside. The bot couldn't get a full assessment if it was alone or not from the little window, but the brig hall appeared to be as desolate as it was just moments earlier.

As much as Brinks didn't want to tamper with a potential scene for Locilette's investigation, it had to get out of there. After a run of a few scenarios passed through Brink's processor, the most likely conclusion flashed across its eye screen in a bright red. The likelihood of an assailant tampering with their investigation was quite evident, and if they closed the brig door behind their escape, the Theseus was a possible target for being compromised. That was something that simply couldn't happen.

The bot's metallic body began to change. The brass plates of armor popped open to allow better ventilation, and two small protective sheets came down to protect the bot's eyes. Thin slits were in the center of them to allow some small visual to be made. The rounded shoulder plates slid up and out to become pauldrons to allow the arms to move a little more quickly. Brinks had entered security mode for the first time since it left the factory.

Brinks brought back its massive brass hand and closed it into a tight fist. With a quick rotation of its hips, the bot threw a lightning fast punch with the calculated precision only a Secure-Droid could muster. Its fist blasted through the window, sending razor sharp pieces of the reinforced glass shooting across the floor. It hammered away most of the surrounding glass to wiggle its other hand through to grab the side of the window frame with both hands, and pulled as hard as it could.

The bot's strength seemed endless. It pushed the door with enough force to push a shuttle across a sandy beach, but it wouldn't budge an inch. Brinks activated a burst of its reserve energy, and hot exhaust steamed from the open vents on its arms. The door began to squeal as it began to move ever so slightly, sparks popping from the electronics grinding trying to keep it closed. With a massive jerk, the door slammed back closed from the centimeters that it allowed.

Brinks stepped back to formulate another plan when the lock clicked loudly as it engaged then reengaged several times. With each cycle of the locking mechanism, the light in the guard's room flashed from green to red in rapid succession. Then, as quickly as it started, it ceased leaving the door unlocked, the weight of it enough to allow it to slowly creep open. It was fully prepared to deal with whatever laid beyond, but was greeted only by the low light of the brig.

Brinks wasted no time. The bot shoved the door open with a powerful shoulder push, then rushed to the main door to the brig. The bot's massive stride allowed it to cross the small hall with enough speed to have it slide across the floor to come to a stop. Just as the cell door, the door to the brig was now completely sealed. The bot ran a quick diagnosis of the situation and pulled back a clenched fist, punching the door as hard as it could. Force didn't seem like it was going to be the solution here. The panel's black screen next to the door was evidence enough to let it know it was offline, but the covered wires appeared to lead back into the guard room.

Brinks shoulder rushed the door, bringing it to fly into the wall with a loud, dramatic thud that echoed the length of the brig. The lights from its eyes scanned the room for any signs of an assailant, but it was just as quiet as it left it minutes earlier. The main door release panel sat on the wall near the window. A quick security assessment led Brinks to believe its purpose was to make the guard get to their feet, and observe before unlocking the door. It was a rather logical idea, contrary to what it assessed elsewhere.

The bot leaned to the side and stretched to push the button without taking its eyes off the brig hall. When it pressed the release button, nothing happened. It climbed over the fallen chairs, and ripped the paneling from around the button. A mangled mess of wires from within coiled around themselves in a fit of chaotic carelessness. This in itself was a blatant fire hazard and would be added to the official report. Brinks pulled a handful of the wires to attempt identification of which one was responsible for releasing the door lock. In one eye, Brinks pulled up various electrician manuals for similar ships, and in the other tried to separate the wires into equal groups.

In a moment, Brinks absorbed the manual's contents. It shut them away to be stored in the deepest shelves of its memory banks to one day be called upon in a situation such as this. The bot identified three wires responsible for the lock release mechanism and flipped open a blade concealed within its hand. The blade sliced through the wires, exposing the copper within, then returned to its home within the brass plating of Brink's hand. It magnified its eyes to get a clearer view. It prepared an electric charge in its fingertip and pressed it against the exposed wiring. Brinks looked up to observe the door, then fired a jolt of electricity through it.

The lights around the door illuminated a dim glow. A loud *click* echoed from around the brig hall. A small bulb Brinks hadn't noticed before lit above the window, which would alert the missing guards that the door was currently unlocked. The door slowly began to slide along its tracks until the faint glow of the corridor lights flooded the entryway. Brinks ceased the charge, ceasing the light in a blink of an eye. The bot pulled the rifle from its back and stormed out of the brig back to the Theseus.

Chapter Five

Locilette's eyes adjusted to the dark corridor that stretched out in front of him. From what he could see, five evenly-spaced doors lined the right side of the hall. The left side was lined with several posters displaying safety guidelines with photos of actors in various awkward poses. In the middle of them was an unlit neon sign that read: *days since last accident.* Locilette couldn't help but chuckle as the dead sign read zero days. An accident that led to the Yanagi floating in the depths of space could lead to some kind of clue as to where her missing crew was. However, if a catastrophic event did happen, a crew member taking the time to change the number on the sign was rather unlikely. He liked to think that someone had a sense of humor good enough to do that, but doubted it.

Dim green lights lined a path on the floor, giving the poorly lit corridor a slight glowing effect. He found it strange how the floor lights were working but the large lights mounted in the ceiling did not. The thought of the floor lights possibly running on a different circuit connected to the backup power crossed his mind, but he wasn't going to pretend like he knew anything about how power distribution worked. What he did know was that the lights were somewhat working in the hangar, so why not in the adjacent corridors, as well?

The thought nagged at him as he started to make his way forward. The lights from the floor flooded his boots with green as he passed, then faded back into darkness. He was curious how the Yanagi's energy distribution was assigned to allow such little energy flow to the illumination of the ship's interiors. He stopped and pulled out his PDA to jot down a few quick notes. *If the Yanagi suffered some kind of damage to her critical systems, it only makes sense that the ship's leadership staff would direct all nonessential energy to those affected systems. Possible star flare?* He typed on an entry.

It was one of the only conclusions he could muster with such little information. With the nearby star a treasure trove of energy, perhaps the Yanagi was hit with a surprise flare that sent her into a comatose state for a while, forcing the crew to abandon ship. It would be one of the only explanations that could explain why there's not a single shuttle in the hangar bay and the lack of power. He noted that idea as well. He wasn't certain of the idea though, which is something he absolutely had to be in order to take the next step with this lonesome derelict.

He approached one of the doors and tapped on the screen. It remained black, but the glare from the dim ambient light revealed an abundance of finger smudges. The paint on the numerical keypad had long since faded from the years of endless tapping. It's not that Locilette expected it to be any different, but he just had to check for himself. He made his way down the hall, tapping on the screens of each door as he passed. He stopped at one halfway down the hall and pushed on the door to hopefully slide it open, but his clammy hands just slid off, leaving a long streak across the metal.

He took a step back and examined the door. There was no inclination of what this room could have been used for. He assumed the room's designation would flash across the door pad screen under normal circumstances, but that really didn't help him now. He knocked on it three times, then stood back to listen. There was a strange feeling of anticipation that rushed through him. He knew all too well that nothing was going to knock back, but what if something did? He imagined the poor lost souls of the missing crew wandering the empty halls of this vessel for the rest of eternity, never finding peace or any form of a happy end to their wandering of the cosmos. They were just destined to float amongst the stars for the rest of time.

Over the course of his lengthy career, he'd heard ghost stories from other Rangers who have witnessed some strange things on derelicts much like the Yanagi. One story he recalled was that of an old freighter that was lost sixty years prior during the establishment of the Weito 1 orbital city. The *Profitable Venture* was a galleon-sized vessel transporting a hull full of colonists to help get the newly commissioned commercial hub on its feet high above the barren, inhospitable surface of the planet. Sometime during the midpoint in their journey, the vessel's life support system malfunctioned, leading to the deaths of 376 men, women, and children. It was an absolutely tragic event that circulated through the entire empire.

A Ranger responder discovered the vessel tucked away behind a large asteroid tumbling through open space. When she did an initial investigation, she could hear something coming through her radio as she tried to hail them. Allegedly, the radio connection was confirmed from the *Profitable Venture* and all that she could hear coming out of her speakers was the cries and pleas of people trapped within. She was said to have conducted an emergency space walk to approach the vessel, hearing the banging of metal as if someone was trying to get her attention. However, when she was able to enter through a service hatch safely, she found nothing but the perfectly preserved corpses of the lost colonists. He shuddered as the realization of that story and where he was now had striking similarities.

Another story hit Locilette a little closer to home. When he was grinding his way through the academy, there was a tale that the senior cadets would pass down the chain to the newer recruits about one of their own. By all accounts, a new Ranger, not but two months graduated, was out on his first assignment when he mistakenly passed straight through an ion storm. It rendered his flight controls useless, sending him spiraling into the powerful gravitational pull of a nearby gas giant. Rangers in the area listened in horror as the Ranger called for help as the heat and pressure consumed his ship. Legend has it that when you pass by that same gas giant, the screams of the helpless Ranger can still be heard over certain frequencies of your radio. Since that incident, every recruit coming out of the academy is required to serve aboard a vessel before being bestowed the honor of operating his or her own responder.

As unsettling and entertaining as such stories were, that's all Locilette regarded them as. Just stories. He doubted the existence of real ghosts, but when he found himself in eerie situations such as the one he stumbled in now, he couldn't help but to give into the fantasy of a haunted ship. Nothing enthralled people's quiet, boring lives like a good story about a ghost ship floating out in the void of space, looking for any living person to add to its ever-eternal crew. As far as Locilette knew, this was no ghost ship, but he shrugged at the thought that he had only been here a short while. There were still plenty of opportunities for whatever lurked in the dark to snag him away. He shook his head and continued on.

He passed by one of the doors in the center of the hall and stopped to give it a second look. It was opened slightly. It was so dark inside that he must have not noticed it. Then again, it was mostly dark everywhere in this corridor. He located his flashlight and clicked it on, delivering a powerful beam of yellow illumination piercing through the blackness.

The door was cracked, maybe a foot and a half. He pointed the light through to see that it must have been the personal quarters of some kind. Directly across from the door was a well-made bed with sheets still neatly tucked from the steady hand of a morning routine. The light slowly passed through the room, revealing several filing cabinets lined up in a tight row. To the far right of the door, Locilette could make out a desk, but his vision was too obstructed by the door to really get a good look at it. He figured that even with his vest on, he could just barely clear the opening. If worse came to worst, it wouldn't hurt to remove it just long enough to get a quick peek around.

He turned to the side and lined himself up with the small opening. He squeezed his way through, but halfway, the front of his vest got snagged on the small metal hook of the locking mechanism jetting out. He carefully freed himself, but as he sat there halfway in the door, the thought occurred to him that doors such as these had enough power to chop someone in half if they were so unlucky to find themselves in a vulnerable position. Just a position he now found himself in. His trained mind forced the thought out, however, he couldn't help but to hurry just a little.

He hopped on one leg as he pulled the rest of his body free from the gap, adjusted his vest, then lifted the beam of his flashlight to the wall ahead. A large dry erase board hung on the wall, taking up a fair portion of it. Flanking both sides were cargo transfer papers tacked to a sliver of cork board lining the edges of it. Each paper had a different colored tag sticking out which Locilette could only assume corresponded with the colored marker used on the board. He moved a little closer to get a better view of the papers' contents, the beam of the flashlight reflecting off the white board, forcing him to squint as he read.

The writings on the board were a confusing mess of words and numbers, but as Locilette predicted, the colors were related to the transfer papers. One transfer request had the Yanagi transport a shipment of oats from Njord 4 to another ship in the Ares system, and another appeared to have a large shipment of wood to drop off directly to an orbital city in the Poseidon system. That particular system, as Locilette knew personally, was rather lacking in natural building resources such as stone, wood, and clay. However, it certainly had an abundance of drinkable water, which he figured was a decent trade off.

He had a few assignments there a few years ago where he was responsible for escorting a flotilla of liquid cargo vessels filled with the precious resource. Oftentimes they would be taken to orbital cities where their water recycling unit was offline. This frequently happened in systems barren of water-producing planets such as Pele and Kagutsuchi. Locilette always found it exceedingly impressive the way the Arkaan commerce system worked. It was like an ever-flowing river of water getting every small drop exactly where it needed to be. Not to mention incredibly efficient. A request for gold could ship across Arkaan space to an electronics factory on the opposite side of the empire in less than four months. Speeds like that were completely unheard of not only twenty years ago.

Locilette did wonder exactly how many shipments didn't make it to their destination. He was standing on such an example. The request for those oats will never arrive at their destination, and he wondered what, or who, that impacted. Would a village of colonists now not eat? Did a wealthy merchant trying to establish his enterprise now go bankrupt because of overhead cost, and no inventory to make his sales? The chain of commerce was certainly impressive, but when one of those links in the chain broke, the thought of the consequences seemed vast. Locilette wasn't an economist though, he was a Ranger. His job was to figure out *why* the shipment would not arrive to these people, and he was more than comfortable staying in that small part of the chain.

He turned, and the light from the flashlight revealed the faces of a happy family. Much like in his own quarters on the Theseus, the wall around the desk showed a lifetime's worth of happy memories forever encased in the moments of the magnetized picture frames hanging sporadically around the office. On the desk sat a picture of an older man in a fine tuxedo, and a younger woman dressed in a long white gown. *A father and a daughter, most likely taken moments after he gave her away to spend the rest of her life with her new husband*, he thought. A single picture sat front and center on the tidy desktop, right where whomever would be spending hours on end here could fondly look upon it whenever things got lonely out in the solitude of space. It was a feeling that Locilette was all too familiar with.

He stared at it for a while. The beams of light from the flashlight created a shimmering glare across the picture's glass. He wondered if the father in that memory made it back home from whatever happened here on the Yanagi, or would his final memories be of the life he left behind amongst these pictures. Locilette hoped that he returned home, wherever that may be, to the loving family that surrounded him in this room. It was a thought that he often had about himself sometimes as he reflected on his own family.

His mind snapped back to the task at hand. He was guilty of letting his mind wander on the job, especially when he stepped into places almost frozen in time. He just couldn't help but let his thoughts take him to another place where happiness was always the end result. It was the only thing he wanted for the man in the photographs that he would never meet.

Locilette broke his gaze away and scanned the little contents that laid on top of the desk. It was all mostly transfer requests that had yet to be processed and a shift schedule that held a list of names for who were slated to work in the upcoming week. He leaned down to get a good look at the date posted in the top left corner of the page. Locilette was a bit surprised that the schedule was posted for eight months ago. The Yanagi had been missing for longer than he had originally suspected. He quickly pulled out his PDA and logged this into his notes.

It was now completely evident why the Yanagi was having such fluctuating power issues. If this vessel had been abandoned for eight long months, it had more than likely burnt through its energy reserves. Most ships had fail-safe systems in place to where when energy was running low, it would automatically pull from non-essential systems without the involvement of her crew. The Yanagi was just trying to survive as long as she possibly could out here on her own.

He began to pull out the desk drawers to rummage through them, hoping to find any kind of information for emergency protocols. There must have been some kind of paper trail to give the slightest hint to where the crew would've gone. At the very least, Locilette hoped to find the locations of escape pods to see if they had been launched. If the comings and goings on the ship would be anywhere, it would be recorded on the command bridge and the Cargo Manager's logs. He would bet that this office belonged to the latter.

The old wooden drawers cried out as he pulled them from their housing. Some of them were sticking, forcing Locilette to wiggle them free from the swollen wood keeping them contained. Most of the drawers' contents were routine paperwork of any staff management, but when he got to the bottom drawer, he realized it was already open by a few inches. Normally Locilette would just ignore something like this, but the fact that everything else was, for the most part, tidy and in their place puzzled him.

He focused the light on the drawer handle and slowly pulled it open. Something within convinced him that a rat was going to jump out at him, but it only made him tug on it faster just to get it over with if there was one. Several orange envelopes were stacked inside, along with a small box near the back of the drawer. The box took up quite a bit of room, so whomever placed it in here had to sit it on top of the envelopes. Locilette pulled it out to set it on the desktop to get it out of the way, then reached for the small stack.

He tossed the stack by the box and flipped the first one over to pinch open the flap. It was prisoner transfer papers. His eyes scanned the names, ages, birthplaces, and eventual destinations of several men and women who have passed through these halls to be handed swift justice. The Yanagi's owners appeared to not waste a single thing about their vessel. Their business model had the crew transporting goods, services, as well as being an armed prisoner transport unit. It was actually quite impressive of the utility this ship could offer. If you needed *anything* moved from one place to another, it would appear the Yanagi was your go-to choice. Locilette just hoped that what was moved here was all legal and nothing off the books.

Just as he was brushing the papers back into a neat pile to return them, one in particular stood out. One of the prisoner transfer forms was almost completely redacted. Black streaks ran over the prisoner's name and other essential information. There were cases where prisoners moving through the witness protection system would have their files redacted so that someone wouldn't tip off a potential aggressor to the movements of a person of interest. However, the amount of information removed was much more excessive than Locilette had seen previously. Even the prisoner's destination was redacted, making him wonder that if the hangar manager didn't know who he was transporting, then who would?

The only experience he had with the transport log being so heavily protected was the movements of a political official. Even then, the media was at least aware of the general area where they would be arriving. This person was completely scrubbed from documentation. At least, in any sort of official capacity. He laid the paper flat on the desk and snapped a picture of it with his PDA. Even though there wasn't any kind of lead on the form itself, its mere existence led to questions of what the

Yanagi was actually moving. It was a question he'd hoped would be answered when he located the bridge.

He slid the stack of papers back into the drawer. Before returning the box to it's home, he gave it a quick look over with the under the beam of his flashlight. It appeared that at one point there was a lock looped around it, but it was removed. With a cautious hand, he slowly lifted the top. Locilette raised an eyebrow as he discovered the box was a gun case, and even more intriguing, an empty gun case. A few magma canisters rolled around the interior, but there was no weapon to be found.

It made sense that someone in the hangar manager's position would have a weapon just in case they were boarded by pirates or had to handle a prisoner escape, but Locilette was puzzled why the box was back in the drawer. If there was an emergency that required the use of a magma pistol, would someone actually have time to return the weapon's case back to the back of a bottom drawer on a desk? He logged that same question into his notes. He began to feel as though there were a few inconsistencies here that would warrant a deeper investigation. He mentally noted to return here if the bridge proved fruitless.

He turned back to face the board on the far side wall. Where were these prisoners heading, and why the secrecy around them? His eyes scanned the board for even the slightest connection, but nothing seemed to link. He made his way back to the door but stopped by a picture that hung magnetized at eye height. It was the same man and an older lady which Locilette presumed was his wife.

"I hope you got out." He nodded. He squeezed his way back through the gap back into the corridor.

As he made his way down to the end of the corridor, he tapped on each of the door panels hoping for a miracle, but the Pantheon were never one to favor him. He stopped just short of the massive metal door at the very end of the hall. Above was an offline light sign that had in bold letters *CARGO HOLD* spelled out on it. He placed a hand on the door; the cold metal ran a shiver even through his gloves. His eyes traced the door then eventually found the door pad, however, this one was different from the others. It had the same screen and keypad as the others, no doubt a later improvement, but also had a dated ocular scanner installed above it.

This wasn't much of a surprise to him, especially on transport vessels such as the Yanagi. Oftentimes cargo holds would have an extra layer of security to protect the valuables they would be moving in case of unforeseen circumstances. Little did most people know, the cargo hold also served an alternative purpose. They also acted as a panic room of sorts, allowing the crew on the edge of the ship a place of refuge in case of any hostile boarding. Cargo holds were usually large enough to hold hundreds of people, as well as being reinforced in the event of hostiles trying to take down the door.

Locilette had to get this door opened, even if he wouldn't like what secrets were kept within. He tapped on the screen above the keypad, but as expected, it remained black. However, Locilette had a theory he wanted to test. In a stroke of luck, he pressed one of the key pad numbers, causing it to light up a dim red. Just as he thought, the cargo hold's lock ran on the ship's auxiliary power along with the life support system. The ocular scanner didn't come to life, sending a wave of relief through him. He tapped a few random numbers, not expecting much to happen, then the entire keypad lit up. It blinked for a few moments before fading back into darkness.

He aimed his light at the buttons on the pad and examined them closely. Three numbers appeared to be just a little more worn than the other six on display. The number facings were faded by the smallest amount that most people with an untrained eye probably wouldn't notice, but Locilette did. The *3, 5,* and *7* were all slightly off-colored, no doubt from years on years of use. However, it did show how well the pad was made that it resisted wear this long. Now all he had to do was come up with the combination. A combination that could be almost endless compared to the little time he had to give this.

The pad lit up as he tapped on the *5* that sat in the middle of the keypad. With no thought at all, he pressed a random series of two numbers that made it blink once more in error. His failure wasn't in vain, what he discovered was the pad forced the error after only three digits were entered. It was rather strange for a vessel's security system to only have a three digit coded lock, but at least it made his breaking in just a smidge easier.

He tapped *7-3-5,* but failed to open. As soon as the flashing ceased, he pressed *5-3-7,* but still he failed. He bent down to get a closer look at the numbers. He wiped off the keypad with his gloves just to make sure that what he thought he saw was actually wear on the keys and not just dust accumulating on the buttons. The slightest signs of weathering remained, giving him a small sense of relief. There were only three numbers he had to work with. If he just pressed a rapid fire amount of combinations, one was surely to stick. His fingers began to thunder on the keys.

5-5-3 Failure

7-5-3 Failure

3-3-3 Failure

5-7-3 Failure

7-5-3 Failure

Locilette's patience was beginning to fade. He straightened himself and eyed the keypad hard, hoping that his intimidating gaze would be enough for the code to come. His eyes drifted to the top right of the pad as he noticed the metal around it was also slightly discolored. It was more than that though. He slowly placed his hand on the same area where the edge of his hand fit perfectly. The cargo manager must have placed his hand in the same spot every single time he would input the code. With that in mind, he let his fingers fall where they were most comfortable and natural-feeling.

3-5-7

The keypad beeped loudly. The red numbers that he had become so used to seeing turned a bright, lime green. The door slowly split open, giving Locilette full access to the Yanagi's hold. It was just as dark in there as the rest of the ship. He stepped forward just a few feet before a wave of horrifying smells assaulted him. He covered his mouth and nose with his arm as he tried his best not to release a guttural gag. He lifted the beam of the light to search around the entrance, but he couldn't figure out where something like that was coming from.

The load of oats that were documented in the transfer papers hugged the wall to the left of the door. They were stacked up four crates high and spanned the entire length of the wall with very little room between. Locilette caught a glimpse at a retractable ladder chained to the nearby racking and pulled it over to the wooden tower. He carefully leaned it against the crates and ascended to the top. The air grew surprisingly cooler the higher he climbed, but a humming of a vent nearby made him whip his head around to find it, eventually spotting it tucked away in the top corner by him. He felt that if the air was a bit warmer that smell would've filled the entire hall, if not the whole hangar bay, as well.

He shone the light down to the crate's lid that had a packing slip tucked away in a window sticker. He tore the end of it and pulled the folded paper out to study where the shipment was actually going. The invoice was written in Arkaan standard as well as the local dialect script of the Ares system. The shipment of oats appeared to be bound for a warehouse on the Ares 3 Orbital City, but had distribution requests for Ares Prime. None of that really mattered now, though. These oats were doomed to roam the vacuum of space until Locilette made the decision to confiscate the vessel. When the time came for that, the

Yanagi would be towed to the nearest space dock to be stripped of all her cargo, then auctioned off to the highest bidder.

It sure beat the alternative fate for derelict vessels. If it presented some kind of risk to life, or carried a disease of some sorts, the ship would be condemned. Locilette would probably be tasked with the responsibility of towing the vessel on a collision course with the nearest star to have it burn away from existence, or if that's not an available option, he'd have to figure out a way to destroy the vessel in space. It was a messy operation that he thankfully never had to do, but if the job required it, he'd do it.

Locilette broke the safety seal on the crate, and unlatched the lock on the front. It creaked as he lifted the lid. It was full to the brim of smaller sacks of portioned-out oats. He leaned down and inhaled deeply, but the stale smell of old oats was enough to give him relief from the rotting smell at the floor level. He almost didn't want to pull himself away, but he knew he had to finish at least a walk through for official documentation. He took one last breath in, then shut the lid, not caring to relatch it. He carefully climbed down, and was once again under the thick veil of this horrendous smell. He tried his best to ignore it.

Crates of every size were stacked high, creating only a small path for someone to walk through. It was astounding how much cargo the Yanagi was transporting during her last voyage. There were crates bound for Anubis, Hera, and even the farthest reaches of Arkaan space with the newly-established Gula Prime, the only planet in that system to feel the feet of people upon its coarse soil.

He had to squeeze between a couple of tall crates stacked on end until he made his way to the receiving officer's desk in the back. This was where he found the source of the smell. It was a sight he wished he would never have seen.

From above, a single dim, orange light beamed down onto the remains of one of the crew members. The body was sitting against one of the crates, slightly slumped to the left where the back wall helped propped it up. Its right hand extended out with a pistol of some kind still snug in its hand, its finger resting firmly on the trigger. The head of the corpse was completely blown to bits, which was what appeared to be a self-inflicted wound from a plasma arc discharge.

Locilette couldn't help himself but to kneel down before the unfortunate soul that rested before him. He rubbed his face with his hands and held them against his eyes to collect himself before progressing with an investigation of the body. He wiped the sweat from his face, but his eyes struggled to look at the scene sitting before him. Things just got a hell of a lot more complicated.

From what Locilette could tell, the body had been there for quite some time. Weeks or maybe even months had gone by since this person had seen their final moments in this dark corner. He inched his way closer as he noticed an ID badge twisted around on the person's chest. Carefully, he reached out to flip it around to put a name, and a face, to the remains.

Kimberly Marloon

Assistant Docking Manager

Arkaan Empire: Yanagi

Crew Number: 47-C

It was almost impossible to tell by the state of the body, but it was a woman that rested here. By the looks of her ID picture she was relatively young, large brown eyes, and dirty blonde hair caked with stains of old, dried blood. He took a moment to ask the Pantheon to forgive her terrible act. Maybe his thoughts would be just enough for the Pantheon to grant her some kind of peace now that she was away from whatever compelled her to take her own life.

Locilette pulled out his PDA and reluctantly began to snap a few pictures of the gruesome scene. He made sure to get a wide shot of the entire body with the weapon still in her hand, as well as a close photo of the deceased woman's ID. He typed a few notes concerning how he discovered the body, and the circumstances around it, but there were still so many questions that remained to be answered. Why was she locked here in the cargo hold? Why would she take her own life without leaving some sort of note to a loved one? Why is she the only crew member he'd found so far, and do they share her fate?

As many unknowns surrounded the Yanagi, there were a few knowns. The ship has been unmanned for quite some time, the lack of damage on the ship's hull indicated there wasn't an outside threat, the full cargo hold proved that the vessel was destined for an eventual end point, and he had one confirmed crew casualty sitting before him. However, he hesitated before logging a cause of death. Something nagged at the back of his mind. Why would she kill herself in the one place of safety that had plenty of food? He tangled with a few theories, but shook the conspiracy theories running through his head. There was a deceased woman with an arc shot through her head, and the weapon was in her hand. He reluctantly logged it as *Self Inflicted Wound.*

Without warning, the single light above him cut out. The ambient sound of the Yanagi's systems ceased a moment later, leaving Locilette completely in the quiet darkness with the body. He turned quickly back to the cargo and darted the flashlight around the hold. There was something unnerving about the absolute silence of space. The only sounds he could hear was the sound of his own beating heart thumping in his ears. He turned to the body, just to appease a biting fear in his brain that the body would miraculously rise and attack him, but it remained slumped against the wall, just as it had done for months now. It's probably where it would be until the end of time if someone hadn't placed a derelict call in. There was something peaceful about that thought.

The sudden sound of the air being pumped through the vents almost startled Locilette. Seconds later, the light blinked a few times before providing the little illumination that was keeping a watchful eye over Kimberly's resting place. He hoped that she had a family somewhere out in the galaxy that loved her and was praying for her safe return home. He would make it one of his top priorities to see that her remains were returned to her next of kin for a proper burial. If nobody claimed her, perhaps this ship will become her tomb once the decision was made what to do with the Yanagi. His hope lay with the former.

Chapter Six

The hangar bay door slid open, but got stuck halfway. Locilette squeezed his way through, putting one leg through at a time. His frustration got the better of him as a few words of displeasure snuck through his lips, but he quickly composed himself as he saw his robotic partner standing ready by the Theseus. The bot's eyes were like shining emeralds that pierced through the low light of the hangar, but switched to its normal visual as it detected Locilette approaching.

"Hello, sir," the bot greeted with a stiff wave, but detected a change in his facial expression. "Are you alright, sir?"

Locilette nodded, ignoring Brinks's question. "Did you find anything?"

"I believe I did, sir. I'm uploading to the Theseus's backup storage now."

Locilette pulled out his PDA and flipped through the bit of evidence he accumulated. There was a confirmed body on board the ship, redacted documents of prisoners, and still no clue as to where the Yanagi's crew was. The more he thought about it, the more he just wanted to hold off further investigations until a few more Rangers arrived to back him up. However, the ship wasn't that terribly big.

He could probably know most of, if not the entire vessel before they even found the correct wormhole gate route to join him.

"Pardon my intrusions into your thoughts, sir." Brinks said, bringing Locilette out of his trance.

"The door you instructed me to go through led to the ship's brig. Most of the notes I compiled are irrelevant until your leisurely review. However, there were two incidents that I concluded would require your immediate attention."

Locilette tossed his PDA on the nose of his ship and crossed his arms. "Alright, let's hear it."

"First, I discovered that one of the cells was covered from floor to ceiling in some strange iconography I could not trace in my files," the bot explained as it projected the pictures through its eyes onto the dark hull of the Theseus.

Locilette examined it closely. He was fairly certain that he had never seen something like that before. There were new religious movements and small cults popping up all the time, which was never a concern. The Arkaan Empire was a vast place that held hundreds of billions of people and their different beliefs. It was a part of his tri-yearly training to catch up on religious and occult happenings throughout the empire, so the only thing that could explain it was it had to be something new. The laws of religious freedoms were very loose, so a random guy out in the frontier regions could claim to be the new savior, and as long as a handful of people believed him, he could register as an official faith. It was a system that he thought was grossly outdated and needed revising. Of course, he could say that about a lot of the archaic laws still floating around since the founding.

"Yeah, I'm not too familiar with that symbol, either. Perhaps it's a gang insignia of some sort? They're very common out here waiting for unsuspecting vessels to travel a little too close into the wrong space. They've been quite the nuisance for decades now." Locilette theorized while studying the picture a little closer.

Brink's eyes flashed back to a solid green. "I did not consider the possibility of it being a gang representation. Please stand by as I analyze it, and compare it against similar ones on record."

"You do that."

Locilette tried his best to give his security bot the benefit of the doubt. He was meant to protect things, not investigate lone derelict vessels in the middle of space. Even an amateur investigator would have checked and ran the strange markings for some sort of gang affiliation. It was the only logical place to start, especially when you worked within the realm of law enforcement. Even if his bot did turn up a match, Locilette failed to see a connection in the greater mystery. A gang member would be in a brig cell on his way to a prison cell on a desolate asteroid somewhere. Exactly where he belonged.

"Nothing in my records shares this emblem's likeness, sir."

Locilette raised an eyebrow. "Nothing in the major or minor gangs in this sector? What about surrounding?"

"No matches. I did a comparison to all active and former gangs documented within Arkaan territorial space."

"Perhaps it could be a lonely upstart?" He paced around for a few moments before going on. "Or, maybe a secret society organization like the *Brothers of Arkaa*, or the *Knights of Neit?*"

"I fail to see the difference between a secret society and a religious cult."

Locilette allowed a brief chuckle to escape his lips. "Who programmed you with humor?"

"I do not understand what you mean by that, sir."

Locilette shook his head. "Oh, forget it. After some consideration, I believe our best course of action is to continue our investigation. With some disturbing discoveries in the cargo hold, I think we should send an emergency call out to any nearby Rangers to assist us post investigation."

"What discoveries did you make in the cargo hold?" Brinks inquired.

Locilette slid the PDA across the Theseus's nose right into the bot's hand. "Have a look for yourself."

Brinks extended a small cable from its chest and plugged it into the device. The bot's eyes glowed green as it downloaded the evidence Locilette had collected. Its eyes slowly faded back to the passive blue as it finished processing the data. Brinks was quiet for a moment, its head tilted off to one side as it studied the pictures and notes that displayed before its eyes.

"The death of the crew member is quite tragic. In your notes you seem as if you knew the deceased individual. Did you?"

Locilette looked serious. "Not at all. Why do you ask?"

"Based on the way you write about her in your notes, it appears that you had some sort of connection with this individual due to your emotional response."

"Oh, well, look," Locilette said, feeling a creeping heat in his face. "That's just the way I write."

"I do not recall the need for emotional additions to official documentation in the Ranger's manual."

"Not that I have to explain myself to you, but there's more to the story than just finding a deceased corpse lying in a corner of a dark room. Who was the corpse? What were their life aspirations? What was their short-term and long-term plan that led them to the moment of their death? Emotions are imbued within the moments of these people's lives. Understanding them as people first and victims second will allow you to see much deeper." Locilette lectured, as he would to any new Ranger. However, this wasn't a Ranger.

"I apologize, sir, but I do not understand."

He nodded slowly, "Yeah, I know."

Locilette made his way around to the extended staircase of the Theseus still open from their arrival. Trying to explain Arkaan emotions to a non-sentient being was like telling a thief not to steal. The matter was simply impossible. He had always felt that every crime is triggered by a motive, and a motive was triggered by an emotion. Those seemed to bleed into each other in most of the criminal calls he had to respond to over the years. Not too many of the newer Rangers these days seemed to have developed an understanding for that. Now that he thought about it, most of the senior ones missed it, as well.

A thief that steals, most of the time, doesn't steal for the pleasure of stealing. He steals bread to feed his starving family on a poor, orbital station in the far reaches of space. The love for his family pushed that man to commit a crime. As illegal as it was, Locilette understood at a core level why that individual would do something like that. A defunct business owner could start to launder money because he is so far in debt his family would become targets of the sharks who placed the bait. He could think of a hundred examples, but the ending would always be the same.

This didn't apply to everything though. There were some people in this galaxy who would do others harm just for the pure pleasure of it. Locilette's theory would still prove to be true, but the emotion would be different. It would be much darker. The emotion behind the motive would be lust. Lust for power, for riches, to see the last moment of someone's life slip away within their fingers. It was this dirty detail that Locilette would dig and dig until he discovered the driving force behind the worst deeds carried out among the citizens of Arkaa.

A curiosity did strike him sometimes when the topic of emotional-driven motives would arise. He wondered if other sentient races in the universe reacted the same to similar situations as the worst of Arkaans get themselves into. The Arkaan Empire's closest neighbor, the *N'Tari*, were beings made of complete plant fiber and produced their own food for their people by all collectively absorbing the light from the nearest star. Did they behave the same as the people who walk the streets of the Orbital cities, or were they just as peaceful and docile as he had studied?

Maybe that was going to be his retirement project. He would travel the cosmos with his wonderful wife, understanding the complex emotions of every known race in the universe to build a deep psychological profile of each one. It would be an incredible series of case studies that he would immerse himself in, as well as be a tool for future generations of Rangers could use when they eventually do cross paths with these intelligent species. The real key to that plan was actually getting his wife to sign on board with that.

He figured she must be getting bored on Kronos Prime, but he knew that she loved her simple life that they built. She certainly kept herself busy. Along with raising their boys, she also enjoyed getting involved in the happenings of local politics on the capital planet of the Kronos System. Perhaps he could hire a group of travelers to compile the information he needed to write the book from home to appease both of their aspirations. Now *that* felt like something he could find peace in.

Locilette made his way to the side of his ship, but stopped as he discovered that the stairs were retracted back into the side. He didn't recall retracting them when they first stepped foot on the Yanagi. Every time he would deploy on foot somewhere, he made it a point to keep the stairs down just in case a chase ensued, or he needed a quick exfiltration off site. It wasn't necessarily a sign for concern, but it was a great inconvenience if he made the silly mistake himself.

"Hey, Brinks," Locilette called out from around the side of the ship. "Did you close the side door on the ship?"

Brinks cocked his metallic head to one side. "I did not, sir. I am quite sure we left it open on our departure."

"I figured I did, but the damn thing's closed now for some reason."

"That's quite peculiar, sir."

Locilette slid open to cover then typed in his pass code on the keypad. It beeped an error code. He shook his head, and typed it in again slower this time to make sure he got it right. Again an error beeped at him. Something about this made his stomach slowly begin to sink. He tried again and again, but every time, the Theseus would refuse to accept his credentials. He snatched up his PDA and attempted to remote link with the Theseus to command it to open the side door. He noticed that the device was connected to upload to the ship's memory, but all access to the ship's remote functions had been disabled.

"Brinks, I can't get in the ship."

The bot stepped beside him to examine the keypad. "Did you enter your pass code correctly, sir?"

"I know my fucking code, Brinks. Something's wrong here."

"Perhaps I can link back up and try to bypass the ship's security systems." Brinks offered.

Locilette gave him a nod. "Do it. Get it done."

Brinks's eyes flashed back green as it entered the system. After a few moments, its eyes returned to normal. Without saying a word it extended a long cable and plugged it into the outlet beside the keypad on the ship's siding. After a few anxious minutes, the bot unplugged itself from the side and retracted the wire back into its chest housing. Brinks took a moment to process the information it collected, then turned back to the Ranger.

"Sir, it would appear that we have been forcefully removed from the Theseus's list of administrators. We are unable to use any of the vessel's systems." The bot explained.

Locilette's expression grew grim. "What the hell does that mean, exactly?"

"Sir, from what I could identify, a third party was able to access the ship's authorized user files and delete them. A single profile was created to replace your deleted one."

"What's the name? Who would be stupid enough to mess with a Ranger responder?"

"That's the peculiar part, sir."

Locilette's patience was wearing thin. "Spit it out, damn it!"

"Sir, the new profile is assigned to a Kimberly Marloon."

A sense of disbelief rose within him. That simply couldn't be. Kimberly Marloon was sitting in that cargo hold dead and had been for quite some time. It's not like her ghost hacked into his ship's onboard computers and locked him out. He told himself over and over how absurd such a thought like that was. No, there was something far more at play here than Locilette originally anticipated. Something much more menacing that had something to do with that poor young woman. Someone else was here with them.

"Brinks," Locilette spoke calmly and clearly. "Is there another way someone could access our ship's systems without stepping foot on her?"

"Negative, sir. Security profiles can only be changed at the vessel's main computer. Do you suspect foul play has been used?"

"Yeah." His head nodded slowly. "Yeah, I do."

Just as Locilette was contemplating his next move the sound of moving machinery broke the silence of the quiet hangar. His first instinct was to draw his pistol. Brinks followed a brief moment later, the bot's eyes turned a dark red as it re-entered combat mode. The tip of the plasma arc rifle pointed to the corner of the hangar bay where a series of numbers were counting down on a large monitor above a door tucked away. The two focused on the door as the number passed from three, then two, then one. There was a loud ding, and the doors slid apart, revealing a tiny space with a buzzing yellow light within.

Locilette and Brinks didn't budge. Both of their weapons were still fixed on the general location as if a platoon of insurgents were going to start pouring out any second. That thought would tick away as the doors remained opened, almost beckoning the two to come inside. Brinks moved up a couple of feet to the left, and zoomed in his telescopic sight to peer within the newly-discovered room. The bot scanned it for a moment, and determined that there were no present hostiles.

"Anything?" Locilette questioned.

"Negative, sir." Brinks responded, its voice now a deep and authoritative boom as it remained in the heightened state of combat mode. "It appears to be an elevator of sorts."

"You have any clue where it goes?"

The bot tilted its head without looking back. "I apologize, but another negative. My best calculations compared to similar vessels would be either the crew quarters or the cafeteria."

"This doesn't sit well with me, Brinks." Locilette warned. "It looks like an invitation, if you ask me."

"An unfortunate agreement, sir."

Locilette moved up to get a better look inside the elevator. The hangar was pretty bare, making his methodical approach feel uncomfortably exposed. He motioned for his Secura-Droid to follow close behind, which the bot obeyed without question. His pistol was extended in front, keeping whatever could pop out of that tiny space in check, but he knew nothing was going to be inside the elevator. The real surprise was going to be waiting for them once they reached the other side of the lift. The question that Locilette had, though, was if he was going to oblige whomever it was who sent it.

"Okay, we're going to go up and take a look."

Brinks's head snapped to the right, "I do not think that is the wisest course of action, sir. Perhaps we should continue to try and get into the Theseus to call for reinforcements."

"In case you hadn't noticed yet, we're already tied into this investigation. We are obligated to move toward potential danger if there is even the slightest possibility that civilians need our help. It's my job as a Ranger, and your job as a Secura-Droid to obey my commands."

Brinks processed that for a moment. Locilette knew what risks came with being a Ranger. Putting yourself in harm's way for the citizenry wasn't just in the Ranger creed, it was a requirement. Any Ranger caught neglecting on his or her duty in the event of a crisis that led to the death of civilians was punished severely. The order took their reputation for being first responders very seriously. If you're first on the scene, then you better make sure you're prepared to do what you must to handle the situation, even if you're out there operating alone.

Locilette only knew of one instance where a Ranger refused to perform his duty. It was a guy who he graduated from the academy with many years ago who found himself responding to an armed hijacking of a small cargo ship headed for an orbital city in the Hera system. The Ranger knew that he was outnumbered and outgunned, but he still had an obligation to keep the situation under control until backup arrived. He allowed the hijackers to escape with the vessel, along with fourteen civilians on board.

After word had gotten around that he failed his duty, he had to stand trial by court martial. He was found guilty and forced to burn his uniform in the presence of the Chief and his graduating class. It was one of the greatest shames a Ranger could ever go through. After his dishonorable discharge, he was banished to the frontier of the Arkaan Empire and barred from ever leaving the poor Orbital City they found best suited to take him in under his circumstances. It was a horrific fate for one who was once looked so highly upon by society. It was a fate that Locilette would rather die than face.

"Weapons at the ready," Locilette commanded. "Let's move."

Locilette stepped inside the elevator first and swept the tip of his pistol over every corner. Brinks followed, having to bend down slightly to enter. It was small and cramped, giving the feeling that this elevator was used mainly for transporting the crew to and from the hangar for various reasons. He couldn't help but wonder how anyone could transport supplies to the mess hall, or even classified shipments in such a small space. Unless it was done in multiple trips, there was no way he could see even moving more than one crate at a time.

The small light that hung overhead showed only two buttons set within the control panel by the door. One had the image of a door on it while the other had two arrows going up and down. Locilette paused just before pressing it. Brinks noticed and turned its head slightly, but didn't say anything. Locilette took in a deep breath and let out a long sigh. He met the bot's red eyes and gave it a nod. He pressed the button and backed up into the back corner, and lifted his pistol toward the door as the Theseus faded away behind the metallic doors.

The elevator was darker now. The red glow of Brink's eyes shone on the walls, giving the small space a foreboding sense of uneasiness. After a few seconds, the control panel let out a loud *ding,* then jolted as it began to move upward. Locilette could hear the cables raising the lift creak and rattle as it pulled them slowly to the next floor. He could feel the sweat begin to drip from his hands as his grip on his pistol tightened after every passing second. Then, with a violent shake, the elevator stopped. The doors didn't immediately open, leaving the two in a suspended state of anticipation. He quickly wiped the sweat from his forehead, and instantly returned his hands around the grip of his weapon.

The sound of the doors unlatching broke Locilette from his intense stare, and the old metal doors separated. The grinding metal sent a disturbing rush through his body that made the hair on the back of his neck stand. A long corridor stretched before them, but both sets of their eyes were drawn to the ceiling. Locilette felt his heart sink, but he steeled himself to not show any kind of reaction.

A large drooping sign with dark, red lettering was there to greet them. Streaks of red trailed down from each letter that at one point dripped into a tiny pool below. The sign appeared to have been created from a torn white bed sheet, and strung up with torn pieces of cloth from the sign. The convenient placement made it ripple as the vent behind it blew the warm air throughout the hall.

"*Welcome to the Party,*" Locilette read.

He quickly lowered his gaze to the rest of the dark corridor to make sure the sign wasn't a distraction. On a closer look, the hall was littered with trash and debris. A plate from the metal walls seemed to have been torn off and now stuck out at a 45 degree angle. Several more long strands of cloth dipped in dark red hung from the ceiling all the way down to the door at the end, like heraldry of crimson.

Every ounce of Locilette's instincts told him to go back to his ship, but a disturbing intrigue took over him. He slowly stepped out, checking the area around the elevator doors. They tried to close as he moved through, but Brinks's hand slid through the gap just in time to force the doors back open. They both crept out, keeping their eyes down the corridor for any kind of excuse to light up every inch of it with plasma arc discharge. The sound of the elevator doors closing behind made them freeze just a few feet short of the banner above them. Locilette began to wonder if this sign was meant for them or someone else who had passed through here before. He began to pray it was the latter.

"Brinks," he whispered while studying the banner. "Can you tell if that's blood?"

The beam of the bot's red eyes darted across the lettering. "I am a Secura-Droid, sir, not a Robotic Forensic Assistant."

"Did somebody program you with sass? Just do it."

"Very well, sir." The bot extended itself higher to get a better look at the sign. It studied it for several minutes as Locilette remained focused on the hall ahead. The red lights from Brinks's eyes flashed green as it processed something, then returned to the crimson of combat mode. "I believe that the words are 90% likely to be written in the blood of an Arkaan."

Locilette nodded. "Alrighty. Things just got complicated."

"Agreed, sir," the bot said, kneeling down next to him.

"Okay, well, let's head back to-"

The elevator buzzed to life and began to descend from behind them. The two quickly trained their weapons on the doors. The bright *2* that showed above the door slowly changed to a *1* as the sound of the lift faded away to the lower level. Suddenly, Locilette and Brinks found themselves back in the quiet of the corridor, but the uncomfortable disturbance still lingered. Locilette's entire body was tense in anticipation for something to happen. The exposed feeling of his back to the open corridor made a rush of adrenaline pump through him, forcing a quick glance back to make sure they were still secure.

He tapped the button on the panel to call the elevator back, but after a few moments, it didn't respond. He pressed it over and over again, but nothing happened. It was as if the elevator had completely died. The button glowed a dim orange, so he was fairly certain that it still had power. It just all of a sudden stopped moving for reasons he couldn't explain.

"Give me a hand with this." He motioned to the door.

Locilette moved to one side of the door, and Brinks shouldered its rifle to move to the other. The two tried to grip the small gap where the two doors met, the fingers only finding enough room for their tips to sneak through. He counted down, and the two pulled as hard as they could. It didn't budge. Even Brinks's powerful robotic strength didn't seem to aid them much. There was a sinking feeling in Locilette's stomach. He quickly began to feel as though he was being funneled like a mouse in a maze, and this was only the entrance.

"Brinks, try and hack it," Locilette said, quickly turning into a combat stance to watch the end of the hall.

The bot obeyed without question, pulling off the elevator control panel to expose the wires within. Brinks analyzed them for a few moments before cutting certain ones. The lights flickered as the wires were tapped against each other, but the door remained closed. Brinks tried to reconnect the wires as they were the best to his ability, then stuffed them back into the wall.

"Sir, apologies, it appears I can not wire the doors to open from here."

Locilette raised an eyebrow. "Why the hell not?"

"My best calculations would point to an emergency halt being implemented into the door's operating software after being commanded to return to the bottom level."

"We're being lured and baited," Locilette said grimly.

"I would say, sir," Brinks corrected, pulling the rifle off its back, "that we have already fallen for their ruse."

All Locilette could do was nod. He didn't know what was happening on this ship, but it was beginning to appear quite clear that it was nothing good. He hated to admit it, but Brinks was right. They took the bait that dangled on the end of a string and stepped right into a trap as perfectly as he had ever seen. One thing he couldn't understand was why here? What really happened on the Yanagi? There was no going back now, so the only way to uncover what happened here was to press on. Even if it meant stepping out of the frying pan and into the fire.

Locilette's entire body tensed as the ship's speakers began to hiss with static. Brinks threw itself against the wall and Locilette dropped down to a knee. His head whipped around, trying to locate the source of the ear-shattering noise. He spotted a small speaker hanging on the corner wall behind them near the ceiling. Almost as soon as his eyes found it, the static stopped. In its place, a soft rumble of a voice came across.

"Hey boys." The voice growled through the speaker. "It's chow time!"

There was a loud click that echoed down the corridor, drawing Locilette's attention. The door on the opposite end now displayed a green light from the door panel that he was certain wasn't there moments ago. They were just being led deeper and deeper into whatever madhouse that had risen here. As badly as he just wanted to stay where they were, he knew that wasn't an option. The only thing they could do is keep moving and figure out exactly who was behind his psycho farce.

Chapter Seven

The dusty metal door slid up into the door frame above. Locilette and Brinks stepped into a small hall with several groups of shelving on both sides. Each shelf was stocked fully with various cleaning chemicals as well as an abundance of toiletries. This must have been one of the crew's supply rooms for necessities as well as a storage place for the janitorial staff's equipment. Based on how little of the stock had been taken, Locilette could only assume that this was a secondary storage space.

It was pretty common for vessels like the Yanagi to have small alcoves dedicated for the storage of non-essential cargo. It was the best use of the sometimes limited space that the crew had to face every day. Every nook and cranny could be useful in some capacity, as long as crew management was just the tiniest bit creative. Finding alternative uses for small, otherwise overlooked, spaces was considered an art out here on long voyages. Not to mention, Locilette found it fun to see where he could convert into place to store his odds and ends.

The Theseus was no different. He had developed a great system for storing the equipment and gear he didn't use every single day. A prime example of this was his food storage. His ship didn't have much storage for rations beyond a built-in pantry that came with the ship when he bought it. His job being what it was had him out in the void of space for months at a time to places that didn't give much opportunity resupply. So, similar to the crew of the Yanagi, he had to get creative.

The tiny corridor that lined the center of the Theseus, he discovered, had a lip that was hidden behind the paneling near the ceiling. It was just a square foot of unused space that extended the entire length of the corridor. Locilette found it silly to waste so much space, so he pulled off each of the panels and installed hinges on them for easy access. He docked at a bustling orbital city and purchased enough canned food and cereals to feed himself for at least six months out there in space. On top of his standard issued Ranger meals kept in the crates in the engine room, he knew he wouldn't be starving any time soon.

He respected the use of space wisely. The crew that walked these halls were experienced enough to know that, so any kind of thoughts of the crew going missing due to being too green for deep space travel seemed to vanish from his thoughts. These were seasoned men and women. His thoughts were interrupted as the skin crawling sound of cackling came from beyond the door that sat closed in front of them. Locilette caught Brinks's plates opening up for exhaust in preparation for an altercation in the corner of his eye. He steeled himself just the same.

They stood on opposite sides of the door, weapons at the ready. Locilette put his ear to the door, trying to hear any kind of movement on the other side, but the ambient sounds of the ship made it near impossible to differentiate between what was around him and beyond. He lifted his hand to the bot and began to count down.

3... 2... 1...

With a final nod, Brinks tapped the button on the door's control panel, making it shoot upward into the door frame. Locilette breached first, moving in to the left, followed by Brinks, who mirrored him. The two swept their weapons around the immediate area, then halted for a few moments to observe. Locilette hadn't done a breaching maneuver in such a long time that he caught his hands shaking with adrenaline. As soon as he was adequately sure that there wasn't an immediate danger, he took in a few deep breaths to calm his nerves.

Locilette's eyes began to scan the expansive room around them. Dozens of long, white tables dotted around the massive room with benches tucked neatly underneath each one. On the left wall was a large opening with a long metal shelf lining the bottom of it. In the corner just beyond it was a table stacked high with plastic trays still awaiting to serve the hungry crew of the Yanagi for a meal that would never come. The opening had a chain link gate pulled down to prevent anyone coming through for a late night snack whenever the kitchen crew was off duty.

Each table had a large trash can that appeared to still be empty from where the two of them stood. The darkness made it quite difficult to make things out, but the powerful beam from Locilette's flashlight brought daylight in small increments around. The empty trash led him to believe that whatever happened to the crew must have taken place between meal times. It was an eerie feeling being in a place that used to host such laughter and conversation that now sat dark and forever quiet. It was a disturbing feeling that he tried to just push from his mind, but it stuck with him as the hairs on his neck once more stood.

"Brinks, do you see a light switch?" Locilette asked, running the beam of his flashlight along the walls.

"Negative, sir." The bot responded.

"Something in here was making noise, so let's stay on our guard."

"Of course, sir. Would you like me to conduct a thermal sweep of the area?"

Locilette looked back at the bot. "It would've been nice to know you could do that earlier."

"Apologies, sir. I was under the impression you were fully aware of what my capabilities are."

"Brinks," Locilette said, allowing a bit of annoyance to slip into his voice, "just do it."

The bot's eyes swapped to the thermal lenses, making them appear pure ebony. The mess hall surrounding them turned into shades of blues, greens, and the occasional red as its eyes drifted past a piece of machinery. Brinks carefully scanned around them, but stopped as a fading heat signature appeared in its view. It took a moment to process what it actually was, but the bot was almost certain what it was looking at. There appeared to be someone sitting at one of the tables in the darkness. Brinks raised its rifle on the heat source, rotating around to the right side to get a better look.

The figure appeared to be laying its head down on the table. The heat signature was displaying mainly parts of yellow, but near the core was a red spot indicating that whoever this was most likely met their end rather recently. The figure had something sitting on the table in front of it, but Brinks couldn't make out exactly what it could be. Locilette breathed a sigh of relief as he seemed to have found the light switch by the serving shutters. Brinks quickly flipped back to its normal optical before the blinding light filled the thermal lenses, possibly damaging them.

A click echoed around the mess hall, but only one light seemed to come to life. Locilette looked around in confusion, until his eyes were set on the horrible sight that sat in the center of the room. The body of a man was slumped over onto the table. Every light in the mess hall seemed to have been busted out except this specific one directly above the grizzly scene. Locilette froze and shot a glance over to Brinks, who was examining the scene from the opposite side. He could tell that the bot more than likely saw it in thermal before as its rifle was still pointed at the corpse.

Sitting just a couple of feet away was a well decorated cake. The icing appeared to be a perfectly sculpted buttercream that showed signs of a careful hand creating intricate designs. The cake itself was tall, sitting just slightly taller than the man's head resting on the table. He crept forward until he spotted the message that was prepared for them written in the same dark crimson as that on the banner. It was clearly written in the man's blood as several tiny trails followed the words back to the poor guy's lifeless head.

Too much sugar will rot your teeth!

"Holy Pantheon, please accept this man into your arms," Locilette prayed. That was all he really could do at that moment.

"Sir, I believe this man was murdered quite recently." Brinks explained. "My thermal optics showed a faint heat source coming from him, but most of the body had already fallen close to room temperature."

He wiped the sweat from his head. "It would seem that the crew, or what's left of the crew, is being used as set pieces in some kind of fucked up perfromance."

"I agree, sir. It would also appear that our assailant is also quite the talented baker."

That one had him stumped. There's no way whoever was toying with them had enough time to bake a cake as perfect as this without plenty of time in advance. Not to mention stage the man up with the cake in the perfect scene to be discovered. No, this couldn't be the work of a single man. Could it?

"Not unless whoever this is isn't working alone." Locilette reasoned.

"A very plausible theory, sir."

"Regardless if he or she is acting alone in this, one thing is abundantly clear…"

The bot tilted its head. "What would that be, sir?"

"We're dealing with a showman, a performer. Everything this person does will have meaning and purpose. Trust me, the devil is in the details. Freaks like this take subliminal messaging to the next level."

"I apologize, sir, but I am not quite sure I understand."

"This is a game, Brinks." Locilette declared grimly. "The pieces are scattered about, but this psychopath is going to want us to put them together to create the picture. There's case studies from similar crimes. This is hardly the first time we've seen this, and it won't be the last."

The bot stared blankly at its assigned Ranger. Locilette could tell it was trying to process what he had said, but he could sense the barrier in Brink's purpose against the situation they have on hand. He needed another trained investigative mind. He needed another Ranger with him, now more than ever. However, if he couldn't have that, he could use the tools he had to their most efficient use to get this madness of a situation under control.

"Brinks, can you adjust your own coding?" Locilette asked.

"I can, sir, but not anything to do with my operating functions."

Locilette nodded, "Perfect. Can you add a code to allow yourself to take in association connected information?"

"I can certainly try, sir." Brinks's eyes began to glow a bright green as it got to work.

The air seemed thick in the mess hall. It felt like the humidity was much higher in this part of the ship than the rest. It made the uncomfortable situation that he found himself in not only emotionally such, but physically, as well. He didn't want it to seem like it was bothering him just in case he was being watched by whomever it was doing these things, but under his combat suit, he was sweating bullets.

Locilette took in the rest of the hall surrounding them. Beyond the scene in the center, it appeared to be just an ordinary cafeteria. Not a single thing was out of place. He looked over at the door directly behind the face-down corpse, but something caught his eye. Something was hanging from the side of it that clearly didn't belong. He tilted his flashlight down to reveal an old combination lock closed around a welded loop. He could tell just by a glance that it was a newer weld done by inexperienced hands.

"You got to be kidding me," Locilette said, letting the lock slide off his hand. It crashed into the door with a loud *clank* that didn't seem to bother Brinks.

The cake that sat perfectly aligned with the corpse was another story. It was made to almost perfection by the hand of a true baking craftsman. It was entirely possible that this psychopath was a talented baker, but a lousy handyman. It began to dawn on him that the cake could possibly be a calling card. From what he understood about the active serial killers roaming the Arkaan Empire, each one excelled at one specific thing. One thing that dominated their persona. It often seemed that a specific craft or hobby became the killer's identity more than his or her actual name.

As he surveyed the scene carefully displayed before him, his mind began to wander to a particular case study he researched at the academy. He recalled a case that pursued a killer from the Selene System. This older man had been active for nearly forty years and would only be caught after allowing the Rangers to close in on his concealed home on a crashed cargo ship on an asteroid. His calling card that he adopted produced some of the most disturbing images he had seen the entirety of his training.

This man the media dubbed *The Funnies Killer* would drain the blood from his victims, then carve four panel comics directly into the flesh of their back. Scenes that would deliver a comedic conundrum for the many characters he would produce followed by a timely punchline would be produced on a canvas of torn meat across the deceased corpses of his countless victims. The imagery used was so light-hearted compared to the brutal acts that were used to bring them into existence. The pictures he saw of those poor victims at the crime scenes haunted him for weeks. The thought of people like that being out in the galaxy made his skin crawl, but it was up to the brave men and women of the Rangers to make sure these monsters are locked away in a cage for the rest of their lives. Now that he stumbled into the path of one himself, he felt a surge of confidence to do what needed to be done.

He pulled out his PDA and began to document the scene. The flash on the front camera illuminated the body, exposing the pool of blood that surrounded the man's mouth and poured onto his lap. Locilette could follow the trail as it stained his pants, eventually pooling on the floor around the chair. He took several shots of the cake from different angles as well as the message that was scribed in the man's blood. He read the message over and over again, trying to piece it together. What could the cake have to do with the man? Could the sugar rotting your teeth be a metaphor for something, or possibly could the calling card have some kind of correlation to a dentist?

Locilette glanced at Brinks who's eyes were now blinking slowly as it applied the new coding to itself. He turned to take another picture at a wider angle, but froze as the dots began to connect. *Too much sugar will rot your teeth...* He placed the PDA on the table and walked over to the man's side. He kneeled down low to get a good look at the man's face, but was startled to see his eyes open. His eyes were glazed over and foggy, as if the life left them quite a while ago.

The man's mouth was closed, but the blood around it gave credit to his theory. The last thing he wanted to do was touch a corpse, but Locilette knew it was his responsibility to follow any leads he may have. Even if it meant opening the mouth of a dead man. He reached under the man's arm that held his head in place on the table and tugged at his jaw. Rigor mortis had begun to set in, making it stiff. He felt his stomach start to turn as he braced against the man's cheek, and with the other hand, he pulled down forcefully.

A disturbing cracking sound came from the corpse's mouth, making Locilette want to turn his head and throw up, but his professionalism and training prevailed. He pointed his flashlight into the man's mouth and his theory proved accurate. The man's mouth was completely bare of any teeth, each one seemingly having been removed by force, leaving only red gums torn to pieces. He prayed that it happened after the man's death, but something in his gut told him differently. He couldn't imagine what this poor man had gone through in the final hour of his life.

"Update completed, sir." Brinks announced from behind him.

Locilette was too consumed with his thoughts to realize that the bot had said anything. He couldn't wrap his head around the removal of the teeth, but not display them in any way. From the little he knew of this killer, or killers, this person wasn't shy to hide their doings. No, there had to be another reason. There was another piece of this puzzle he was missing.

He stood up and began to look around the table, his eyes moving in the dark like an owl searching for an unsuspecting field mouse. He dropped down on his knees, looking underneath the table, but nothing seemed to be out of sorts. He tilted the beam of the light upward to examine the underside of the table above him, but there was nothing more than someone scratching *Kellender is a whore* into the table. There was nothing quite like a space faring crew expressing themselves on the property of their employers that would remain until the ship bought new tables. Locilette knew that was a rare occurrence, so this message would more than likely live on, even if the one who wrote it is now another victim of this soulless mad man.

"Is there something I can aid you in, sir?" The bot offered.

Locilette climbed back to his feet, his gear feeling heavier. "Yeah, check this out. The teeth in the man's mouth have been removed."

"Too much sugar will rot your teeth."

Locilette nodded. "Yeah, there has to be a connection with a rot of some kind. Maybe he is referring to a bad character within the crew that created a rot among them?"

"A very plausible theory, sir."

"Or, maybe *he* could've been the rot that was removed." He continued. "But what about the sugar? What in the burning hell could that represent? Love? Passion? Both?"

"Could the cake potentially be the sugar in the puzzle? Cakes are made with an exuberant amount of sugar, are they not?" Brinks theorized, pointing a long metal finger at the desert sitting idle.

"Well, I think-" Locilette thought for a moment. "Pantheon above, please tell me it's not."

He unclipped his combat knife from his thigh, and pulled it out. He hesitated as his eyes burned into the icing of the cake. He prayed to anything that was listening that he wasn't going to find in there what Brinks suggested. He couldn't even imagine how something like

125

that could even be possible, but he brought himself back to reality. When dealing with people like these, absolutely anything was possible.

He gripped the rubber handle of the six inch blade tightly. His hand began to sweat creating an uncomfortable, moist feeling inside of his gloves. He took a deep breath, then angled the knife's razor sharp blade a few inches above the cake. Very gently, he pressed it down, cutting a clean line straight through it. The blade tapped against the metal table beneath it. Locilette carefully pulled out his knife, and angled another cut to slice a perfectly-shaped triangle.

He slid the knife under the slice of cake, and delicately removed it from the rest of the whole. He pulled it out a few inches, and the dread began to creep into his stomach. He pushed the disturbing thoughts to the back of his mind, and steeled his mind. In one fluid motion, he grabbed his flash light and aimed it down on the slice of cake. The light illuminated a yellow interior, but there was more within. More than enough to make an untrained man vomit in a horrifying blend of fear and disgust.

Within the three layered cake sat white specks dotted throughout the perfectly baked yellow interior. Locilette leaned down, and used the tip of his knife to pick out one of the specks from the top layer, and drop it on the table. It clicked as it hit the metal, and recoiled back a bit as he discovered that it was just as he feared. Baked inside the cake was the man's teeth.

"That is indeed a tooth from an Arkaan male, sir." Brinks observed.

"No shit, Brinks. It's the teeth from our friend here, no doubt. The only question is how does figuring that out help us?"

"I would say it does not at all, sir."

Locilette raised an eyebrow. "What makes you say that?"

"According to my calculations, we are on a predetermined path orchestrated by an individual who is capable of causing much harm to others. We were led into a closed environment where our movements are restricted, and our path forward is controlled by this individual. Based on these circumstances I would place our odds for survival at around 9.7%"

"Wow, you doubt me that much?"

"I am simply reading the results, sir."

Locilette shook his head, turning back to the cake. "We'll figure it out. If this person wanted to kill us, we'd more than likely be dead already. There's an overarching story here that we've yet to reach the climax. Why else would someone go through so much trouble just to send us to the grave with the rest of the Yanagi's crew?"

"That is based on an assumption that the crew is all deceased. We have yet to find certain proof of that fact, sir."

"That's very true. Though, I would say the number of dead would be pretty high for this guy to do what he has done uncontested. In fact-" Locilette stopped as it came to him. It was like turning on a light in the endless dark.

The numbers. The numbers were the key, not the message.

"Are you alright, sir?"

"The cake," Locilette pointed with his knife. "The combination lock on the door…"

The bot's head turned to examine the door behind the body. The blue eyes looked closely at the vertical number slots lining the right side of the lock. Brinks rotated the numbers until they were all facing on 0. Each one of the slots displayed a single digit. Brinks tugged at it to see if brute force would be sufficient enough to get them through, but the tungsten metal was just too strong to break.

"Sir, I am failing to spot a connection," Brinks relinquished, allowing the lock on the door to slide from its hand.

"Look at the lock," Locilette said, pointing his knife at it. "There are three numbers in a vertical descending line. This is a three layered cake. I'd bet my life on it that the number of teeth baked into this is going to give us our combination to get the hell out of here."

The bot's eyes flashed green for a moment. "The average adult Arkaan male has 28 teeth in their mouth. By that figure, the combination we seek is *028* or *280*."

"Try it." Locilette instructed with a quick nod.

Brinks turned quickly and grabbed the lock. It looked so tiny in the bot's massive metallic hands, but its fingers worked with precision to turn the numbers. After a few seconds the first code was lined up on the pad. With a quick tug it didn't budge. Brinks reset it, and tried the second group of numbers, but still the lock failed to open. The bot straightened up to look at the Ranger for further instructions.

Locilette couldn't help but fold his arms. He began to pace around the table running the entire scenario again and again in his head. If the average Arkaan male had 28 teeth, shouldn't that be it? Unless this particular man did not have all of his teeth, meaning Locilette would have to pull every single tooth out to count. That was something he would dread doing, but he couldn't just sit in here forever and wait to be slaughtered by a mad man. He had to figure this out.

He took a deep breath, and leaned forward on the table. Brinks stood by the lock, staring at him with its big blue eyes, but it didn't seem to break Locilette's concentration. He needed three numbers from a three layered cake. He was fairly certain the combination had to result from the number of teeth in the cake, but was it the cake as a whole? Was it the total number of teeth? No. There were layers for a reason.

Locilette sprang up with enthusiasm. "It's not the total number of teeth that's in the cake! Each number represents a layer. We're going to have to separate each layer and count exactly how many teeth were baked into each one individually."

"Very well, sir. Standing by."

Without a second thought, he carefully removed the top layer of the piece he removed and set it to the side. As he flipped it over, it made a grotesque plopping noise as the icing hit the table. He turned his attention to the rest of the cake and slid the blade of his knife in the gap the piece left. He followed the thin line the icing between the layers made with delicate precision. The last thing he wanted was to accidentally cut too deep where the number of the teeth would be thrown off.

As soon as he was confident in the cut, he lifted the knife to remove the top layer. The sticky icing made it slightly more difficult than Locilette would've hoped, as the rest of the cake lifted with it for a moment, but it eventually gave in. He flipped it over, allowing it to land icing side down just like the sliced removed from its whole. He sighed deeply. With his clean hand, he quickly documented what his findings were, and what he was about to do. The other Rangers weren't going to believe this. After a few notes, he tossed it to Brinks, who caught it in midair with lightning reflexes.

"We're going to have to document this as best as we can," Locilette said, preparing himself to break apart the layer.

"Sir, I can also document evidence, as well. Would it not be redundant to record the same thing twice?"

He glanced up at the bot. "Normally, yes. But since we can't link with the Theseus at the moment, we have to act as each other's back up for evidence storage."

"I see. A completely valid point. I will begin double recording at once, sir." The bot replied, holding up Locilette's PDA to begin.

With a quick nod, Locilette began to dissect the cake. He found the white teeth dotted throughout the layer, some covered with thick icing, and some buried within the fluffy yellow cake. He wondered how the heat from the baking process didn't discolor the pearly whites in the slightest, but he wasn't an expert on forcefully removed teeth either, so he let the thought slip away.

Before him sat a mangled mess of sugar. As much as he tried to stay focused, his mind began to wonder to a happier time. A time where he was home enjoying one of his boy's birthdays with a smash cake baked by his wife. The boy covered every inch of his high chair with icing and chocolate cake, but the pure joy on his face made the clean up worth it. It took at least forty-five minutes after their family left to get that mess cleaned, but not for a single second did he complain. He loved every bit of it. He wished he was home.

"Nine teeth. The first number is nine." Locilette announced.

Brinks turned the number until the nine faced out. Locilette carved his knife into a wide circle in the middle of the two remaking layers to separate them. He lifted it up, but cursed loudly as it collapsed onto the table. He breathed a sigh of relief that it landed a few inches away from the mess of the top layer. Without wasting a single moment, he dove his hands in, feeling for anything small and hard. One by one he pulled out the teeth and lined them up neatly beside the layer. He counted them several times just to make sure he got it right.

"Alright, we have seven teeth here." He called out, wiping his gloves on the edge of the table.

"Seven." Brinks repeated, inputting it into the lock.

That just left the last layer. Locilette was beyond over this sick game. It felt quite belittling to cover himself with icing like he was some kind of child. He imagined what he would do to whoever was doing this when he found him.

He began to pull the bottom layer apart. One by one he found the man's teeth buried deep within the blend of cake and frosting. Just like the other two, he lined them up for easier counting once he was certain it was all of them. As the cake and icing started to move around, Locilette caught a glimpse of something underneath the cake. He stopped for a moment just to confirm if what he was seeing was real. There was more writing under it.

Trying not to lose his place in the search, he focused on retrieving the teeth until globs of cake and frosting covered every free inch of space on the table. With a wide swipe on the table top, he pushed away the mess to reveal another message. This time, the Ranger felt a shiver run up his spine. He could only guess what the meaning behind it was, but if he was going to be honest with himself, he probably didn't want to know.

"Hey, Brinks," Locilette called out. "We have another message here."

"Another clue from our assailant, sir?"

Locilette shook his head. "I don't think so. It feels more like a threat. It says: *Is it getting hot in here?*"

"That does sound quite foreboding, sir. I would advise that we prepare ourselves for possible conflict."

"Agreed." Locilette sighed, then counted his line of pulled teeth. "Last number is eight. This guy only had twenty-four teeth, it would seem."

The bot rotated the numbers until eight faced. Brinks pulled up on the lock, and to Locilette's surprise, it actually popped free. Brinks removed it from the door and tossed it to the side. It pulled its rifle off its back and stood by the door in a breaching stance, awaiting for Locilette to join. He slid off his frosting covered gloves and tossed them on the table, freeing his sweaty hands from their protection. He upholstered his pistol and stacked up on the other side of the door.

He unlatched it and pushed hard with his shoulder, causing it to swing out hard. The two rushed in, weapons raised high to meet whatever threat awaited them on the other side.

Chapter Eight

It was cold. It felt like the climate control in this part of the ship wasn't quite working the way it was supposed to, but if Locilette was being honest with himself it didn't surprise him one bit. His opinion of this ship was quickly declining the further they made their way through it, and it wasn't just the murderous psychopath that was funneling them into his web of horrors. Even if you removed that from the situation, which seemed quite impossible to do, the ship was running on minimum power, which would leave lasting damage to the ship's important systems and the evidence of that was already showing.

No, he was pretty convinced that the Rangers were going to send the Yanagi to the scrap yard. With a confirmed suicide in the cargo hold and a murder in the mess hall, there was just too much baggage that came with it. There could be a decent opportunity to auction it off to some merchant start up, but even then, how could any self respecting Arkaan sail the stars knowing there was so much death within these halls? Locilette knew he wouldn't be able to eat in a mess hall ever again after what he just had to do. However, if a future crew wasn't told of such things, would it even bother anyone?

Locilette wasn't afraid of the truth. There was going to be more death to come here on the Yanagi. His only hope was that the poor souls forever bound to this tin can could have a proper burial. A proper send off that every spacefarer deserved. Not sold to some sketchy merchant who will paint over their blood, throw away their possessions, and erase the memories that these people had. That wasn't going to happen as long as he had anything to say about it.

A shiver ran through his body as he stood with his back against the freezing metal wall. Brinks mirrored him from across the corridor, not taking its eyes away from the other end. It astounded Locilette with how many corridors and halls this ship had. It felt like a maze of long passages that were separated into large blocks. He wondered if that was by design, or how the owners of the Yanagi organized it. Regardless, it seemed to fit perfectly for just this occasion. Luring someone deep into the belly of the beast.

One thing that caught his eye was that this hall appeared to be shorter and thinner than the others. He could tell from where he stood that the corridor turned off to a sharp right at the end. Locilette counted six doors, three linking each of the walls going down. Written in bold black on the silver door was a letter. The left side of the hall had *A, C,* and *E* while the other side held *B, D,* and *F.* He prayed this was for an administrative reason and not another sick puzzle.

Locilette skirted along the wall until he arrived just short of the *A* door. He tapped his hand on it, checking for any kind of booby traps, then flipped to the other side by the door pad. Brinks lightly jogged across the thin hall a short distance, then stacked up on the other side, ready to breach and enter. Locilette could name plenty of complaints about his bot, but the one thing he couldn't say was it was incompetent of tactical action. It knew exactly where the most advantageous position would be without Locilette having to think of it himself. He considered that a great asset, especially in the dire circumstance they found themselves in.

He gave a quick nod to the bot, who returned it, then drove his elbow into the button by the door. Faster than he expected, the door shot to the left side, exposing the room. Brinks rushed in low with its rifle trained on each corner. Locilette went in only a moment later. They both occupied a separate corner, anticipating a barrage of gunfire, but none came. At least he could say the Pantheon was looking out for them this time.

Before them appeared to be the well-lived in quarters of some of the Yanagi's crew. Pretty fitting living standards for the rank and file. The room was long and well lit. It was quite the opposite of what Locilette was used to on this vessel. There were two rows of eight bunks lining both sides of the room. Each bunk was a stack of three beds, with the top one barely allowing the occupant of the bed to sit up. From where he was standing, that one seemed to be the premier one as some opened up the hollow walls near the ceiling for additional storage. Looks like Locilette wasn't the only one with that idea.

Clothes and other personal belongings littered the floor. The four trash cans scattered about seemed to not have been changed in quite some time. He peeked in the one closest to him to make sure no one was currently using these bunks, but most of what he could see was just old food wrappers with long passed expiration dates. He even caught a glimpse into a notebook tucked underneath some crushed drink cans and a sock that was crusted with something he simply didn't want to give a guess for the substance. He carefully maneuvered his hand around the trash and pulled the notebook out.

Scribbled on the blue lined paper were several drawings of oddly-shaped penises. Some were big, some were on the smaller side, but there was one in the bottom right corner of the paper that was circled several times with a small note beside it that read: *Just right.* Locilette caught himself grinning as he forced himself to get back to his search. He noticed that every bunk had some sort of nickname written on the same notebook paper, and taped to each of the bunk frames.

One bunk was assigned to a man named *Nibbler.* He could only imagine how someone could possibly get a name like that, but something told him that he didn't really want to find out. As he and Brinks made their way down the center of the room, they came upon a bunk stack that had *Guzzler, Harlot,* and *Please* written on them. It was pretty rare for male and female crew members to be bunked together in the same room, but as Locilette rummaged through some of the belongings, it was clear that this must have been the case on this vessel.

He couldn't help but appreciate the raunchy sense of humor the crew seemed to have developed collectively.

With male and females living so close together out here in the distant void of space, things were surely to develop amongst them. However, by the looks of it, they seemed to overlook such stereotypes and keep the environment one of good nature and amusement. Now that he could get a better look at the names, most of them had to deal with some kind of sexual reference. Ten years ago, he would've cracked up at such things. However, these days his sense of humor had faded away to nothing more than a slight smirk from the hard years.

Locilette and Brinks made their way back into the hall where the cold bit him harder than a few minutes prior. If he had a clue that the ship's climate control would have any kind of issue, he would've prepared better. He wished he was home. He wished he and his wife were watching the two suns fade away under the horizon of the Kronos Prime sky. The warm air blowing a calming breeze through the tall trees that surrounded his home.

He wanted it so bad he could feel it. He could feel the soft skin of his wife's hand in his. The sounds of the branches swaying in the wind and the smell of the cracking fire from the stone fire pit filling the air. Knowing their two boys were safe and sound in their beds would allow them to finally breathe a sigh of peace as they would settle in for the evening to do what they've always done. Just be together.

"Are you alright, sir?" Brinks asked, noticing the Ranger miles away in his thoughts.

Locilette looked up. "Huh? Oh, yeah. Just a little chilly, is all."

"I did read that the temperature has dropped significantly. I believe I spotted a coat in the previous room. Would you like me to go acquire it for you?"

"No, I'll be fine. Let's just get through here. Let's hit this door real quick and move on." Locilette said, nodding toward the door on the opposite side.

Brinks tapped the open button on the door panel of room B and allowed the door to slide into the wall. Locilette chose not to conduct any kind of breaching maneuver on this one, but hesitated around the door frame before entering. Even though a breaching rush would be good combat practice to keep themselves sharp, he didn't believe whoever is at the helm of this charade was the kind to stand and fight. Still, he wasn't going to risk anything, either.

He lowered himself down halfway of the door frame and slowly inched his way to see. The sight of the metal turned into another bunk room, however, this one appeared to be much darker than the last one. Locilette clicked on his flash light and quickly aimed the beam into each corner of the long room to check if anyone was waiting to ambush them. It all seemed clear, but an unsettling feeling rushed through him. The bunk room looked like the people occupying it were here one moment then torn away, dropping their things right where they stood. It felt like he was walking through a ghost town.

Locilette motioned for Brinks to enter. The bot lowered the barrel of its rifle, but kept it tight against its shoulder to be used at a moment's notice. Locilette heard the loud clicking of Brink's optical flash lights fire up, allowing it to see.

"All clear, sir." Brinks's voice called out in a low, calming voice.

B room appeared to be in a higher state of living chaos than A. The beam of his flashlight caught the sight of several desk lamps dotted around on top of wooden end tables by the bunks. He wondered why the crew would need an additional light source when he shot the light up to the ceiling and got his answer. He was surprised to find that there were no lights in the ceiling at all. Not even a fixture for one. This led him to wonder if this was once a storage space of some kind that was converted into crew quarters.

The members of the Yanagi's crew that called this room home didn't let the lack of lighting hold them back. In fact, Locilette was quite impressed with how they set up their space. Beyond the moody desk lamps that sat between the bunks, long strings of twinkle lights were woven through the top beds in a web of clear bulbs. He squinted his eyes to find the switch for them hidden on one of the beds. His eyes followed the string all the ways back to the other side of the room where a green switch sat magnetized to the wall.

He clicked it on, and the many bulbs that hung from the drooping strings burst to life. They filled the room with a relaxing aura of a low, yellow glow. Only a few of the bulbs didn't join the rest, but in no way did it break the calming tone that the room's occupants would have enjoyed. They shone like the little stars that surrounded the Yanagi on its voyage through space.

Locilette found himself absorbing the calm nature of the bunk. The lights reflected off Brinks's metallic body, making the bot look as if its body was adorned with tiny sparkles. However, Brinks didn't notice. He knew that the bot was incapable of seeing the beauty within this ugly situation. In no ways did he blame Brinks for not being able to see things through the emotional lense of an Arkaan, but it did send a wave of loneliness through him, much the same as he would get on his long, intergalactic travels. Brinks was good enough company. Especially when he needed his back watched here in a hostile environment.

The bunk room was messy by normal standards, but that seemed to be the feeling of the crew. It appeared that the officers of the Yanagi allowed the crew to govern their own cleanliness standards. For someone that was trained to military code, Locilette couldn't help but feel a bit uneasy by that thought, but he could certainly see the value in it. It could've been a way to empower the crew to improve morale on these deep space voyages. When it came to crew morale, it was either you brought out the whip and cracked it once and a while, or you gave the crew more freedoms that other vessels would only turn their noses up at. He didn't necessarily agree with it, but he understood the theory.

He began to toss blankets and kick loose articles of clothing around, looking for anything of note. Brinks observed him for a moment and then began to replicate it. The two of the Theseus worked in tandem to find even a shred of evidence as to what happened on the Yanagi's final night, but the bunk room was barren of even the smallest of leads. Locilette pulled one of the end table drawers and found the contracts of employment for three people assigned to this room. He looked over the cluttered beds and wondered if these three were the ones that slept here.

Attached to their contracts was an extensive group of resumes. Locilette was a bit impressed by how well-traveled they were. Very rarely does an Arkaan have a chance to leave the planet or orbital city where they were born unless they joined the military, merchant crews, or the Rangers. These three were experienced, veteran star sailors. Locilette's eyes widened with surprise as he read that one of these crew members, a man named Vaseil Nubberon, was a part of a merchant fleet that Locilette himself escorted many years ago. It was a successful delivery that netted the merchant guild owners a substantial profit. He only hoped that Vaseil got a fair cut of that.

He instinctually placed a hand on his chin as he read over the man's contract details for this voyage. They were indeed headed for the Ares 3 orbital city where it appeared that Mr. Vaseil Nubberon was scheduled to depart for a three week shore leave. His contract had him scheduled to make 12,000 Astrids, which wasn't a terribly bad payday considering the short route he was on. Locilette wondered what he was going to do with that money. Would he transfer it to a family somewhere in the vast Arkaan Empire? Or was he just another stereotypical contract worker that blew his earnings on booze and loose women? He hoped that it was the former.

Now that the room was brightened a little more, Locilette could see the walls were covered with various strange, but familiar tapestries. Some were green with black tribal designs while others were a royal purple with various geometric shapes patterned around it. It added a bit of flavor to the room that was almost like a complete contrast against the rest of the ship. The people stationed in bunk room B appeared to be pretty keen on making it into a haven from the day to day. Something deep within him felt almost a shred of peace in this room. It was a great relief.

Brinks made its way to one of the bunks in the center of the room. A long, green crystal necklace hung from one of the beds. The gold chain sparkled as the bot's lights struck it, creating tiny dots of light to shine against the nearby wall. Brinks cocked its head to the side as it examined the stone. The bot's large metallic hand wrapped and lifted it close to its eyes to do a quick scan. The only matching information in Brinks's database was that of a mineral quite uncommon in Arkaan Space. The references that flooded the bot's vision showed most come from asteroids floating in the empty void between systems.

"Sir," Brinks said, keeping the stone in its hand. "What is the purpose of this mineral adorned upon a golden chain?"

Locilette glanced over and immediately recognized the piece. He smiled, "It's a juminite necklace. Legends say it wards off the evil spirits that are said to prowl through the darkness of space. You place it over your bed to protect yourself while you sleep."

"Evil spirits, sir?"

"Yeah, like aether demons or something like that. I don't know, I've never seen one so I couldn't say." Locilette shrugged.

"Is it a religious item?"

He had to think for a moment. He turned to the Secura-Droid and eyed the necklace. "Well, not exactly. It's more like a superstitious thing that sort of ties in with the Arkaan Pantheon."

Brinks's eyes flashed green for a moment. "Like a folk religion?"

"Precisely."

"Do you believe in the stories of this stone, sir?" The bot asked.

Locilette was caught off guard from the question. Not that he was lost of an answer, but that his bot had the capability to even ask such a thing. "I believe that the Pantheon watches over us out here. That I know in my heart. I don't need a silly stone to drive off demons when I have the big ones looking after me and my family."

"Big ones? Interesting wording, sir."

Locilette pointed up to the ceiling. "You believe in them, they believe in you."

Brinks looked up to the ceiling. The bot held its eyes there for a moment before they flashed green again for a few seconds. Its head returned to the stone, then back to Locilette, who was observing the bot in a way he hadn't done so before.

"Does the Pantheon look after me, sir?" Brinks asked.

For once Locilette didn't have an answer. Was it for him to say if the Pantheon favored things that weren't actually alive? He really didn't know. He liked to think that the big ones upstairs had enough love and guidance to spread to not only organic beings, but machine ones too. If a being that was created by the god themselves create a being, wouldn't that being also receive the blessings, as well?

"I'd say the Pantheon looks over everyone in their domain. Even non-organic beings," Locilette said with a shrug.

Brinks clutched the necklace in its hand. "Why would someone place the stone on a neck chain and not simply mount it above their sleeping space?"

"It's a keepsake, Brinks."

"I am afraid I do not understand. Keep for the sake of what, sir?"

Locilette tossed some blankets around to see if anything was hidden underneath. When he was satisfied, he turned back to the bot, who's stare remained fixed on him. "Why all the questions?"

"I apologize, sir," Brinks said, allowing the necklace to slip out from its hand. "The new additions to my coding compels me to do so. I can revert the changes if you wish."

Locilette shook his head. "No, no, I didn't mean it like that. A keepsake is an item that reminds someone of home, or another person that means a lot to them."

"Do Arkaan have such bad memories that they forget the things that mean the most to them?"

"That's not really what I meant. I mean that these things can invoke feelings of love, longing, and safety. It reminds people that there is something waiting for them after their time out here traversing the stars is over. It's very common on long distance transport vessels like our Yanagi here. According to some of these contracts, these star sailors have been on assignment for six months to a year. That's a long time to be away from home, Brinks."

The bot paused for a moment. "Do you long for home, sir?"

A smile popped in the corner of his lips. "More than anything, Brinks. More than anything in this entire galaxy."

The bot appeared to be processing something. Locilette let the quick thought of his family pass through his mind as he turned to get back to work. The only keepsakes of them that he had was on his ship. The ship he was currently locked out of, which motivated him to get this figured out as soon as he could. He just wanted to be locked in his quarters with the happy faces of his boys surrounding him. He figured that they've probably grown a foot since the last time he saw them. That thought alone made his heart ache more than anything on this investigation. He tried to refocus his mind on the task at hand.

"Alright, Brinks, let's move on. I don't think we're going to get anywhere here. These people didn't leave much of any trace except dirty laundry and pseudo-religious items."

"As you wish, sir."

Locilette prompted the door to open, but in the corner of his eye he caught Brinks taking one last look at the crystal that hung on the bed. He hesitated before stepping out into the chilly hall. With a deep sigh, he scooted his way past the bot back to the bunk. He unlooped the gold chain from the small hook where it hung, and stepped up to Brinks, putting it around its head. The bot looked puzzled as Locilette stepped away.

"There, now it's your keepsake." Locilette smiled, slapping its metal arm.

"Sir, is this thievery?"

"Nah, trust me. The person who owned that would've wanted it to go to a good cause. I'm sure of it."

Locilette could tell by the bot's silence that it had no idea how to react to an act of kindness. If he was honest, he preferred it that way. He motioned for Brinks to follow as he made his way to the door. Brinks immediately snapped into combat mode, falling in line behind him with his rifle drawn. They both jogged into the hall. Locilette just wanted to warm himself up as the cold air nipped at his exposed hands. He started to make his way to room C, but something unusual caught his eye from down the hall, making him hault.

The last door on the right looked as if it had been beaten to hell and back. Locilette shot a quick glance back to Brinks, then drew his pistol. They crept down the hall, the sight of his breath in the cold air was deep and heavy. He tried to not let it distract him, but his hands felt like they were dipped in an ice bath. The regrets of leaving his gloves back in the mess hall filled his mind along with the intrigue of what laid before them.

There was a battered F on the front of the door that was framed by several dents from something Locilette had no idea could cause. Scorch marks dotted around the silver door, leading him to believe they were remnants of a discharged weapon. He ran his fingers over them and felt a sizable dent in the metal. The tips of his fingers rubbed off some of the black char as he pulled his hand away.

"Magma bolts." Locilette declared, wiping off his fingers on his pant leg.

"Agreed, sir. It would seem that an altercation transpired here at some point."

Locilette slowly lowered his beam to the floor where a red streak ran from the door. His eyes followed it until it wrapped around the corner in a wide arch that continued on into the darkness. The bot caught his eye as he motioned for it to take a peek around the corner. It leaned out slowly, then fully stepped around the corner to follow the trail. A moment later, the blue glow of Brinks's eyes came out of the dark, followed by the bright reflection of Locilette's light on its copper body.

"This peculiar trail leads to another door that appears to be offline, sir." Brinks reported, running a quick diagnosis of the red streak by its feet. "My data states that this is 98% Arkaan blood and 2% various dirt particles."

He placed a hand on the back of his neck to massage the muscle. "Any idea how old it is?"

"I apologize, sir, I do not have the necessary instruments to properly date it."

Locilette kneeled down to examine it a bit closer. It was quite apparent that the streak had dried a while ago, but his only thought was *how* long ago. The one thing he was missing in this ordeal was a timeline of events to even begin building a solid report. He had his certainties, such as there was someone conducting a string of homicides with a motivation of showmanship. Then there were the uncertainties that frustrated him too much to even begin to list.

"What the hell happened here…" He spoke softly, gripping his flashlight tightly.

"Sir, I think it is worth noting that the weapons that are supposed to be kept within the guard's station in the brig were missing. Perhaps these were the weapons used in this confrontation?"

Locilette climbed back to his feet and traced the streak again with his light. "That makes sense. Arkaan law prohibits the casual concealment of weapons on registered merchant vessels. Even if the crew members were to bring a personal defense weapon on the ship, more than likely it would've been kept there."

"Precisely, sir," the bot said, examining the battered door again. "Perhaps a minority group within the Yanagi's crew acquired the weapons for unknown reasons?"

The thought hadn't ever crossed his mind. He looked over at Brinks with a sense of eureka. "A mutiny!" He exclaimed.

"The current combination of evidence is pointing to that most likely outcome, sir."

How could he not have thought of that before? The missing crew, the suicide, the playful murder of one of their own, it made complete sense. However, every rebellion needs a leader, and a leader needs a purpose to drive the masses. What could've possibly happened on this ship to make the crew turn on their employers? He had to get into the F bunk room and see what exactly this mob was after.

"Brinks, try the door," Locilette instructed.

Brinks reached a finger out to tap on the door panel, but it was completely smashed in. The bot observed the door for a moment before it placed both hands on the surface and pushed hard. The metal began to squeal as the locking mechanisms fought back against Brinks's force, but the bot's hands slipped on the metal, sending it tumbling off to the side.

Before Locilette could say anything, Brinks processed a plan. It pulled off the rifle from its back and leaned it against the wall by the door. The bot turned around to face Locilette and slammed itself into the metal. Locilette raised an eyebrow as the sound of Brinks's magnetized back holders activated, connecting it to the door like hardened cement. Its powerful mechanical legs pushed as hard as they could muster, and to Locilette's surprise, the door began to slowly move.

A loud grinding wail filled the quaint hall, making Locilette wince and cover his ears. Immediately recognizing the amount of noise they were making, he dropped to a knee and watched both sides of the corridor the best he could while his partner worked. The last thing he needed was an ambush when Brinks's was stuck to the abused slab of metal. Locilette found a brief sense of comfort knowing that direct conflict didn't seem to be their perpetrator's strong suit, but what if that in itself was a ruse? He shook the hypotheticals out of his head and refocused on the happenings around him.

The door was opened just wide enough for them to sneak in when Brinks stopped. The bot looked around for a moment and realized that forcing the door open wasn't going to keep it open. As soon as Brinks moved, the door was going to slam back shut like a stretched rubber band.

"Sir, we need to wedge something in the opening to prevent it from closing." Brinks instructed as it leaned to the side, propping its leg up on the door frame.

Locilette quickly looked around for anything of use, but it didn't seem like there was too much that could withstand that kind of pressure. He quickly raked his eyes across the previous rooms with no luck. The only thing that could keep that door open was already there.

"Alright, our best bet is for you to keep that door open while I do a quick look around. Sound good?" Locilette asked, sizing up the gap.

"As you wish, sir. However, I must advise that you will be alone."

"Operating alone is something I've grown accustomed to over the years. I'll be fine," he said, stepping over the bot's leg. The vest scraped against the door as he scooted his way through, but he leaned back out before continuing on. "Oh, and Brinks?"

"Sir?"

"Please don't leave me trapped in here." His voice came across as more of a plea than a command. Brinks's blue eyes locked onto his, but it didn't respond. Locilette knew the bot was trying to process how to react to such a comment, but there was no time to waste.

He gripped his flashlight tightly as the beam illuminated a chaotic scene stuck in time. Around the door was a barricade of chairs and overturned beds stuffed with various heavy items to pack as much weight on it as possible. Bunks were stacked with thick books, and the end table drawers were filled with containers of liquid that had mold growing on the sides of them. The entrance looked like a war zone, and the more he examined the bunk room, the more he started to feel like that might have been the case.

He ducked under a cabinet that was propped up by a stack of chairs and what looked like the remains of an old water fountain. When he was free of the barricade, he turned to the sight of all the pieces that seemed to have been pushed off to the side at some point. Whoever wanted in here that badly appeared to have gotten their wish. Locilette just prayed that the defenders gave them a hell of a fight before their eventual breach in their barricaded defenses.

The light reflected the shining sparkle of metal on the floor around the barricade. Locilette kneeled down, and to his surprise, there were crude, bladed weapons scattered around him. Trickles of blood caught his eye, then the more he followed the drips, the more he found. Swipes of blood covered the barricade, and several dried pools with shoe prints encased within seemed to carve trails that pointed in every single direction around him. Just by the look of things, he knew this skirmish didn't last too long after the aggressors breached. He raised the light around the bunk room to confirm a suspicion. The glow of the flashlight ran the length of the wall until it double backed to a gaping hole in the metal wall.

It was quite ingenious, Locilette thought. Whoever these defenders were had enough of an engineering mind to use the resources they had available to them. They removed the thin sheet of metal wall, cut it into strips, then appeared to have shaved the edges to make a blade. At the bases of the desperately crafted swords were torn shirts tied tightly around the bare metal to allow for some kind of grip. However, the looks at some of the handles showed signs of blood, making Locilette guess it wasn't the safest weapon to handle.

Locilette slowly came to his feet and took the entire scene in. This must have been one hell of a fight. He pulled out his PDA and began to document the area as best as he could. Flashes from his camera filled the bunk room like the distant cracks of lightning of a Kronos summer storm. As soon as he was about to return to his awaiting bot, the final flash exposed something on one of the bunks that made him double take. He quickly raised his flashlight. Half buried in the sheets was a PDA. It was a few models older than his own, but still easy enough to learn to operate.

He sat on the edge of the bed and held the power button, not expecting it to show life. A smile of shock flew across his face as the screen lit up in an orange display of manufactioner's branding. The first thing he saw in the upper right corner was the battery icon flashing. He worked quickly to get to the last uploads on the device. At the top of the list was an audio recording dated five months ago. He tapped the play button and turned up the volume as high as it could go.

"Hey there, Kellium." A man's voice rolled out of the device's speaker with a strong accent. "Daddy isn't going to make it home for Saint Omania's day this year. I have to-" loud shouting could be heard coming from the background. "Daddy has to work just a little bit longer than he expected, but I'll be sure to bring you something from Ares! I wish I could take you there, and I intend to soon. After we pay off our cottage, we'll be able to actually get out there and explore our galaxy! It's what Mom would've wanted, huh? I miss her. I miss you."

The man's voice was interrupted by another's. "Branx, they're about to tear down the door! Get your ass over here before they kill us all!" His voice was full of the panic of a man that was about to meet their end.

"Well, Daddy has to go now." The first man's voice came back on. It was noticeably more calm than the others screaming as the bangs heated repeatedly. "I'm sorry I haven't been here like I should've been when Mom went to heaven to be with Grandma. I promise you this will never happen again. When I get home, it's just going to be you and me. Be nice to your aunt Loucinda. She's kind enough to take you in while I'm away. I love you, Kell, and I can't wait to see your face-" The recording stopped, leaving Locilette in the lonely silence.

He sat there in the dark absorbing the man's final message. He went into a haunting presence knowing that most of those people, including the man, were probably killed during that final hour, leaving behind loved ones and this empty room where they made their final stand. Locilette needed to know why the crew of the Yanagi fractured so deeply that it led to bloodshed among the people they've traveled with for months. He got up and tucked the PDA back where it was, just in case.

"Let's get moving." Locilette said, passing by the bot.

Without question, Brinks released itself and allowed the door to slam shut. It was now the tomb of final wishes, final thoughts, and final goodbyes to loved ones that have no idea what happened on this ship. They will know. Locilette was going to see to that personally if it was his dying action.

Chapter Nine

"Officer's Quarters," Locilette read the sign above the door. The sign, like most of the others, was unpowered, only visible by his and Brinks's combined lights. "If there would be any information, surely it would be in here."

"I agree, sir. I will note that the trail marks appear to lead past this door. We should prepare ourselves for possible altercation."

Locilette nodded. "Always ready. However, it seems like our demented little friend here doesn't want to have a face to face chat. The way I'm feeling at the moment, that might be a wise decision on his part."

"May I remind you, sir, that our highest priority is to seize and detain, not harm the perpetrators."

"I know my job, Brinks." Locilette snapped, feeling a little offended. Even though he knew the bot was just stating the obvious based on what he said, he didn't need some machine reminding him what his duties were. He had done this for far too long.

He took in a deep breath and let it out slowly. He was allowing himself to become way too emotionally connected to this investigation. There was just something so haunting about this place that he couldn't shake. The words of the man's audio recording just replayed over and over in his head. He couldn't help but put himself in that man's shoes. The thought of his boys growing up without hurt stung like a stab to the stomach. He just couldn't handle that thought as his eyes became slightly blurry with tears.

Brinks didn't notice. Could he notice things like that? He wiped the corner of his eyes with the back of his hand, then lifted the narrow beam to the door. This whole part of the small hallway remained in complete darkness as he noticed the light above them had been smashed out; glass covered the floor like a rug of glittering shards sparkling in the glow of the flashlights. It was more than likely done during the skirmish that took place here. Locilette placed a hand on the cold metal and gave it a little push. He quickly retracted his hand in with surprise as the door actually moved. There was no way it was going to be that easy.

"Door's unlocked," Locilette whispered, his hand grasping at his plasma arc pistol that sat high in the holster from constant removal.

"This is a breach in standard Arkaan merchant vessel protocol. All senior staff on merchant vessels must have a secured, well defined space in order to protect sensitive information on the contents of the cargo. This will be noted for future reference."

"Brinks," Locilette said, almost letting a smile across his face. "I really don't think the owners of the Yanagi are going to care about a door being unlocked at this point."

"Would you like me to cease similar observations?"

He answered, still whispering. "Just record information that pertains to our investigation. Let's get moving. The longer we stay here the more time our perp has to act on his plans."

"Of course, sir."

With Brinks standing by his side, plasma arc rifle at the ready, Locilette pushed open the door with ease into its housing in the wall. It was pitch black. The darkness that came from within was like staring into the void of space without the guiding light of a star to navigate you through. Could the power be completely out in this section? Could this be another black out like before?

The lights from Locilette and Brinks darted around the interior of the next section in the ship. From what he could make out, it was another long corridor. Of course it was. Yet this one felt different from the others. The light pierced the darkness, exposing heraldry of a merchants guild that he had seen before. The blue banner was adorned with zig-zagging patterns going down the sides of it, and in the center was a hand with a pen surrounded by leaves. Each leaf descended around the hand, creating a framed emblem that the guild used on most of their official documents.

They were that of the Josakk Merchants Guild. Named after their founder who had been dead for hundreds of years now, but still practiced the same shady business. Locilette had the pleasure of working with this guild before. They seemed to favor traveling through the more unsavory parts of space that the long reach of the Arkaan authority sometimes couldn't get to so easily. It wouldn't save them any time on travel, but it was avoiding the cargo inspections from system authorities that was the cause. It was no surprise that a vessel operated by this guild would be in the position it was.

He lowered the light to illuminate the flood just on the other side of the door frame. Another message from their gracious host lay stained on the floor. The words were written in a script not commonly used by the average Arkaan, which caught him more off guard than the bloody words scribed on the floor. Locilette wasn't very well versed in it since school only taught it as an elective, but what he did know was that a lot of the early religious texts of the Arkaan Pantheon were written with it millennia ago. The dread crept up on him as he quickly realized that not only was he dealing with a deranged, psychotic killer, he was also dealing with a potential academic. The combination of those two meant only horrifying results, as it appeared to be the case on the Yanagi.

"Brinks, can you translate that?" Locilette inquired about his bot's abilities.

"Of course, sir." Brinks's eyes flashed to a bright emerald. The green glow passed over the words several times before its eyes returned to their normal blue. "It is written in an archaic script of the proto Arkaan language. The text appears to be pulled from the Arkaan Pantheon's third volume of *Lords of the Sundering* spiritual text. It would appear to be from the story of King Howettez's conduct towards the common people of the fledgling Arkaan Empire."

"Perfect. More riddles from a book known for its puzzles and word play. What does it say?"

"Peasants and serfs begone, ye villains!" Brinks recited in both the original speech and the translation.

Locilette shook his head in disgust. He moved in with Brinks just a few steps behind him. Soon after they entered the dark hall, the two froze as the fixture above them cut on like a spotlight, illuminating a single actor on a large stage. Brinks threw itself into the wall, as Locilette dropped down on a knee, his pistol extended out towards the other end still capped in black. He listened closely. Something was on the other end of the hall.

"Brinks, thermal scan, *now.*" Locilette commanded, not allowing his eyes to drift away.

Just as the bot was about to swap visions, the next light above them sparked to life. Then the next, and next, and next. One by one the lights traveled the length of the hall until the last one. There was an uneasy pause that left Locilette in a disturbing sense of anticipation. Finally, the last light illuminated the end of the hall, revealing someone sitting in a chair. From the distance away, he could see the person's head jerk up to look at them.

"HELP ME!" A female's voice cracked, bouncing off the metal walls like the wails of a banshee.

Without a single moment of hesitation, Locilette broke out in a full sprint. Brinks followed soon after, the bot's steps pounding heavily on the floor even with the pads on the bottom of its feet. The woman's big eyes welled with tears as the two approached. Her arms struggled against the restraints that held them tight to the arms of the chair. The woman wore her trauma on her face like a photograph. Locilette knew this woman had been through absolute hell without her muttering a single word.

"Ma'am, my name is Locilette. I'm with the Rangers and I'm here to help. What's your name?" Locilette asked, trying his best to calm the woman's shattered nerves while diagnosing the situation.

She didn't answer. Her bloodshot eyes were wide as she watched Brinks move around the chair. Her head darted back and forth from the bot to the strange man that stood before her. Locilette slowly slid his pistol back into his holster and raised his hands up to show her that he wasn't a threat. He carefully kneeled in front of her, her deer-like eyes following his every movement.

Her wrists were bruised and bloody as she appeared to have fought against the people who forced her into the restraints. Near the edge of the chair arms was dried blood caked all around. It was unclear if it was this woman's or from somebody else that found themselves in the same unfortunate position. His eyes dropped to her feet as the same straps bound them tightly to the legs of the chair. She didn't seem to fight as hard against those since her blue pant legs showed only a little blood around the straps.

"Seems like you're in a pickle here. Wanna tell me who put you in this?" Locilette asked, trying to slip a finger into the straps to test the tightness against her ankles.

She shook her head furiously. At least he got some kind of communication from her. The last thing he needed now was someone inflicted with shock, trapped in a zombie-like state. That would make extracting her back to the Theseus that much harder. If that was even an option at the moment. That was something he would have to figure out later, now he had to get this woman out of this chair.

"Ma'am, can you tell me your name?" He repeated.

"Zes-" She choked back her tears, "Zesper."

Locilette gave her the warmest smile he could force given the circumstances. "Alright, Zesper, let's try and get you out of this. How does that sound?" She nodded slightly.

"Okay, Zesper, where are you from?"

"Poseidon Prime..." She let out with a whisper.

"Oh yeah? I have a good friend that comes from the Poseidon system. Tell me, do you know where you are? Do you know what ship you are on?"

"We're..." She struggled to get the words out, her entire body erupting in a trembling fit. "We're on the Yanagi."

Locilette smiled. "That's right, Zesper." His eyes darted to the side and caught a glimpse of Brinks examining the strange device that seemed to be attached to this woman's chair. He was so focused on responding to her cries that he hadn't even noticed that there was something abnormal sitting just off to the side of her. It didn't really seem like she knew it was there either, and by the way things seem to be going here, that was probably for the best.

He motioned to her wrists. "Mind if I take a look here?"

She nodded, but her eyes trailed his hands all the way. Locilette tried to slip a finger under the straps, but she winced in pain as she moved them. They were tight, but he was certain he could cut through them with his combat knife. The only thing he was wondering now was what was he going to do with her once she was free? Was this meant to happen? Is she a pawn on the board to slow his progress? It didn't matter if she was or not. He still had a duty to help her any way he could.

The hair on the back of his neck began to rise at the thought of him taking more bait into another trap, but his training pushed him through the doubt that crept in. He slid the knife out of its sheath. She looked confused, but when Locilette moved to start cutting away the straps, she let out a horrible wail of fear. Zesper thrashed around in the chair, her wrists now dripping the crimson blood onto the silver floor. He immediately put the knife away and raised his hands again.

"NO!" She cried. "No! Put it away, NOW!"

"Hey, hey, take it easy. I'm here to help you get out of here."

"You don't understand! If you cut the straps he'll kill me! He'll fucking kill me!"

The look of concern washed away his calming smile. "Who, Zesper! Who is going to kill you?"

She leaned forward to look into his eyes. "I can't say… He's listening. Even now. He's always listening." Her eyes began to dart all around her. Left, right, up, as if something was flying around her head.

Locilette looked around them, his eyes focusing on each corner, hoping to find some camera or even a simple listening device. He found nothing. This poor woman had probably been through hell, and she was way past the point of breaking. He didn't blame her for a second. The things he had seen to this point would make any untrained mind crack. He was fortunate in those regards.

"May I have a word with you, sir?" Brinks asked, the hydraulics in its knees squeezing slightly as it pressed itself off the floor. Locilette nodded and stepped to the side a few feet. Locilette leaned into the bot, trying to ignore the burning stare of the woman.

"Sir, I am almost certain that the device attached to this female's chair is a modified immolator," Brinks explained, its voice coming out as a low hum so only Locilette's ears could pick it up clearly.

"What do you mean? What does it do?"

"Sir, an immolator is a common device on long range vessels that dispose of waste via extreme blasts of heat," Brinks said. "It appears to have been mounted to the chair on which she sits. I identified several possible triggers that would activate the device."

Locilette wiped his forehead with his sleeve. "How the hell do we get her out of it, Brinks?"

The bot paused. "I am unsure as of present, sir."

He could feel his heart begin to pound in his chest. Locilette wasn't equipped to handle something like this. Could he handle gangs? Sure, he's done that plenty. Aid the Arkaan Military in busting up some rebel cells? All in a day's work. Disarming an explosive device was not in his list of expertise. The Rangers deployed specialized units to deal with threats like these. Men and women trained for months to be able to safely disarm devices, or at the very least extract the hostage safely. How was he going to potentially do both?

Locilette stepped away from the bot. He found himself pacing around, only stopping when he met the terrified eyes of the woman sitting before him. He couldn't let her die. No, he wasn't going to let her die on this ship of the damned. He breathed a deep sigh to calm himself, then gave her a reassuring smile. Her face remained the same, but he just had to give her the illusion that he was still in control of the situation. Even if he was panicking internally.

"Forget the device." Locilette commanded in a whisper. "Find a way to remove her as safely as you can. Get it done."

"At once, sir."

Brinks sprang into action, and took its place behind the chair. Locilette kneeled back down in front of the woman slowly, hands slightly raised on his way down. She did a double take, trying to see what Brinks was doing behind her, but her restraints held her tightly to the chair. Her breathing quickly began to accelerate and her fingernails dug into the arms of the wooden chair. She looked like a scared cat in a crate being taken to a strange new place for the first time.

"Hey, Zesper," Locilette said, grabbing her attention. "Tell me what your home is like."

Her eyes dropped to the floor. She remained silent, almost as if she was trying to recount a life before she was imprisoned here. Something cracked behind her chair, making Brinks freeze for a second, but then continued back to what it was doing. Whatever it was didn't seem to break Zesper from her thoughts of a safe place far, far away from here.

"Me and my boyfriend have an apartment in Braenor." She spoke softly. "It's a city in the western hemisphere of Poseidon Prime."

"Oh yeah, my friend I mentioned earlier has a little property outside the village of Syrane. I believe it's a hundred miles from Braenor or something like that. I always hated to visit Poseidon Prime, but his house was so beautiful. It's a little cottage that overlooks the western sea, settled on a long ridge line. He got it for a steal since it was in the path of so many hurricanes when the season rolled around. Every time I would see reports of a major hurricane forecasted to hit that area on the news, I would always be sure to give him a call to see how he was doing," Locilette explained, his hands gesturing with every word.

He noticed that her eyes were now fixed on him. His attempts to calm her seemed to have been working. Even a little bit was worth gold at this moment. He continued, "He would send me pictures of the storm slowly coming into view on the horizon like a rolling black mass in the sky. It was frankly terrifying, because it takes three days for messages to travel the long spans of space along the network of satellites and comms buoys. Usually by the time I received them at me and my wife's house on Kronos Prime, the storm would've already passed. It was like receiving a warning for something that had already happened. It was eerie."

"I miss the storms…" She managed to say. "I miss the way the wind would rip around me as the daily rain would wash over the land."

"Oh, the Poseidon System and its water planets."

A smile cracked the side of her mouth. "Yeah, it's not for everyone, but it's a great place to connect with nature. There is nowhere like Poseidon."

"The last time I think I visited, I took my family there." Locilette recalled. "As soon as our ship dropped through the atmosphere, we found ourselves right in the eye of a major storm. I don't think I've thrown up so much in my life."

"Rookie mistake." She chuckled.

It was refreshing to hear her laugh. It was refreshing to just hear somebody laugh at all in this wretched tin can. Locilette believed that humor could be found just about anywhere. Even in the dark corridors of a derelict ship with a murderer guiding them on a path that is most likely destined to see their deaths at the end. That was a problem for later on. This woman was his priority at the moment, and her shaky nerves were a liability that he couldn't afford to have break.

"So, Zesper," Locilette started, catching a glimpse at Brinks removing something and carefully setting it to the side. "What was your job here on the Yanagi?"

"I was a cleaner, well, the official title was *Sanitation*, but I'm really just a janitor." She sighed with an eye roll.

Locilette raised an eyebrow. "A janitor? So, you just clean up after the rest of the crew?"

She nodded slightly. That was it. That was the reason she was chosen to be a pawn in this killer's murderous game. Locilette tried his best to not show his thoughts on his face. He pulled out his PDA and added a new note section under the current investigation.

Peasants and serfs begone, ye villains…

She was the peasant being referenced in the message. Her job aboard the Yanagi was considered to be the lowest of the low for unskilled laborers of an interstellar vessel. Most crew members were either highly trained engineers, mechanics, security personnel, or accountants to control the ever-flowing stream of money coming and going. Then there were the unskilled positions. The positions that hard-working Arkaan filled to feed their families, but this psycho would refer to them as *serfs*. The sanitation personnel, the cargo movers, and the meal preppers all served a great purpose for the officer class. Why force a class struggle into this twisted narrative?

"Hey, can you tell me how it was working for the officers on this ship?" Locilette inquired.

She shrugged. "I mean, it was a job that paid money. There was never a time where I felt uncomfortable or anything."

"Do you think you were ever looked down on?"

"I mean, in terms of importance, I'm pretty low on the food chain here. But that would be on any merchant ship, I suppose." She shrugged again.

"Did the officers ever try to shut you out of something because of your low ranking job on the ship?"

"I don't think so…" She thought for a moment. "At least not that I was ever told to my face. I knew my place here, as did everyone else on the cleaning staff. I didn't poke my nose into any of that money stuff because I don't understand it anyway. I'm here - *was* here to help my boyfriend pay our bills. I didn't want this! I just clean tables and sweep. Why did he do this to me!?"

He…

Their perpetrator is a man, it usually is in cases like this, but it was nice to have a confirmation. Brinks looked up to connect with Locilette's approving gaze. The bot recognized that piece of evidence too. He was proud of Brinks for using the new update to its processing he demanded earlier. Perhaps this bot was useful for more than just shooting things after all. Just like everything else on the Theseus was automated by him to some extent, maybe Brinks could be a useful asset in the future if he decided to continue with his career with the Rangers. He logged the findings in his notes.

"Zesper, who is doing this?" Locilette asked. He didn't want to upset her more than she already was, but he had to know.

"I can't say his real name. He hates his real name."

"Who? Tell me."

Her eyes locked on to his with an intensity that sent a wave of unease through the Ranger. "He's the chosen one."

Locilette's face fell into a serious expression as he scooted closer to the woman. "Tell me, Zesper, who is the chosen one? I can end this nightmare for you, but you have to tell me his name."

"How do I know you just aren't a part of his-" She stumbled on her words. "His fucked up thugs? His disciples."

Disciples. There's more than one as he had anticipated. It was a bit far-fetched to think one man could be capable of taking over a vessel of this size, but it wasn't unheard of. One person with the proper knowledge of a ship's schematics and crew routines can have a vessel flipped on its head in a matter of hours. He had the feeling something along those lines happened here, but it appears to have been on a much larger, quicker scale. By the little evidence of a struggle through the parts of the ship he's visited so far, he could only assume that the take over was fast. The officers probably didn't know what was happening until it was far too late.

"Who are his followers?" Locilette grilled. He was done beating around the bush. He needed answers, even at the expense of her sanity.

"No, I can't say any more. Don't make me say any more!" She pleaded.

Locilette grabbed her shoulders as she began to thrash around in her trash around in her chair. "Zesper! Get a hold of yourself! The only way we can beat them is together. If I know *exactly* what I'm dealing with, I can have them behind bars before they can hurt anybody else. I need your help with this, okay?"

Her eyes showed enough torment to service several lives of hardship. The pools formed in the corners of her eyes, but only a single tear managed to escape its captivity down her dirty, pale cheek. Locilette felt her whole body tremble in his grasp.

"Please don't let me die." She managed to say.

He gave her a reassuring smile. "I'm not gonna let anything happen to you. It's what I do, after all," he said, pointing to the Ranger emblem on the front left of his tactical vest.

"I've only met him face to face once. It was during the overthrow. He was meeting everyone one on one, trying to convince them to throw themselves against the few security officers that were barricading the bunk rooms."

"Why was he organizing a coup?"

"All he told me was that after we take the ship, he would be able to be the bridge for us to become something incredible. Something immensely revolutionary that would bring forth a new era in the galaxy."

"I don't understand," Locilette said, stroking his chin. "How could this guy turn a majority of the Yanagi's crew against their employers? Did he ever say what this revolutionary thing was going to be?"

She shrugged with a deeply defeated expression on her tired face. "You just can't understand. He had such a powerful presence about him that demanded your loyalty. If his charm didn't influence you, he found other ways of forcing your loyalty."

"Where did he come from? Was it the brig?" He asked, seeking confirmation of his theory.

She shrugged again. "I don't know. All I know is that his voice had been spreading dissent for a while around here, but he showed up personally just before the takeover. It was like he was a mythological character. Until he wasn't. It was like hearing the stories of the Pantheon, then seeing one of them actually stand before you. It was surreal and powerful. I don't know…"

"Is there anything else you can tell me? Even the smallest pieces of information can change things."

"I don't know…" Her gaze trailed off as her mind spun with thoughts. "The insignia. His stupid insignia he uses."

"What about it?"

"He forced the ones most loyal to him to carve-"

An alarm started to ring out from all around them. Brinks launched to its feet and pulled the plasma arc rifle off its back in anticipation for combat. The bright lights that filled the room now turned to a dark shade of red, surrounding them in a veil of crimson glow. Locilette spun around to check their rear, but as far as he could tell, they were still alone. He could feel the biting in his stomach as the thoughts that something really bad was about to happen eclipsed his mind. Zesper started hyperventilating, making him do a quick glance back to the contained woman.

"Pantheon almighty, please, I'm sorry, I'm sorry. Please don't let him take me back!" She cried to the ceiling above her.

The alarm ceased. The three stayed in silence as Locilette listened intently at their surroundings and beyond the red room they found themselves in. Brinks pushed into the corner and kneeled down to allow a more favorable tactical position. He appreciated the bot's proactive approach, but seeing it do that made him feel more uneasy. It meant that Brinks probably calculated that their chances for conflict had increased significantly. As much as he wanted to adopt a similar posture, he still had to care for the woman still strapped in this nightmare.

The ship's intercom buzzed around them, then a voice came across that chilled Locilette to his core. "Seems like you all are being unfairly cold towards me. We haven't even met yet! How quick we are to pass judgment based on hearsay. Oh wait - I know how to beat your cold attitude. How about I just warm you up!"

Zesper's terrified scream echoed through the corridor. "No! What does that mean! Please don't hurt me anymore!"

A hissing sound began to come from her chair. Locilette looked over to Brinks, who was examining the sound. The bot began to back up, and as Locilette tried to move past it, its large metal hand stopped him from going any further.

"Brinks, move!" Locilette ordered.

"Sir, a flammable material has begun to discharge from the back of the device. I cannot allow you to put yourself in danger."

Zesper's thrashing stopped only for a brief moment as a new panic began to set in. "I feel something wet on my back. What do I do? What do I do!?" She met the Ranger's worried stare. She repeated, "What do I do…"

"Brinks, we have to get her out now! That's an order from your Ranger!" He barked at the bot.

"Of course, sir. At once." Brinks rushed behind the chair and began to tug at any loose parts it could find.

Locilette pulled out his knife again, but this time the woman didn't protest. It appeared her current animalistic state overpowered the fear she previously had at the sight of his combat knife. He started at the bottom, and slid the blade between her feet to start sawing at the restraints. Her legs were kicking as every breath she took led to an ear piercing shriek of terror. Locilette braced one of her legs with his free hand just to allow him to cut away without slicing her in the process. Then, a loud ding that reminded him of an over timer rang loudly a single time. Several clicks started going off under her chair.

Locilette put his face on the floor to try and get a glimpse of anything underneath the chair, but it was concealed behind the rest of the housing for whatever was attached to it. It sounded familiar. The clicking gave him a sense of nostalgia that he couldn't quite place, but it was certainly of home. His home on Kronos Prime. His home in the warm sun of the Kronos Star, out enjoying an afternoon with his family. Him grilling freshly caught fish from the nearby lake.

The grill!

"Brinks!" He called out in a fit of panic. "It's a fucking pilot light! Get her out *NOW!*"

The bot's eye turned red as it switched to security mode. It began punching the device around connected to the chair, as Locilette resumed slashing at the woman's restraints. Something caught his eye, making him slow for a moment. Zesper had stopped panicking. When they made eye contact, he met the gaze of someone who had given up. Someone who knew she wasn't going to see this to the end. Someone who has made peace with the inevitable. Then it happened. Locilette's greatest fear manifested into reality.

The final click ignited its flame, sending a wave of fire rushing up the chair in a fraction of a second. The wave of heat made Locilette stumble back as the sight of the woman's engulfed body wildly thrashed around in her chair filled his disturbed eyes. Her scream was something that he could only imagine in his worst nightmares. It wasn't a scream for help, it was a scream to show her mercy and end her suffering. He couldn't let her torture continue. Without a second thought, he drew his plasma arc pistol and fired the bolt through her head, sending a spray of blood on Brinks still working behind her.

Her suffering had finally come to an end.

Chapter Ten

The corridor, still encased in the veil of a red glow, smelled like charred meat. It was a smell that made Locilette want to gag every time he breathed it in, but he grew more used to it as the hour ticked on by. Zesper's body remained with her head thrown back from the blue bolt fired from his own pistol. It stayed just like that as he watched it slowly burn away by the intense flames that consumed it.

It was a revolting smell. It was a smell that reminded him of his failure. He failed to protect her, breaking not only his sworn duty, but breaking his word, too. He promised her that he wasn't going to let her die, but it was by his own hands that she met her end. Given the circumstances, he knew he did the right thing rather than to just let her suffer in unimaginable agony until the flames took her, but that did little to calm his thoughts.

He now had three victims. Each person having a family and a life they wished to get back to, only to see their lives cut tragically short by some fucked up mad man who wanted to play inspiring rebel leader on a merchant vessel that nobody cared about. Locilette clenched his fist tightly as that thought played through his head. These were *real* people dying here only to satisfy some freak's game. It frustrated him more that he didn't even know what the game was at this point. If he was a serial killer, then he could sort of understand the playful motive, but Zesper made it seem like this was some kind of strange cult following led by this guy.

Locilette just couldn't wrap his head around it. Why bring people to your cause only to slaughter them for amusement? If this was some kind of cult, would that have made it easier for him to kill from the flock he created? No, that just didn't add up. Why go through the trouble of leading a coup of the ship's leadership if you were going to just murder the people who helped you, and even if that was the case, wouldn't other coup leaders see what was happening to stop you?

All of these questions swirled in his head, but the answers remained just as mysterious as the person orchestrating this nightmare. After jotting down some quick notes into his PDA, he tried to clear his head to think. He needed to come up with some kind of plan to get to this psycho and bring him to justice. He took a deep breath in to calm his mind. Big mistake.

The smell of the scorched flesh of the body filled his nose, forcing him to lean over and empty the little he had in his stomach on the floor. He spit out the rest, then unscrewed the cap on his water canteen to rinse out his mouth. He had to get out of this room. If he and Brinks kept following this predetermined path set out before them, then they were going to meet the same fate as the three souls he stumbled upon.

He couldn't let that happen. His wife and boys were waiting for him at home. The thought of them waiting and waiting for him to walk through that front door hurt him deeply. His boys would grow up waiting for a day that would never come. His family would end up like the families of these poor souls trapped on this hell-ship, wondering and praying for the safe return of their loved ones. Their prayers would fall on the deaf ears of the Pantheon, keeping the universe moving in the cosmic ballet. He couldn't let his fate fall into their hands.

Locilette looked down at his PDA's screen still lit from the notes. He clicked it off and brought up the audio recorder screen and contemplated what his next couple of hours were about to be like. He's been doing this a long time, so he wasn't naïve in his hopes. The odds were already greatly stacked against him now. If he had taken more time to thoroughly inspect the Yanagi then maybe, just maybe, he would have avoided being trapped in this game. He shook his head in frustration. There was no use in beating himself up now. Surviving this and bringing this fucked up group to justice was the only thing he wanted consuming his thoughts until he was back on his own ship.

His hands grew sweaty as he continuously stared at the screen. What was he even going to say? How does someone just say goodbye to their family? He rolled his eyes and glanced at his bot, who was like a statue against the metallic wall. The only thing distinguishing it from the background was its glowing green eyes and the copper-colored plating. His eyes lowered just a little to Zesper's blood splattered over Brinks's chest plate. It was a reminder of his failure and his mercy. He nodded to himself. He needed his family to know that he was out here saving lives, even if it might cost him his own. He tapped the record button below the screen, and brought the device up to his mouth.

"Hey, it's me, Locile-" H stumbled on his words for a moment, the thought of his kids listening to this. "It's Dad. Things here aren't looking too good for me, so I just wanted to record a message just in case, well, just in case anything happens to me."

He tried to avoid using wording that would cause too much worry, or reveal how much suffering he had seen up to this point. He just wanted them to know his love for them, and put his stupid, macho pride aside. "You know, I've been thinking a lot about home recently. I feel like I've been away for far too long, and that's killing me. After this op is finished, I'm thinking about applying for a desk job in Kronos, or even a change in career altogether. I want to be with all of you. I want to be on our patio watching the clouds fly by, and I want to listen to the sound of our way too many wind chimes clinging away with every breeze."

The door behind Zesper's body clicked as it was remotely unlocked, but Locilette ignored it. "Boys, you be good to your Mom. You are both the men of the house while I'm away, and I expect nothing but gentlemen-like behavior. This galaxy is full of wondrous and incredible things that are like a door wide open for the both of you. I know deep in my soul that you two are destined for greatness in whatever it is you both choose to do with your lives. Don't let anything hold you back, even if it's me not being there..." he said, his voice cracking.

That hurt him to say out loud. He didn't think this was going to be so hard, but goodbyes are never easy. He could feel the water start to cloud his eyes, but that just frustrated him even more. He reminded himself that this wasn't an official goodbye, but a message just in case the Yanagi becomes his tomb, as well.

"Marla, our years of marriage have been the greatest thing to ever happen to me. I mean that from the bottom of my heart, and you know that. I just need to remind you, because sometimes I don't feel like I say it enough. Our life together is better than anything I could ever dream of, and I'm so thankful for the time you have invested into me. I know it's not easy raising two young boys, but watching you take that on with grace has been incredible. You are incredible. I miss you, and I hope if you never see me again, my final thoughts were of you, our boys, and our home. The home you've made with your love. Thank you for believing in me. I love you, Marla." He ended the recording.

He hated doing that, but the last thing he wanted was leaving his family with no words at all. He scoffed at himself, because he knew he wasn't very good at doing things like that, but it made him feel just a bit better. He inputted in the settings for the message to be sent in 72 hours when the soonest connection is established as a fail safe if he in fact did die here. If he made it back to the Theseus, it would be almost like a reward to delete the recording and tell his family he loved them in person. That was a gift to motivate any man.

Brinks did a double take as it reexamined the chair that held the charred remains of Zesper. It kneeled and reached underneath where the pilot light ignited the execution. The bot pulled out a strange device half burned by the inferno. With a quick scan, Brinks identified fairly quickly what it was. Even with the extensive damage to it.

"An Eavesdrop, sir." Brinks announced. "Attached to the bottom of the chair."

Locilette nodded a defeated nod. "That must be how he could hear us, and if Zesper revealed too much. Probably to listen if the pilot light was actually working, as well…"

Locilette slowly found his way to his feet. Brinks followed his movements and readied itself for the next room ahead, however, the Ranger's eyes were on the ceiling rather than the door. There had to be a way to get out without moving deeper into the jaws of the lion. Then he spotted it. The vent to the air duct hung in the middle of the corridor behind them with an opening that he was sizing up to actually squeeze his frame inside.

"Sir, I recommend we breach the next room and the next as hard as we can muster. Based on my projections, we should be nearing the administration side of the vessel. This would logically be the sectors of the ship that are the most heavily defended." Brinks advised, running a few scenarios through its internal processors.

"No," Locilette declared without taking his eyes off the vent cover. "It's time we take the initiative, Brinks."

"That would be most wise, sir. What did you have in mind?"

He pointed to the vent. "See that up there? I know you can't fit, but I'm pretty confident if I lose the vest I can just sneak through."

"Sir, I do not advise operating alone. I will not be able to lend additional aid if you were to fall into a skirmish."

"I understand that, but we need to start thinking outside the box here. This guy has us locked down, and if we keep on this path, we're going to die, too. I know you're a robot with little to no survival instincts, but trust me. You do not want to follow the breadcrumbs of someone who wants to kill you."

"You are most correct, sir. I do in fact lack the necessary risk of life as you do. This is why Secura-Droids were created to assist rather than lead. I humbly apologize."

He shook his head. He wasn't quite sure why he felt bad, but he did. It wasn't Brinks's fault his programming didn't allow him to understand the risk versus reward of life out here in the field. Especially in an active, dangerous investigation.

"Forget it, Brinks. Let's strategize for a moment." He motioned to the bot to come closer. "Here's the plan. If his eavesdropping device is out of action, then we have a rare opportunity to make the next move."

"Agreed, sir. You mentioned something about the ventilation?"

"Yeah, that's going to be my ticket out of this corridor. Step one is going to be concealing ourselves just in case there's a camera hidden somewhere in here. We're going to bust out these lights, then I need you to rip off the cover of that vent."

The bot's eyes momentarily flashed green to process something. "Step two is I need you to give me a boost so I can get into those vents. I'll crawl to the next section of rooms and do a little scouting. I'm going to go as far as these air ducts will let me, then try to find a way to get you to move up. You clear each corridor as we push forward, then rinse and repeat until we locate this bastard. "

"A scouting sweep maneuver. Creative use of military strategy on a micro scale, sir. I contain a full library of Captain Neville's studies in my files who created that tactic."

Locilette smirked. "I get to do a lot of reading on these long voyages."

"And is there a step three, sir?"

"I'll figure that out when we get to that point. In the meantime, let's go dark. Let's save as many cartridges as we can. Can you jump high enough to reach the ceiling?"

Without a moment of hesitation the bot squatted down, then rocketed into the air, busting out the glowing red light above it. It came down with a shower of broken glass that spread around the floor. Brinks landed with a loud muffled thud as the pads on the bottoms of its feet impacted the metal floor. It swept some pieces of broken glass off its shoulder plates and moved forward to the next one.

One by one they made their way down the corridor, Brinks wiping out every bit of red light that surrounded them. The farther Brinks got, the darker it became, allowing Locilette plenty of time for his eyes to grow more accustomed to the dark. As soon as the bot busted out the final light at the opposite end, full darkness followed. He felt the hair on the back of his neck stand with the thought of Zesper rising from her chair to take revenge on his broken promise. He took a deep breath to clear his mind. This wasn't the time for childish fears.

The sound of Brinks's footsteps crunching on the glass grew closer and closer, its eyes like two bobbing blue orbs dancing in the darkness. As soon as it got near to him, it switched on a very dim light from one of its eyes, allowing Locilette to view his surroundings. His first reaction was to look around his feet. Shards of glass and bulbs were spread around them almost evenly, like a bed of jagged edges. He cleared an area around the base of the vent, pushing it into a big pile against the wall.

"We are concealed, sir." Brinks announced, looking up to make an estimate of how to get his Ranger up there as safely as possible. In a lightning fast movement, Brinks jumped up as high as its motor powered legs allowed and pulled off the vent cover. The bot landed with a loud thud from the foot pads still holding strong on the bottom of the bot's feet.

Loiclette nodded and began to unstrap his tactical vest. He knew there would be no way he could fit in that cramped space with it on. It made him uncomfortable not having any of his gear within a hand's reach, but this had to be done. They had to get out of this before it was him strapped in a chair like that and Brinks probably reprogrammed to be some kind of nightmarish murder-bot. That was the last thing this psychopath needed at his disposal. As engineer minded as this guy was with his murder devices, he wouldn't be too surprised if he had already developed something like that just waiting up ahead from them. He just prayed that his bot was a better shot.

He hoisted the hefty vest over his head and laid it down against the wall. It slouched over just a little, but the thick armor plates inside helped it keep its shape. Locilette felt thirty pounds lighter. He was confident that his slender build could squeeze through the ducts, but a new concern filled his mind that he hadn't considered before. What if the air ducts were trapped too? Wouldn't some serial killer pseudo-genius think of every possible angle of approach when crafting a murder maze?

He could only imagine it. Methodically pulling himself through the tight ducts, then suddenly nerve gas gets sprayed in his face. Or worse yet, a row of sharpened metal javelins shoot out from somewhere, leaving him to slowly bleed out, his resting place being forgotten about in the last place anyone would ever look for a body. Just fears and uncertainty, he thought. He had a plan, and he had to stay committed to it.

Locilette rummaged through the ammo pouches on the side of his vest and pulled out a handful of cartridges for his plasma arc pistol. He figured that at least a few rounds would be better than nothing if it came down to it. He certainly wasn't looking for a fight, but he sure as hell was going to be ready if, and potentially when, the situation occurred. He slid them into both pockets, trying not to make either one too bulky from the cylindrical plasma rounds contained within each one.

Both pockets bulged out farther than he would've liked, but it should be fine enough to allow him to traverse the tight spaces above. He's never been in a situation like this before, so he never gave the size of plasma shots a second thought. Never would it occur to him that he would ever have to discard his entire set of field gear. Even though he felt the literal weight lifted off his shoulders, he also felt horribly exposed. It was like being caught in the rain without an umbrella, or forgetting your winter coat during a blizzard. It felt unnatural for a Ranger to operate without any gear.

Everything would be okay. It just had to. Locilette gave himself one final check before nodding to the bot awaiting his orders as patiently as a statue. There would be no better time than now. For all he knew, their captors were on the move as well, so time appeared to be of the essence.

"Alright," he said, steeling his nerves. "Give me a boost up."

Brinks kneeled down just below the vent in one fluid motion. Locilette drew in a deep breath, then placed one foot on the bot's shoulder. The dim light from Brinks's eyes reflected off the metal floor, giving him just enough light to find his footing. He grabbed the bot's copper head and pulled himself onto its other shoulder, trying desperately to keep his balance centered. Slowly, Brinks raised him up to the now exposed duct above them. Locilette reached up, grabbing the sides of the duct interior. His arms burned with over exertion, but he quickly threw his elbow inside to give him the leverage to crawl in.

The darkness of the air ducts made it seem like there was an endless void around him, but just moving a few inches reminded him that he was contained in such a small space. It unnerved him in a way he had never felt before. He knew it must have been the circumstances he found himself in rather than the actual fact his body was trapped within a 5x5 box of metal. He fully extended to distribute his body weight as evenly as he could. Even though the ducts were well supported, he didn't want to take any chances of his plan, and himself, crashing down.

Little by little, inch by inch, he pulled himself through the tight length of the ventilation system. He heard the system kick on and a rush of cool air blasting oxygen in his face with a speed that reminded him only of a mid-season storm. Locilette's eyes burned from the intensity of the blowing air. He resorted to just closing his eyes as he moved his way forward. It wasn't as if he could see in the darkness anyway. He decided before coming up here that it would be the wisest move not to alert anyone of his presence with a flashlight more than he probably was while moving above them.

The further he moved, the more a distant memory began to play before his eyes. Shortly after he and his wife bought their house on Kronos Prime, they started hearing a faint noise coming from underneath their floor. They tried their best to ignore it, brushing it off as miniature moles that are native to Kronos, protesting them cultivating the thirteen acres that surrounded their property. Marla couldn't stand it anymore and asked if he could get into the crawlspace under their house to flush them out. As much as he just wanted to relax during his time off, he would do anything for her to relieve the pressure of raising their then infant boy.

He opened the crawl space door on the side of their house and crawled into the dark underbelly of their cottage home. He pulled himself little by little until he reached the point that he was certain was under their bedroom. Tucked away in the corner was a litter of Kronation cats, huddled around their tired, starving mother. He already knew what he would have to do when he told his wife. Every single day before he was sent back on assignment, he would crawl in that dark space to make sure that mother was taken care of. In a strange way, he saw his wife in that silly cat. While he was off traversing the stars, Marla was alone here with their baby. It was his duty to see them both thrive in his absence. He never asked what became of the cats after he left. He made a mental note to ask Marla if, no, *when* he got back home.

It felt like he had been in this claustrophobic space for hours, but in reality he was sure it had been only a few minutes that had passed. Now that he had a moment to reflect on his situation, he was acutely aware that the Rangers Academy didn't properly train him on handling situations such as these. There is no section in the field manual that states how to flank an enemy via air duct on a derelict vessel. He allowed himself a brief, quiet chuckle. Most of the work he did lacked any *real* training, but that's one of the reasons he enjoyed doing what he did so much. He was quite literally making up the rules as he went along, which gave him a sense of empowerment.

A sliver of light illuminated the small area up ahead, showing the many years of dust and dirt accumulation on the sides of the duct walls. With that sight, he pulled the high neck of his shirt over his mouth to avoid breathing in as much of that as he could, however, dirt and dust was the least of his concerns at the moment. He just kept his eyes trained on the light ahead as he carefully pulled himself inch by inch.

The shadow the light was casting on the wall had several horizontal lines of black reaching across its entirety. It had to be the vent covering from the next section, he thought. As he neared it, the sound of a man's cries began to echo off the walls around him and travel down the dark duct in a continuous plea of help. Locilette froze and tried to focus his hearing on the vent. There were sounds of an intense struggle, then a loud crack, like the whipping from a leather belt across a hard surface. The man begged for someone to stop, but the struggle seemed to continue on.

Locilette pulled himself to the vent and peered through the small openings in the bars. A large, well lit auditorium with a raised platform at the end came into view as his eyes adjusted to the brightness. There were decorative pillars lining the walls where several rows of chairs sat.

The heraldry of the Josakk Merchants Guild draped down from the pillars with only a single banner of the Arkaan Empire held high above the stage. It appeared to be some sort of congregation place for the Yanagi's more religious crew members and perhaps a place for crew-wide meetings, as well.

His attention was immediately drawn to the center of the stage where two men were struggling with another, who thrashed in their tight holds. They eventually were able to subdue the man long enough to wrap a noose made of cables around the man's neck. Locilette's heart sank into the pit of his stomach. He was going to witness a man's execution if he didn't act fast. His plan to just scout ahead seemed to already fail as his morality was being called into check. If he intervened, he would just fall right back into this psycho's hands.

One thing did appear to be clear now. The killer wasn't working alone. Something in his gut told him that any one of those two men weren't the actual guy, but the enforcers of whatever cult ideals he integrated into their psyche. He knew that if he was to get involved, his cover would be blown, especially if these goons failed to show back up. But he couldn't let this man die before his eyes. His life's work was to protect people, and he sure as hell wasn't going to break his oath of defending the citizens of Arkaa now.

Without another thought, Locilette rolled on his side to slide out his pistol. This wasn't going to be an easy shot. On top of that, he knew he was extremely out of practice, but this was the best bet he had. He placed the barrel between the bars on the vent, his eyes locking on to one of the men who moved a lot less than the other. He took in a deep breath and held it in his lungs to slow as much movement from his own body as he could.

His lungs burned, but he held strong. The hesitation started to creep into his mind as his target began to walk around the man strung up. He started yelling insults at him, and smacked him in the face, leading to more pleading from their victim. It was now or never. With one more micro adjustment, Locilette slowly squeezed the trigger. A blue bolt ignited from the tip of the pistol, making a bright blue flash surround him in his tiny hiding space. The bolt of lightning speared through the air, striking his target in the back and sending him falling to the ground like a sack of meat.

The other man's head glanced at his fallen partner, then began to whip around in search of the shot's origin. Locilette let the air escape his lungs as he expelled the spent cartridge into the duct, then in a fluid motion, he inserted another into the loader on the back. As soon as he closed it with a loud click, a burst from a magma bolt struck the side of the air duct just behind him. Reactively, Locilette looked behind him to see the gaping hole being melted away in an expanding orange glow. The molten metal surrounding it began to drip uncomfortably close to his boots.

He punched at the vent cover, but it didn't budge. If he couldn't get out of this duct, he was going to be the next thing bubbling in a molten mess. With everything in him, he punched it over and over again until it started to bend, then popped out onto the floor below. He started to pull himself out, head first, but when he turned his head to locate the gunman, all he saw was the orange burst from the end of his barrel. Without a single thought, he let go of the sides of the vent opening, and allowed himself to free fall down to the floor.

He crashed hard, the impact knocking the wind out of his lungs like a punch to the gut. Where his senses lacked, his training took over. Obviously dazed, he still managed to take a quick, calculated peek at where the shooter was. He was in the midst of reloading the magma musket, stuffing the bolt down the thin barrel. Locilette quickly whipped his pistol around with both hands and fired a lightning arc across the massive assembly room. The blue bolt struck him in the chest, sending him flying into the wall several feet behind where he stood.

All was quiet for a moment. The man with the noose around his neck began to whimper from underneath a hood made of a brown sack. Locilette hastily climbed to his feet, his vision blurring for a brief moment. He shook the dizziness out of his head, then quickly reloaded his pistol shot without taking his eyes off the motionless body across from him. The barrel of his weapon stayed trained on it as he approached. The musket had fallen from his hands during the impact, along with the round he was attempting to load into it.

The man was dead. Blood began to pool around him from his chest. Locilette kicked away some of the scorched clothing to see the gaping hole created by the arc bolt. It was a disgusting wound that bore deep within the gunman's chest, exposing his obliterated ribs within. It was a wound that would kill anything that didn't have a sliver of armor on. Taking a life was never a goal, but he saw value in this. He could tell just by looking at both of the men he had to put down that they were the farthest thing from an organized militia. He had seen some rebel factions better equipped than these two. It gave him a well-needed sense of relief that these were just civilians attempting to play soldier.

"Is someone there?" The man spoke out, his voice trembling with fear. "Please don't hurt me anymore."

Locilette walked over to him and pulled off the hood. The face of a man who had been through hell stared back at him. His greasy blonde hair ran down the length of his shoulder, but his bright blue eyes were red from the tears he shed. His clothing was nicer than the other people he'd seen to this point, well, the corpses he'd seen, at least. It resembled that of an officer's uniform, which would probably explain why he was in the predicament he was. This killer had a thing for rebelling against authority, so making a public display of his death would solidify his position aboard the Yanagi.

"I'm Locilette, fifth degree Ranger, I'm here to help."

"Oh, thank the Pantheon! My prayers were actually answered!" He cried to the heavens. "I pleaded - I begged for someone to come, and you actually did!"

"What's your name?" Locilette asked, helping him out of the noose tied from a braided cable.

"I'm Phillip, navigation officer here on the Yanagi. Please, these people are fucking nuts, we have got to get out of here now."

"Believe me, I know. Who were the men that attacked you?"

Phillip scoffed, "A bunch of psychos is what they were. They're a part of that wannabe's band of disciples, just a couple of blowhards that were given guns. This is why guns need to be banned on *all* merchant vessels. Bunch of lowlife crooks, if you ask me."

Locilette ignored such an ignorant statement, especially when it was his own firearm that just saved his life. "Can you tell me anything about the wannabe that you're referring to?"

"Not much beyond him targeting the officer staff when he led his little coup d'etat. I've been kept in a cage for months, paraded for all the other nut cases to see. Please, sir, can we get out of here? When these two don't report back at the top of every hour, they'll send a search party to locate them. Trust me, you do *not* want that to happen"

"Yeah, but I have a problem I need to find a solution to before we can make our escape. Whoever is behind this nightmare somehow hacked my ship sitting in the hangar. He completely locked me out of all my systems."

Phillip shook his head with disgust. "Markus…"

"I'm sorry?"

"His name is Markus." Phillip explained with a look of pure hatred on his pale face. "He was on my staff in navigation. A brilliant kid that has a knack for computers and other electronics. He bought into the Chosen's garbage about achieving immortality with the Pantheon and other crap like that."

Locilette raised an eyebrow, "Do you think he was the one who hacked my ship?"

"Not a doubt in my mind the little fucker did. He used to hack my own comms as a prank whenever I would be in a private conversation with Josakk heads."

A connection began to form before him. Why would a low-ranking navigation officer want to hack the communications of the Yanagi and the heads of the Josakk guild? His first thought was this kid was trying to get involved with some potential inside trading with the guild's stocks, but that didn't seem like something a young officer would do. At least, not on the surface. No, he was sure it had to be something else.

"Mr. Phillip, why were these men trying to string you up?" Locilette asked, examining the magma musket.

Phillip was silent for a moment. He placed a hand on the marks around his neck, and breathed a deep sigh. Locilette could tell it wasn't a sigh of frustration, but a sigh of relief. He was proud that he chose to intervene to save this man's life.

"I was the next prop to be used for his display for who they referred to as *Spoiler*. I'm assuming they were referring to you. He is a big fan of your ability to solve his puzzles. He acted like a child in a cupcake shop when you figured out how to solve the teeth game. Fucking sick-"

Voices started coming from the half opened door behind the stage. "Quick, we need to hide!" Locilette barked, pulling the man behind one of the pillars. He hid himself behind the adjacent one, and held his pistol close to his chest. The sounds of several footsteps came pounding towards them.

Locilette held his breath. The sound of his heart began to pound in his ears as the door burst opened, but they didn't rush in. He could hear one of their heavy breathing as, he assumed, was taking in the scene that Locilette left for them. He made eye contact with Phillip, and slowly raised a finger over his lips. There was no telling how many men there were, and Locilette did not want to find out. Phillip returned a shaken nod. The poor guy looked as if he was about to crack. If Locilette was being honest with himself, he knew if it wasn't for his training, he would be, too.

"We gotta go," The voice of a frantic man exclaimed. "The Enlightened is gonna need to hear this. He might have to expedite our ascension to the next stage!"

"Glory!" The combined voices answered in unison. Their feet padded back off into the direction they came, leaving Locilette with ever more questions.

What was the next stage?

Chapter Eleven

Locilette watched as the last bit of his water poured over the face of Phillip. He carelessly poured it into his mouth like a man who hadn't drank a drop in days. He could only assume that these terrorists weren't the best at treating their prisoners with respect, like most armed religious movements, so he allowed the man to take in whatever liquid life he had left. Hopefully he could get back to his ship soon to get a drink himself.

Phillip wiped his mouth with the sleeve of his blue officer's uniform. His eyes were glazed over with the expression of a man whose thoughts were thousands of miles away. Locilette could relate. He felt like every few minutes he was forcing himself to forget home so he could stay present to the dangers around him. To forget home on this floating tomb was to keep himself alive so he could actually return to the home that awaited him. He wasn't trying to keep that a fantasy, he *was* going to make it out of this, one way or another.

Brinks peeked through the door to the corridor beyond. Just after the group of armed men left to tell the Enlightened One of their discovery, Locilette deemed it safe for his bot to make its way to their position. Brinks had the plasma arc rifle at the ready and remained in security mode just in case they came back. It was only a matter of time before they stumbled into a skirmish, and Brinks was going to bring everything it had to protect the new civilian attachment, as well as the Ranger who led them.

Locilette examined the magma musket closely. He had never actually used one before, but he knew the basics of it. The shot is loaded down the muzzle as the firing mechanism was too bulky near the stock to allow a break-action weapon. It may have taken a few seconds longer to load, but it was one hell of a devastating weapon. He couldn't help but wipe the sweat from his face just thinking how close he was to melting alive from the splash damage this thing caused.

"You ever used one of these before?" Locilette asked.

Phillip shrugged. "Nothing beyond basic weapons training, but I'm not an expert shot or anything."

"That's good enough."

Locilette extended the musket, along with the pouch of magma shots that were slung over the shoulder of one of the dead men. Phillip's hesitation caught his attention. He held it there another couple of seconds before noticing Locilette's confused stare. He smiled with a nod before promptly grabbing both from the Ranger. He examined it closely, as if he had never touched one before. His eyes traced the long barrel all the way to the opening where a magma shot was presently loaded.

Locilette tried to hide his bewilderment the best he could, but was shocked when the officer actually looked down the barrel. He closed one eye to look down then nodded in approval. He wondered what exactly Phillip was approving. Did he not think someone of his experience and skill could properly load a basic muzzleloader? He couldn't help but feel slightly offended by that thought, whether it was actually the case or not. He risked his life to save this man, so the last thing he wanted was some sort of criticism for a weapon he knew was handled properly.

Locilette shook those thoughts out of his head. He was sure this man didn't mean any offense by it, but it bothered him nonetheless. He gave Phillip the benefit of the doubt that the things he'd been through the past few months must have been hell, so trusting a complete stranger handing him a weapon must have been difficult to do. This investigation, this environment, this ship was starting to get to him in more ways than he was comfortable with. He had been in some dire positions before, but none quite like this. He just needed to keep his head straight and his objective in focus. He needed to get off this ship.

"Mr. Phillip," Locilette began, taking out his PDA to record some notes. "What can you tell me about this *Enlightened One?*"

Phillip sighed deeply. "The man is one of the most brilliant men I've ever met. I mean, he *actually* convinced most of the crew to turn on the ship's officers. I've never seen anything like it before."

"How did he pull off such a stunt?"

"From what I know, he was a prisoner being transported to the Ares System to stand trial for the murder of some missionaries on some far off planet that I've never even heard of before. Since that system's population is still too low to support its own judicial branch, he was transferred to the closest system equipped to handle such a case."

Locilette nodded while typing away on the device's small keyboard. "Was it a premeditated murder or opportunistic? Crime of passion?"

"No, it's actually a seriously fucked up story," Phillip said, his face taking a grim appearance. "This guy invites these Pantheon missionaries to his estate in a barely habitual region, then proceeds to ritualistically kill these holy young people to, well, it's super fucked up, like I said."

"No, please, anything could help me build a profile on this guy."

Phillip turned, his eyes almost glazing over as he recounted the details. "He allegedly murders these young people similarly to how he did the people of the Yanagi. Games, murders masqueraded as some fucked up games where there is only one winner: him. There was some other nonsense about ascending to the Pantheon or something crazy like that."

"What position was he hoping to take in the Pantheon? The texts are clear that in order to join, one of the eternal beings must willingly give it up, or be slain by another equal entity." Locilette asked, genuinely intrigued by this killer's thought process.

"He said that he was going to carve out his own spot amongst the eternal Pantheon. He was going to establish a new seat of power among the souls of the stars."

It was a disturbing thought that kept running in Locilette's head. Trying to find logic in a serial killer's motives were a waste of time, but it still made little sense. Did this guy truly believe he could ascend to the heights of the Pantheon by simply murdering people? It was a fool's errand to put himself in the mind frame of someone so disturbed as that, but he had to try to understand him if he was going to end his crusade of death.

"I'm curious," Locilette stopped typing for a moment. "Why were you singled out to be hanged?"

He shrugged. "I didn't conform to his fucked up little cult or his party of maniacs."

"Wait, you mentioned the word *party*. Is there some kind of significance to that ?"

Locilette caught Phillip's hesitation. He knew something more than he was letting on. The sight of the first bloody sign he witnessed as he stumbled into this maze of torment flashed in his mind. *Welcome to the Party.* He figured that this psychopath was referring to a party-like event, it never crossed his mind that he could be referring to a group of people. It would make perfect sense with the information he had now.

"Can you go a little more in depth about the party?" Locilette pushed again.

"The most loyal of the Enlightened's followers. They were there for him in the early days, some even committing vicious crimes just to be aboard the same ship as him to enact his plan."

Again, Locilette looked up from his PDA. "You're telling me that he had followers with enough foresight to get themselves in trouble, because they knew they would have to be extradited to Ares with him?"

Phillip nodded grimly. Locilette again found himself rather impressed by what this man could accomplish even without being directly involved. He knew that most cult leaders were masters of manipulation, but this was something on an entirely different level. However, his mind began to float back to the sign. Why was it welcoming? Did this man seriously think he could persuade someone like him, a Ranger, to participate in his gory deed to achieve his dreams of joining the Pantheon? It made him sick to his stomach to think about.

"Tell me, was he planning on trying to convince *me* to join his party?" Locilette asked directly.

Phillip's eyes locked to his. "You have no idea what he had planned for you."

Before Locilette had a chance to ask a follow up question, the sounds of feet storming down the corridor, echoing off the walls. The three tried their best to conceal themselves as the armed men came running by, stopping only briefly to look into the room. One man leaned in, then pulled out a brick of a radio from his pocket. He switched the frequency with the knob on top, then brought it up to his mouth.

"Hey, you were right. They're dead. Looks like they took his magma shot too, keep your eyes peeled." He spoke into the device.

Only static came through as the group awaited a response. Locilette leaned out just enough to see them. There were seven men standing near the doorway to the auditorium, some with similar magma muskets, others sporting various types of make-shift melee weapons forged from the Yanagi herself. However, that wasn't what really caught his eye. All seven wore a mask that appeared to be cut from the metal walls of the ship, just as their weapons. Each mask was different in small ways, giving them a sense of individuality, or at least the illusion of it.

"That's no fun. Make sure they don't get to the bridge. If they figure it out, then kiss your eternal ever-after goodbye." A voice broke through the static. The voice sounded familiar. Locilette was sure it was the same voice that had come over the ship's intercom just before Zesper was set ablaze.

"Of course."

The man stashed the radio back into his pack, then waved his squad forward. They jogged up the corridor and turned the corner out of sight. What was in the bridge that needed such a safeguard? He didn't have much time to think of a theory as Phillip caught his eye with a look of helplessness. As bad as he wanted to get to the bottom of this, his first priority was always the care of civilians. Brinks rose from behind a wagon full of dirty laundry to make sure all was safe.

"Sir, I would advise we form a plan with haste. The likelihood of another patrol passing through here yet again is quite high." Brinks counseled, its eyes flashing green with calculations.

Brinks was right. They couldn't just stay here waiting for the inevitable. His first thought was to tell Phillip to stay put, but if he was being honest with himself, he wasn't confident that he could keep himself hidden long enough for he and Brinks to finish their investigation. No, the safest course of action would be for Phillip to tag along for extra firepower in case of an altercation, but more importantly to keep a safe eye on him. Even if it would put the civilian's life in danger, that's just the risk that had to be taken if they were going to make it through this in one piece.

"Alright, here's the plan. We're going to follow those guys, because whatever they're going to protect, that's where I want to be." Locilette stated.

"Wait," Phillip responded with a look of horror. "You want to go the *same* direction as them? That's suicide!"

"Keep your voice down! Look, I understand you're scared, but I still have to get to the bottom of this."

It was as if Phillip shrunk as he leaned against the wall. "Man, you just don't understand. These people will hurt you in the most disturbing, violating ways you can imagine. I- I can't go back there."

Loiclette took a moment to think. He didn't want to put this poor man through a triggering event, making him become a liability. But time was of the essence, and if he didn't find out what the ascension event was soon, he had a strong feeling that it would be irreversible for this ship and her inhabitants. Himself being among them.

"Mr. Phillip, believe me, I've seen some pretty messed up things in my career, but we have to get to the bridge. If I can piece together who this guy is and what his motives are, we can build a case on him that'll put him away in a prison where he'll never hurt another soul again. I'm going to need your help to do that."

Phillip pondered his situation for a moment then sighed deeply. "Man, please, don't let me die."

It felt like a knife to the chest, but he couldn't let it show on his face. It was Phillip's words, but it was Zesper's voice that bounced around in his head. He promised that once already on this ship, and he failed horribly to protect her life. He wasn't sure he had it in him to make that promise again and truly mean it, but he had to try. That's all he could do was try.

This was a chance to right that wrong. Zesper was dead, but Phillip was alive and looking to him for guidance. He couldn't let the past hold him back from what he needed to do. He refused to feel sorry for himself. That woman was brutally murdered under his care, but there was no way under the Pantheon's stars that recent history was going to repeat itself. They were *all* getting off this hell ship together.

"Hey, I'm not gonna let anything happen to you. We're going to get out of here one way or another. Okay? You just have to follow my lead, and please, please try and keep as quiet as you can." Locilette reassured.

Phillip nodded, his face paled from what Locilette could only assume was the horrors he'd been through playing over and over in his mind. He wasn't far from cracking. As much as he wanted to get that man off this ship, if his mind failed him and he drew too much attention to himself, it was on him. Locilette had to continue on with or without him.

"Brinks, let's get going. You take point."

The bot moved ahead of them without a word, the plasma arc rifle held tight against its metal shoulder. It came to the turn at the end of the corridor where the group of men ran off and leaned ever so slightly around. The corridor went on ahead for a little bit further, but there was a set of double doors to the right where one masked assailant stood. He stood there stoically like a statue of a war hero, weapon held firmly in his grasp.

Brinks found Locilette's gaze, and held up two fingers to its eyes, then followed it up with one metal finger raised. *Eyes on one hostile.* Locilette motioned for Phillip to hold, and placed a quick finger over his lips. He crept forward on his stomach to get a good look around, keeping as low of a profile as he could. The guard on the door had the same metal mask on as the others that passed through here. He wasn't entirely sure if this guy was a part of that patrol since he didn't get a great look at all of them. He wondered if this was his posting, then that meant there was something in that room worth guarding.

Locilette tugged at his bot to get his attention and whispered as softly as he could. "I'll distract him, you neutralize." The bot responded with a thumbs up.

Locilette fished around in his pocket for a single cartridge, only now realizing that he had forgotten about his vest in the previous section of the ship. There was no time to worry about that now. He would just have to handle business with the ammunition he had on him currently. If it came to it, he could just take the magma musket from Phillip.

With an unspent cartridge held firmly in his fingers, he lifted himself up slightly and tossed the cartridge of concentrated plasma across the open corridor. It sailed over the guard's head, and clanked several times before coming to a rest at the end of the hall. The masked man's head whipped to the side. With lightning reflexes, he shouldered his magma musket, and observed for a few moments. Slowly, he started to make his way toward the noise.

"What's the word?" He called out. "If you don't say the Enlightened One's word, I swear I'll blow your fucking lungs out your back!"

The only thing he heard was the pounding of heavy footsteps. The stock of Brinks's rifle struck the back of his head with enough force to send his unconscious body falling into the wall. The bot stood over him for a second, assessing whether or not to deliver another blow, but deemed it unnecessary. He was lucky if he wouldn't have permanent damage from the strike. Another hit would surely kill the man. It was an act he was incapable of, unless specifically commanded by Locilette.

"Nice work, Brinks," Locilette said, quietly walking up behind them.

He kicked the musket away from the man and searched him for any extra magma shot they could use. Crumpled up papers with prophetic words of the Enlightened and the badge of a female officer was the only thing he could find. It seemed a bit strange to not have more than one shot for a weapon that is notorious for its long reload time. Could their ammo be so limited in supply that they can only allow one shot per weapon? As unlikely as it seemed, it wouldn't be that much of a surprise.

Merchant vessels usually only had enough firepower on board to keep the peace in the event of a mutiny. He wondered if the merchant guild operating the Yanagi relied on the decommissioned guns on her hull to discourage pirates from getting too frisky as she sailed by her lonesome in space. Keeping a ton of weapons on board was seen as a liability for these money hungry guilds, so it was safe to assume that the stockpile was low to begin with. When these people overthrew the ship's officer staff, there's no telling how many shots were expended in the initial skirmish. With that thought, it made a lot more sense as to the abundance of makeshift melee weapons.

Phillip jogged up behind them, the barrel of the musket pointed straight in front of him. Loiclette rolled his eyes and pushed the barrel up to the ceiling when he got close. He nodded without uttering a word. He was out of his element, but Locilette forgave his inexperience.

"What is this room used for?" Locilette asked, motioning toward the door before them.

Phillip thought for a moment then shrugged. "I'm not entirely sure to be quite honest. We stored weird things in weird places sometimes. One job, this may have been a supply closet, then another it could store chemicals."

"Whatever it is, these guys want it protected. Let's get in there quickly before another group starts wondering where their guy is. Brinks, get this door open."

Brinks magnetized the rifle to its back, then kneeled down to examine the door panel. The bot knew it was highly likely that it would be locked, but it tapped the open button anyway. As expected, the light on the panel blinked a bright red. It pulled the panel off the wall, exposing the electronics within, then extended the short cable from its chest. It snapped into the small insert on the back of the panel to begin processing its hacking features.

Without warning, the floor beneath them began to vibrate with a rumble coming from somewhere else on the ship. It was enough to catch Brinks's attention for a moment, its eye reverting back to the standard blue to glance around. An unsettling feeling ran through Locilette to see his bot reacting to something like that. It more than likely meant nothing good for them, which would be on brand for how things have been going.

"Brinks, what is it?" Locilette inquired to his Secura-Droid.

"I apologize, sir, but I am unable to answer that question. I am unsure as to what it could be at this present time. Would you like me to investigate?"

"No, let's get get in there-"

"It's the engines." Phillip interrupted, his eyes glazed over. "We're moving."

An expression of concern flooded Locilette's face. The Yanagi was supposed to be a derelict. Derelicts are incapable of moving. He felt a sinking feeling in the pit of his stomach. He thought that it was stepping off that elevator in the hangar bay that sprung the Enlightened's trap, but now he was reconsidering that thought. What if the mere act of responding to the derelict call was the trap being sprung? What if it was always his destiny to end up here to stop a false ascension?

No, he couldn't allow his thoughts to be clouded. He took an oath to not allow his own personal religious beliefs to come into conflict with his duties. He was here because of a responder call, which he had done numerous times before. This was no different. The Pantheon wasn't driving him to be here, nothing was beyond his obligation to serve the people of Arkaa. He prayed, no, he hoped that was truly the case.

Locilette put everything into blocking those thoughts out. He carefully crept to the corner at the end of the hall and leaned to do a quick look out. A short hall capped by double doors at the end was thankfully all he saw. A small window was at eye level on both sides of the door, allowing him to at least get some kind of idea what was coming before they hopefully saw him. It was quiet for now, but something in his gut told him that their luck was eventually going to run out here.

He squinted his eyes to get a better look at what awaited them on the other side. From where he stood, all he could really make out was three massive windows that appeared to be pointed to the front of the ship. The stars were moving rapidly off to the side, confirming that they were turning to the Yanagi's port side. He didn't know where they were going, and he sure as hell didn't want to find out. They were going to have to expedite their push to the bridge even at a heightened risk.

Locilette turned back just in time to see the door Brinks was working on pop open. However, his eyes darted down the hall from where they came from as six armed, masked men turned the corner. Everyone stood motionless for a moment as the two groups eyed each other down. They stood quite a ways away, but Locilette could tell most of their eyes fell on Phillip, who was cowering behind Brinks's massive frame. Their hesitation was Locilette's initiative. Without another thought, he quickly drew his plasma arc pistol and sent a bright, blue blot of crackling lightning thundering down the hall.

"Brinks!" Locilette yelled, dipping back behind the corner.

The bolt streaked across the air, striking the lead masked man in the arm. He yelped out in pain as he spun around in the air, cupping the charred wound with his other hand. The long, sharpened piece of metal tumbled against the wall with a long clank before landing by his feet. The others reacted to the fallen comrade, one taking him by the arm and dragging him away back down the hall. Three more lifted their magma muskets and fired a volley down the hall toward the fleeing bot covering Phillip with its metallic body.

One of the bolts grazed the back of Brinks's leg, making it callpase to the floor. Brinks pushed Phillip around the corner to safety, then struggled to take its footing. With a lightning quick diagnosis of its leg, the damage was severe to the motor functions in the joints. Without warning, Brinks was pulled hard around the corner by Locilette, giving every ounce of strength he could muster to save his bot from more damage.

Locilette quickly ejected the spent cartridge, then slid another into the insert. Exhaust from the sides of his pistol bellowed out white smoke. A green light illuminated from the weapon's handle, telling him that it was now safe to use. In a fluid motion, he placed one hand on the wall to anchor himself, then leaned out to fire another shot. The blue arc of electricity erupted from the barrel, but sliced between two of the men. It struck the wall behind them, leaving a charred hole in the metal paneling.

"Brinks, you alright?" Locilette asked, his voice struggling to overcome the blasts of the volleying magma musket fire.

"I am adequate to continue performing my duties, sir." Brinks responded, preparing to fire a shot. "May I advise we exfiltrate as soon as possible?" The bot leaned and fired a quick shot as the men pounded the magma down their barrel. "One hostile KIA, sir."

He had to think fast. Phillip tried the double doors behind them to the room with the large windows, but it was no use. He resorted to pounding on the glass with the stock of the musket, but still wouldn't give way. These windows were designed to handle possible breaches within the sections of the ship. If by chance the hull of the Yanagi was punctured on either side, the other would remain safe from the vacuum of space.

"Come on out!" A voice called out from beyond their safe haven. "Toss out your weapons, and step out with your arms raised. Nobody else has to die here today. The Enlightened wants to meet you in person, Ranger Locilette."

The sound of his name leaving that psycho's lips felt like nails on a chalkboard. If they knew his name, he was worried about what else they knew from rummaging through his ship. Did they know his kids' names? His wife? Worst of all, did they know where he lived? He couldn't imagine putting his family in danger. If he was to get captured, there wasn't a doubt in his mind that this so-called *Enlightened* would find his family just for the sport of it. His eyes darted around for a moment, instinctually looking for some kind of way out. The door.

"Okay, fine!" Locilette responded. "You have to promise not to harm us."

"The Enlightened does as he wills. Come out!"

"Alright, listen guys." Locilette whispered. "We're going to make a run for the door."

"You're fucking insane! They'll kill us!" Phillip protested as quietly as he could manage.

"Look, if we stay here we *will* be killed. This is the best chance we have. Make sure everything is loaded, and when I count to three, we're going to make a run for it. As soon as you clear the corner, fire at them. Hopefully we'll catch them off guard long enough to make it."

Phillip began to tremble. "Die by my flesh melting from my body, or being tortured to death. Both are just wonderful ways to go."

"Here we go. One…Two…Three!"

The three burst into a full sprint. As soon as Locilette cleared the corner, he saw the orange flash of the magma shot launch at him. He responded with a quick shot of his own, and a fraction of a second later, a second plasma arc bolt trailed by a magma bolt followed suit. In the corner of his eye he saw the men drop down for cover, giving him plenty of time to pass through the door. He glanced behind to see Brinks standing in the doorway, but the screeching cry of Phillip came wailing behind him. He spun around to see the Yanagi Officer laying on the floor, clutching his leg. From where he stood he could see the extent of his injury, but a moment later the group rushed him. They started beating him with blunt weapons, and as soon as they noticed Locilette and Brinks standing in the doorway, they charged.

"Brinks, close the fucking door!" Locilette yelled.

Brinks punched the door panel, making it slide closed. One of the men's fingers got stuck in the gap, but his screams in agony ceased as he managed to pull it free. The Ranger and the bot stood there in silence as they listened to the horrified cries of Phillip being dragged away to meet a fate that they couldn't save him from. The only thought he could manage was that he failed once again to protect a life.

Chapter Twelve

Locilette tried his best not to move a muscle. He made himself as small as he possibly could to conceal his body from the approaching band of enforcers. The rhythmic sound of their footsteps echoed through the hall, causing him to tense with every step. He had to calm his nerves if he was going to pull this off the way he planned.

It became apparent that simply evading these madmen wasn't going to get him off this ship. No, it was time to take the fight to them. He and Brinks situated themselves in a small closet just off the main corridor of the ship's administration. He wasn't completely sure where they were, but he would bet his life on it that the bridge couldn't be too far away from where they were. And he certainly was about to risk his life on that bet.

Drastic situations like this demanded drastic actions. Locilette and Brinks prepared themselves to launch their ambush from the dark closet that appeared to have had its door removed for reasons he didn't want to consider at this moment. It was the perfect spot. If they were responsible for the door's removal, then they wouldn't be suspicious of the obvious opening. He was confident that they could take on a small group, but what if it was more than that? What if they came fifteen strong, or however many they had brainwashed into their murderous club? It didn't matter anyway. As soon as they passed, the two would surely be spotted and killed on the spot.

With slow and steady movements, he wiped the sweat from his head. He lowered himself into a crouch, then carefully extended a piece of broken mirror from the trashed bathroom nearby he managed to scavenge. They had to duck in there momentarily to allow a pair of men carrying the almost lifeless body of a woman to who knows where off within the inner ship. He pushed the glass out just enough to see the group approaching.

Four. Only four men. He knew that he could do this, but it was going to require precision he knew Brinks possessed. It was his own aim he worried about. He was by no means a bad shot, but his job wasn't all about shootouts and raids like the media would like the public to believe. He had to pass an annual firearms assessment to be able to carry his weapon of choice into the field, which he did every year. No, this wasn't the time to be doubting his abilities. They were going to be no more than ten feet away.

He pulled the mirror shard back in and left it by the door way. He signed to his bot of the approaching men, which Brinks responded with a sharp nod. It raised its rifle to its shoulder, its barrel sticking out far from its body in anticipation to deliver a fatal shot. Locilette followed suit. He backed away from the doorway and slid his pistol from his holster. He lifted his weapon to eye height. His hands were sweating worse than he had ever experienced before, but his arm held firm and his hand steady.

Locilette could hear his shaky breath as he drew in a deep sigh. With that realization, he could feel his hands begin to tremble under the weight of his pistol. This place was getting to him much more than he realized. Although his extensive training and career experience shielded him from a great deal of the trauma he had witnessed to this point, everyone had their limit, and he was almost at his own.

The real nagging feeling that crept into his mind was what would he actually do if he couldn't get the answers he sought on the Yanagi's bridge? Would that even help him get off this evil place, or would it just be another stupid puzzle he had fallen into? This psycho can't be that good, could he? His thoughts panicked at the possibility that this, too, right where he stood in ambush, was another step in an overarching game crafted just for him. His stomach tightened in a tight knot. He prayed over and over, begging the Pantheon to give him just a brief moment of reprieve. Where his emotions failed him, his training took over like the switch of a light.

Entering his vision from the right of the doorway, the lead masked man entered. He wore a bright orange jumpsuit that resembled the standard uniform for transporting prisoners. Clutched loosely in his hands was another magma musket with its hammer pulled back. He was expecting a fight, but there wasn't going to be a fight today. No, Locilette was going to be the one slaughtering these animals this time.

Locilette didn't have to adjust his aim a bit. The man walked directly into the path of his aim. The iron sights found its home on the man's ear, and like a reaction, Locilette squeezed the trigger, sending a bright blue flash expelling from the tip of the pistol. The closet flashed with the light of the electric bolt cracking through the air. It struck the side of the man's head in a fraction of a second, sending a gut wrenching display of blood and brain matter on the opposite wall.

"Whoa!" Was all the next man could get out before he met the same fate from Brinks's shot.

Locilette darted from the closet at a full sprint and jumped over one of the deceased men. His body was still twitching abnormally as Locilette hurled himself over it to shoulder tackle the stunned man behind. He broke out of his shock a fraction too late as Locilette crashed into him, sending both flying into the wall. They wrestled briefly before the masked man was able to kick off the Ranger long enough to whip out the sharpened metal blade he had tucked into what appeared to be a sheath made of a burlap sack.

He swung it wildly in the air, Locilette only managing to dodge it by a hair each time. His panic began to set in, but in the corner of his eye he saw Brinks shed off a blow before wrapping its large metal hand around the last man's throat. His cries were distraction enough for Locilette to close the distance on his attacker, and grabbed the weapon with both hands. The masked man tried to wrap his arm around his throat, but Locilette sunk his teeth down as hard as he could into the man's exposed arm. He wailed in his ear, and tried to pull away, but Locilette used the distance to grab the man's sleeve, and threw his hip into his stomach.

He gasped as he flipped over the Ranger's shoulder, falling flat on his back. He tried to jump back up to his feet, but was met with a tip of Locilette's boot smashing against his face. He went limp and slumped over to the side, blood streaming from his nose. Locilette shot a glance back to see the life in the last man's eye fade away as Brinks had strangled every ounce of oxygen out of him. When the bot deemed it satisfied, it released the man, letting his motionless body go crashing to the floor.

"Did you kill him?" Locilette asked between heaves of breath.

"I did not, sir. As per my programming. He may have severe memory loss and a possible concussion, but his life should be intact by a margin of 99.879%."

Loiclette nodded. He didn't really care if the man survived or not, the only thing he was concerned about was getting any information that he could to figure this out. He waited for a moment just to see if anyone else was going to come, but none appeared to have heard the commotion. However, he knew that it could change in a moment's notice.

He observed the bodies scattered around him. All four had the metal masks on, all different in some small way. He kneeled down to the man he knocked unconscious and examined it more closely. Now that he had a moment to actually look at the man, he could see that he had an unkept beard that curled around the edges of the metal. It was designed to almost resemble an animal face. It was feline in nature, but had two long metal ears jetting out from the sides. It sent a chill through him seeing a grown man wear something as juvenile as this for such horrendous reasons.

He slipped his fingers into the corners of the mask, and slid it off the man's face. He looked like his face hadn't been washed in weeks. Black dirt, crusty scabs, and the blood from Locilette's final blow littered the man's wrinkled face. What intrigued him even more was what was just above his brow. Seared into the flesh of his forehead was the emblem that Brinks discovered in the brig by the hangar. It didn't seem to show signs of recent healing, which made him wonder when it was done.

He went around to the other three men to see if they held the same markings. Each one of them had the emblem of the Enlightened burned into their foreheads, but what Locilette struggled with was why. If the symbol was hidden behind a mask, then what power did it hold? If nobody was able to see your dedication towards your cult's leader, then why even go through the process of getting it done? Then it hit him. It wasn't something to show other people at all. Instead of showing others your allegiance to the Enlightened, it was meant for you and you alone. It was a silent dedication only meant to remind *you* that you were his. It was a brilliant use of manipulation that made each one of his followers more than likely feel a personal connection to him, only reminded by the fact when they were alone, and most vulnerable.

Locilette rose to his feet and began to take photographs of the burned emblems with his PDA. He jotted the notes on design as well as his theory as to what they could be used for. He couldn't help but wonder how long the seeds of this scheme had to have been sown to deliver such unheard of results. He knew he was in quite the predicament now, but *when* he got out of here, this would be the case new Ranger recruits would study for generations. He just prayed that it had an ending where he too could look back on it.

A quiet beeping came from behind him. Locilette spun around to see Brinks's eyes flashing yellow. It was something he had yet to see from his Secure-Droid, which made him apprehensive. The flashing went from quick successions to a slow pace where seconds would pass by with its eyes being a solid black. It eventually faded into the bright green he was accustomed to seeing, then blue as the bot turned to him.

"Sir, there appears to be a Ranger cruiser nearby responding to your drone's message." Brinks announced.

A flood of surprised confusion swirled within him. "How did the message get through? I thought you were locked out of the Theseus's comms?"

"It appears that I am able to access our ship's basic communication systems via the connection the drone and I share with it. I am able to conduct simple functions remotely at this present time, sir. However, I am unable to say how long I can maintain this connection."

This was beyond a stroke of good luck. Maybe the Pantheon was looking out for him after all on this evil tomb of a ship. He couldn't help but let a wave of relief flow through his shaken, tired body. For the first time since he stepped off that elevator, he felt hopeful. He felt like survival wasn't the endgame anymore, but bringing all these psychopaths to justice.

"Can you activate the Theseus's SOS beacon?"

Brinks sent a message to the drone, which was responded to in a fraction of a second. "Yes, sir. It appears that I can."

"Do it!" Locilette instructed, his excitement briefly getting the better of him. "Make it a primary alert for any Ranger units in the area."

Brinks got to work on his request. It would take some time for the cruiser to reach them, but the thought of backup coming invigorated him to finish this before they arrived. When they did locate the Yanagi, he wanted all the cult's leadership already bound for transport to meet the justice of Arkaan law head on. This horror show was about to end here and now. If he could find the so-called *Enlightened One*, he could use the threat of impending Ranger reinforcements to end this as peacefully as possible. If he didn't take the bait, then Locilette had zero problem taking justice into his own hands.

With that thought, he slid his hand into his pocket, seeking to reload his empty pistol. He didn't like what he felt. Only a single plasma cartridge remained. He was going to save this shot for the most extreme emergency, but lucky for him, Brinks appeared to still have a pouch full of larger cartridges for his rifle magnetized to its hip. At least they weren't completely defenseless.

"The Theseus's SOS beacon has been activated, sir. The arrival of the Ranger cruiser could be within the hour," Brinks said.

"Nice work, let's get-"

The echoes of Phillip rang out nearby. Locilette and Brinks both turned down the hall where the group of men they just incapacitated came from. Another group was coming, and from the sound of it, they had a familiar face in tow. There wasn't much time to think of a plan. There was no way they could conceal these bodies in time. He was going to have to wing it.

"Brinks, I need you to lay down and shut off until they pass." Locilette commanded.

The bot cocked its head to the side. "I do not understand, sir. You wish for me to deactivate myself in the midst of a skirmish?"

"The point is that there won't be a skirmish. We're essentially going to play dead. Hurry!"

Locilette reluctantly dipped his hand in the pool of blood forming around the head of the man that he shot. He pushed all thoughts out of his mind as he smeared the blood on the back of his neck, and lathered it through his hair. It was beyond disgusting. Not just because the blood of one of these deranged people was on him, it was the simple fact that he just didn't know what kind of diseases these men carried. Regardless if there was or not, at least he would be alive to seek treatment.

He watched as Brinks sat down on the floor and leaned back against the wall. Its bright, blue eyes started to blink for a moment as it powered down, then faded completely to black. Locilette followed suit, lying next to the lead man he killed. As much as he didn't want to do it, he knew that laying his own head in his blood would sell it even more. He steeled himself. Slowly, he laid his head down, the warm blood coming in contact with his cheek made him want to vomit. His stomach held firm as he relaxed his body as best as he could.

All he could smell was the lingering smell of electrical heat from his fatal shot still burning the side of the dead man's head. The wound was close enough to him where he could feel the slight heat still radiating off of it. Now that he was down here, he had a slight sense of envy for the man eternally resting here. No longer did he have to worry about the hardships of the life he chose for himself. There would be no more violence he would have to witness, or deliver by his hands. Perhaps death was the only true way people could have peace. At least for people like him.

Locilette shut his eyes as the stomps of several feet came thundering at the end of the hall. This was it. It was either they were going to live to fight another day, or die here along with these men. Just as they were on top of them, Locilette drew in a deep breath, and held it in his lungs. He just needed a minute and a half. That's the longest he could guess he could hold his breath without gasping for air. Especially in this recycled oxygen created by the Yanagi's life support system.

The footsteps stopped just shy of the messy scene. Locilette could hear the wimpers of Phillip, as one of the cultists demanded him to stop. His heart began to pound. He could feel one of the bodies being shifted on the floor, then being slumped back down. Now, a whole new fear rose in him. What if the men they knocked out wake up? Panic slowly began to rise within him, but it took everything he could muster to not let it reflect on the outside.

"Fucking hell," one of the men sighed. "That's Darius there. It wasn't supposed to happen like this!"

"Keep it together. He's going to be waiting for us on the other side, just like Kellenger. This is almost over."

Locilette placed the sound of clanking metal around where Brinks sat itself down. "You think we can do something with this metal man?"

"It's a waste of time. We're getting close to the final act, there's no place for soulless robots where we're going. Leave it. The soul of the Ranger will join us as we take the next step."

"Oh, the Ranger's part isn't finished." This voice was different. It was wicked sounding, unlike anything Locilette hadn't heard before. It was familiar, like the voice from the murder of Zesper. It was him! It had to be the Enlightened, standing only a few feet from him. It took every ounce of self control not to spring up, but he knew that would be suicidal. His time would come. Sooner than he possibly could know.

"Let's get moving." The same voice commanded the others.

It was hard telling how many there were, but the sound of the echoing footsteps began to fade away. Locilette waited just in case one hung back to keep an eye on the bodies. Slowly, he opened an eye to observe his immediate area, then being satisfied with that, he lifted his head. They were gone. They just left the bodies of their comrades to rot in this hall without a second thought, which wasn't a real surprise to him.

"Brinks," Locilette whispered sharply. "Power up."

The bot's eyes flashed momentarily, then sprang to life at his command. It took a moment to assess things, then sprung itself off the floor with a massive push against the wall. Without wasting any time, Brinks rolled one of the bodies on its side to retrieve the plasma rifle it hid just before entering sleep mode. Having unloaded it prior, it cranked open the break to slide a fresh cartridge in, then dropped down to a knee ready for combat.

Locillete couldn't help but feel slightly impressed. Not only did it identify the value of concealing the only reliable firearm they had left, it did it in a way that would least likely be found. For a Secura-Droid considered obsolete by most other standards, Locilette couldn't have been happier with the one standing by his side and watching his back.

"Come on, let's get moving." Locilette called out.

As quietly as they could, they moved in the same direction as the large group that passed by. Locilette crouched just as they reached the corner, then leaned to watch as the last member of the group was walking through the door at the end of the corridor. Every light was busted out, but strings of multicolored lights weaved in dips every few feet, giving the hall a joyful glow. It was like an abandoned toy store with colorful decorations, but trash and debris scattered all about. Trays from the mess hall with rotten, half eaten food littered the wall, some stacks rising near the ceiling.

Locilette's nose flared as some horrendous smell hit him like a wall. It resembled the smell of some livestock that had been rolling in the mud after a late summer rain. There were few things that came close to the smell of dirty stables, and that was death and ungodly fumes produced by a sanctions trash planet. What disturbed him most of all was he had now smelled two of those three on the Yanagi. However, he didn't see any animals being transferred in the hangar bay manager's notes.

He motioned for Brinks to follow. Carefully, quietly, they maneuvered their way down the hall. He gave a quick glance back at Brinks, who's metal reflected every light, bathing it in a glowing rainbow aura. The blue eyes that scanned around only blended into the dancing sparkles off its body.

"Sir," Brinks said, grabbing his attention. It extended a metal finger at a door off to the side, tucked away in its own small walkway. It was too dark to see it clearly, but from where he stood, he could tell there was some kind of writing scribed on the door.

"Brinks, give me a light." A bright flash of blue illuminated the dark alcove, revealing the door.

The Unfaithful Ones was written on the door in the signature dried crimson blood of someone most likely long gone by now. A thousand different scenarios played out through his head. With a group of people as homicidal as these, and the lack of bodies everywhere, it made sense that they would have a single place to stash away the corpses after they served their use. What their various uses were, Locilette felt nauseous at the possibilities.

Brinks did a quick thermal scan of the door, but it was too thick for its sensors to penetrate. As the two approached, it was clear that whatever was kept inside was important enough to keep the others out. A heavy lock was looped through a welded latch that seemed to have been done by an unskilled hand. The lock appeared strangely familiar. Locilette was sure he had seen similar ones keeping sensitive goods protected in the cargo hold. With reusing the locks to the blades crafted from the Yanagi's metal walls, Locilette had to give these psychopaths credit. They were certainly resourceful.

Locilette crept forward to approach the door, but the closer he got, the stronger the mysterious odor got. Every instinct told him to turn away, but he knew that whatever was behind that door was going to just add to the mountain of evidence collected against the people. He was more than confident that he had enough to put the Enlightened and his party behind bars for multiple lifetimes, but the more incriminating pieces he could collect, the less likely that man could claim insanity.

Insanity was a word that could be applied to this man. However, in the eyes of Arkaan law, that would mean care and comfort as the doctors work through his multitude of mental illnesses to understand what made him tick. No, that just wasn't the justice that was fitting for this nightmare. The Enlightened was in complete control of his actions, and was more than self-aware. Any man that could take the time to craft a multitude of horrifying puzzles for a responding Ranger to play through was more than competent to stand trial. Locilette prayed deeply that the case would skip the lower courts and go straight to the courtroom of the King himself. That would be a fitting end that could help him sleep a little better after this ordeal.

As disturbing as the writing on the door was, it appeared to be a newer addition to the Yanagi. Most of the walls and doors in every section of the ship showed the wear and tear of decades of hardship in space. Patches of added metal to cover a repair, or the occasional rust spot from the humid air passing through the ship was common, but not this one. The entire small walkway appeared to have been added within the past two years, if Loiclette had to guess. It felt somewhat out of place compared to the sad state of improper maintenance the rest of the ship experienced.

He took the massive lock into his hand and gave it a tug. It was made of strong steel, but like most key locks, a simple shot of a plasma arc should be sufficient to break it. His only fear was alerting someone to their presence, but it was now or not at all. Before he turned to give the command to his bot, he noticed that the door didn't have any sort of panel to allow it to open. It was just a sliding door with a lock. It was almost as if it was installed, then simply forgotten about. As cheap as some of these merchant guilds were, it was hardly a surprise to find a job like this half done. If it wasn't directly generating profits, it was likely thrown on the back burner.

"Take out the lock, Brinks." Locilette commanded, taking a peek down the hall to make sure the coast was clear. "Let's see what these people are hiding."

"As you wish, sir." Brinks placed the tip of its rifle a few inches away from the thick metal loop, then squeezed the trigger. The blue light from the shot flashed in the tiny hall like the flash of a camera. Locilette could smell the electrical burning odor from the plasma discharge, then turned just in time to see the lock crumble away to the floor with a loud clunk. He glanced down the hall one last time before approaching the door and kicking the smoldering lock remains off to the side.

Locilette tried to slide it open, but the door didn't budge. Something was preventing it from gliding on the rails which it sat on. After several more attempts, a thought came to him that it wasn't that something was preventing the door from sliding, rather the door was incapable of sliding at all. If this was a new addition, perhaps even the motor that allowed it to open wasn't installed yet. Motors like that have emergency features to allow any door to be manually opened if the electronic door brakes weren't activated by someone on either side of the door. It was the only logical reason he could come up with.

"Sir, perhaps if we lift the door together, we could potentially raise it over the rails enough to move it." Brinks suggested.

Locilette nodded. "Alright. It's worth a try. Something is in here, Brinks. This door is incapable of opening, so why put a lock on the outside?"

"A plausible theory, sir. Perhaps a weapon stash?"

"No, I don't think so." He scratched his head, but it dawned on him that Brinks wasn't able to detect odors like he could. "I think it's going to be something far more incriminating. Let's hurry and get this open."

Together they both found the best hand grip they could, then Locilette counted down from three. When he got to one, they lifted the door. Locilette immediately felt the burning in his arms as he strained to lift the hunk of metal. His eyes were shut tightly and his teeth gritted as he gave every ounce of waning strength. The sound of Brink's gears grinding wailed as the bot bore most of the weight. More slowly than he would've liked, the door gradually rose. The two crept over just over a foot before Locilette's arms gave out, leaving Brinks to push the door another couple of inches before its exhaust fans were pushing steaming hot air.

Locilette's arms felt like rubber. He couldn't help but to lean on the door just to stop himself from falling over. Sweat dripped from his head even as the cold from the flowing air nipped at the back of his neck. He straightened himself up, then drew his pistol by instinct, and moved past his bot to take a peek inside.

The smell from the room's interior hit him like a train. It was definitely the same thing he had been smelling, but only amplified ten times. Brinks aimed its blue lights into the room, but immediately froze as it took it in. Before Locilette could look inside, Brinks's eyes flashed as it took several pictures. Something wasn't right. He could just feel his stomach brewing with a disturbed churning of anticipation. He placed his sleeve over face, then stepped in front of Brinks to observe for himself. When he saw what was kept within, his mouth dropped open, despite the disgusting odor assaulting him.

Huddled around the room were people, dozens of them, all with their back turned to the door in fear. They didn't dare turn to see what Locieltte could only assume was their captors. It was almost pitch black in the room with the only light seeming to come from a single tea light candle that was used for the worship of the Pantheon on any normal occasion. Here, it was used as a beacon of hope for these unfortunate members of the Yanagi's crew.

Locilette quickly tried to get a headcount, but they all seemed to blend together when he crossed forty-one. Several corpses were piled up in a corner, covered with several articles of clothing in an attempt to fight off any kind of contamination that the decaying flesh could spread. Brinks's light slowly panned the room to the corner where seven buckets filled with urine and feces overflowed onto the ground in heaps of liquid. This was truly one of the most gut-wrenching things he had ever had ever seen.

The people's hair seemed to be falling out from abuse and malnutrition with the light reflecting off their oily bald spots. Locilette's heart ached for these poor people. It took him a moment to even process it, but what this was truly the most grotesque things he had seen a people do to their fellow Arkaan. Not only that, but to another living creature. There were protections in place to even shield beasts of burden from this kind of treatment. Seeing it done to people was on a level that Locilette couldn't possibly imagine.

One of them was brave enough to quickly steal a glimpse at the two standing in the doorway. The person revealed a man whose face showed the horrifying scars of survival aboard the Yanagi. His skin was dotted with large blotches of brown spots that appeared to be oozing some sort of substance that Locilette didn't even want to take a guess. His eyes were deeply sunken with the only color coming from the dark rings that surrounded them.

The man did a double take before his eyes sat upon Locilette and Brinks like a hawk finding its prey. His cracked lips began to quiver as the realization that they weren't his torturers washed over him. The last bit of liquid in his body manifested in the corners of his eyes as he turned around fully to them and started walking with his arms raised. The pain in this man's eyes was going to be something that Locilette would never forget, but the overcoming of emotion that came across his face was too one he would always remember.

"Save…" The man's voice cracked. "Saviors!"

One by one, each of the people turned to see the Ranger's silhouette standing in the door frame. They all turned and followed the man in the chants for their savior, some wailing out cries as they crawled on their knees. Their voices all seemed like a jumbled mess that slowly climbed to a point that started to make Locilette worry. There was no way such noise had come from these people in weeks. If the Enlightened's men heard them now, they'd certainly come to investigate.

"Listen, please, you have to keep it down." Locilette stressed, waving the mob down with his hands.

Their voices were now in a unison of whines. "Savior. Savior. SAVIOR!"

"No, everyone, please - you have to be quiet! I have a cruiser coming shortly to get you all to safety, but for right now, you have to play it cool if we're going to get out of this."

They erupted in cheers and cries. Locilette shushed them as he took a look down the hall to make sure nobody was coming. These people were going to get him killed! He understood the relief they must be feeling, but they wouldn't be able to get off this ship at all if the armed group came back and slaughtered them all. He had come too far now to let these people drag him into the pit of horrors with them. He knew what he was going to have to do. He was going to have to leave them here back in their containment. At least until the Ranger cruiser arrived.

"Please, everyone back against the wall. The Ranger recovery team will come find you when they arrive." Locilette commanded sternly.

"Wait, you're just going to leave us?" One woman asked from somewhere in the mob of people inching closer.

"He's going to fuckin' leave us to rot!"

"That's not what I'm doing! I can't operate with three dozen people trailing behind me. I need to get to the bridge to figure out what's going on here, but I assure you that when the cruiser gets-"

"Liar!" A man spat from behind the front rank. "You're a filthy little liar!"

"I'm not lying, sir, I'm being realistic. Now, back up so I can close the door. Trust me, this is the only way. You just have to hang on for a few more hours."

"LIAR! LIAR! LIAR!" They all shouted, their voices ringing in his head like the piercing sound of a screeching cat.

They kept approaching inch by inch before Locilette started to get the feeling that if they got any closer, they were going to do to him what they've probably only dreamed of doing to their captors. They spat and cursed at him as they neared the door. Locilette felt Brinks's metal hand lay on his shoulder and tug him back to get him out of harm's way, but that wasn't going to solve the issue. They were going to come pouring out of there any second to maul them both like a pack of starving animals, which wasn't too far off the mark.

Standing his ground, he drew his pistol and pointed it at the approaching mob. They stopped immediately, some looking offended that he would even resort to such a thing.

"Listen," Locilette tried his best to explain as calmly as he could. "We're going to close this door, and as soon as we get things under control here on the Yanagi, we're going to come rescue you. You have my word."

"You're going to die here with the rest of us, Ranger," the first man said, his voice lacking any of the emotion that he just displayed.

A chill ran up his back. Something was wrong here. These people were sick. Their minds had been broken several times over by the abuse from the Enlightened's hand. He prayed for their recovery in the future, but right now he couldn't help them. Their salvation was determined by his success to gain control of the Yanagi on the bridge, and their outbursts already caused enough ruckus.

"I'm sorry. We'll be back for you. Brinks, shut the door, now!"

Brinks bolted to the door, and with every ounce of power it could muster, it lifted the door. The mob wailed out in a shrieking battle cry as they charged the ever-closing gap of the doorway. Locilette fired his final shot through the gap, a streaking blue bolt of electricity striking the floor in front of them, sending bursts of sparks upwards. That was enough to slow them for a couple of seconds as Locilette rushed to the bot's side to help. He pushed with all his strength until he felt the door settle back down in its original place.

They both backed away slowly as the pounding on the door turned into blood curdling screams. Something told him that whatever was happening behind that door was something that nightmares couldn't replicate. He prayed for them. He prayed that peace will come to each and every one of them either in this life, or in the everlasting peace of death. For some of those poor people within, that would be the only way.

Chapter Thirteen

Captain Bellenor studied the reports neatly stacked on his desk. Each one spelled out in great detail the various damaged systems that sustained his vessel. The dim light of the Captain's quarters wasn't the best for reading the small print of the lengthy assessments, but it was how he preferred it. He was a man that liked to do things his way.

He viewed his quarters as an oasis from the hustle and bustle lifestyle that was commanding a Ranger Cruiser. Every moment of his time was taken by someone else needing him to solve an issue that really could've been passed to the next in charge, or even the person below that in most cases. This wasn't the kind of leader he was though. Bellenor liked to be in the thick of it with his crew, getting his hands dirty to solve the day to day issues that arose. In his opinion, it was what kept the job interesting.

When he became a second degree Ranger a couple of years ago, he was immediately offered command of the Ranger cruiser Harriet. Her former Captain was retiring that year, so the Chief was looking for fresh blood to captain the best and only cruiser in this sector of Arkaan space. He accepted it without a single thought otherwise. Opportunities like this didn't come too often. He would've been a fool to decline it. It was an honor of a lifetime to take the reins of this ship, but now she was battered and bruised. Her hull scarred from her most recent engagement.

Twelve hours ago, he received intelligence that a small flotilla of small cargo vessels turned makeshift gun ships were operating in this sliver of the sector. Being the only Ranger capital ship in the immediate area, it came to the Harriet and her crew to respond to the threat. It appeared that the pirate flotilla, if you could even refer to them as such, had been harassing merchant vessels passing through the area between wormhole gates. Where the pirates and thugs lacked in pitched battle prowess, they were experts of targeting lines of logistics. It wasn't enough to bring the Arkaan military into the fold, but just enough of a nuisance to force the Rangers into responding.

It was never military logistics they targeted, which Bellenor found the most dishonorable. It would be a simple shipment of vegetables for a fledgling colony in a neighboring system, or a hull full of raw ore being shipped to a refinement station. Things that were relatively invaluable in the grand scheme of things being targeted just for the sake of making a tiny splash in a massive ocean. Now, he could understand if there were citizens under the influence of these criminal factions that were starving, but most impoverished systems and planets on the outskirts of Arkaan space were more times than not completely agrarian. These weren't the actions of a starving people. No, these were the actions of a group of dirty savages looking to shed blood wherever they could.

The Harriet was able to conceal itself decently well as she approached the flotilla sitting just off dock of the Apaosha 3 Orbital city. Even though that's what it was classified as, it was a shanty station at best. It was notorious for attracting some of the worst people that Arkaa had to offer. It was no surprise to anybody that it would be among the group of planets to fall into the clutches of the criminal organizations that plagued Arkaan space. It was always those who were given the most from the government that appeared to be the first to pull away when the idea of obtaining wealth by faster means popped up. Bellenor often wondered what these people would do if the support from his Majesty was pulled.

He couldn't help but to find that thought a bit humorous. The farthest planets and colonies had some of the highest rates of investment and social funding in the empire. It was standard protocol that ran with the economic theory of the Colonial Holdings Act created by one of the former monarchs of Arkaa. They would receive vast amounts of investment capital to create a sustainable, self-sufficient domain under the Arkaan banner. Slowly, the funds would be pulled away to encourage the Count or Countess of the planet to explore free trade and production under their own industrial capabilities.

This theory didn't always work, however. Even though having a single executive leading a planet, or an orbital city revolving around an inhospitable one, had its strengths, it also had its apparent weaknesses too. If the Count of a planet happened to fall under the sway of corruption, then funds were destined to be misused. When money is misused, proper investment into the planet isn't made, leading to the population to suffer and go without. When citizens go without, they turn to organized crime to fulfill their needs. When organized crime took root in the foundation of a society, the only way to cleanse it is with fire, and Captain Bellenor was more than happy to be the flaming fist in this sector.

When the Harriet came within radar distance, all hell seemed to break loose. Most of the time these smaller vessels would fire a few pop shots then turn tail back into the safety of the darkness of space. For some reason, this group of pirates thought it was time they tried their luck to score a bigger prize: the Harriet herself. In a surprisingly competent coordinated assault, they all fired their rockets, targeting a multitude of the Harriet's systems.

Bellenor was fortunate to have one hell of a helmsman on his staff. With the finesse and grace of a trained dancer, the helmsman maneuvered the massive beast of a warship through the first wave. A few rockets found their home, but they were superficial wounds at best. It was time for Captain Bellenor to respond. He commanded every battery lining her hull to open up on the flotilla as they circled around for another run. From his command chair in the center of the bridge, the flashes from his cannons lit up the darkness surrounding his ship, with only moments passing before the sight of several small explosions blinked off in the distance. *These half-witted pirates didn't stand a chance*, Bellenor thought.

Without a single warning, the Harriet rattled violently as the smaller rockets peppered the ship's hull. He would've been thrown clear across the bridge if his combat straps weren't secured in observance to general quarters regulation. As soon as the red alert went up, all officers on the bridge were required to find their seats and strap in for a potential skirmish. It was times like this where Captain Bellenor understood that the creation of policy comes from necessity.

Out of a nearby asteroid belt, a corvette-sized vessel emerged to meet her exposed aft. Another barrage of small rockets pelted the engine as well as the rear hull where the Harriet had little to no armor. It was a brilliant tactical decision that the Captain couldn't help but to crack a grin at. It was like playing a game of Kannoes with a child, but the child surprisingly made a move that put him in a favorable position. At the end of the day, the child was going to lose, but seeing a glimmer of thought that he placed in the move was not only shocking, it was a fair bit of sport, as well.

The Harriet swiveled half her cannons aft. Each one completed the 180 degree turn in fifteen seconds or less. If the corvette was any smaller, or maybe if it had just a more powerful engine, she would've escaped her fate. Despite getting the jump on the massive Ranger Cruiser, the corvette made a vital mistake that would spell her end. She left her broadside exposed. Even with only half of the Harriet's firepower bearing down, it was more than enough to get the job done.

In an incredible display of overwhelming force, Captain Bellenor commanded each of the cannons to fire non-stop until the corvette was nothing more than micro pieces of metal floating in the void of space. From the bridge, he could hear the sounds of the guns echoing up and down the halls of his ship. That was more satisfying than watching the grainy camera feed pointed off the Harriet's aft on the small monitor. He had to squint his eyes to even enjoy the separation of the lower deck from the engine compartment. In a matter of moments, the corvette broke away into six different pieces, all of which floated in opposite directions.

A few rockets from the other smaller gun ships found their mark as half the gun crews were focused on the other threat. The floor beneath his feet shook as one seemed to have struck a vital component with the ship's artificial gravity. His feet involuntarily rose in the air along with several stacks of papers and cups, but all shot back down to the floor as the engineers quickly appeared to get a jump on the situation before it got worse. Within only a few minutes, the Harriet had taken out a few more of the pirates, forcing the rest to abandon their friends and escape with the little they had left.

The Harriet wasn't going to be the prize today, but she was left to lick her minor wounds from the brief skirmish. It wasn't entirely necessary to head back to the nearest port for repairs, but Bellenor thought the crew needed a little leave time. Their rotation was coming up in a month, so he figured that if they get it in now, they could spend the rest of the month wrapping their assignment up in one solid stretch.

Just as they were about to pass through the wormhole gate, they were met by a Ranger drone rocketing out. After a connection was made remotely to the drone, the call for additional units to support in a derelict call came across the comms officer screen. Normally a vessel the size of the Harriet was completely unnecessary for such a small call, but as he was the first to receive it, he felt some obligation to respond. Even if it was just brief, he would be able to sleep just a little better on leave knowing he didn't leave a fellow Ranger in a rough position.

He felt his stomach wretch as the Harriet dropped out of the gate back into normal space. He remained as stoic as ever. Even though it was just him in the office, he wouldn't allow himself to show any sort of weakness to wormspace travel. It was a part of the job, so the only way to not simply complain about it all the time was to just simply ignore it. He let it become just another unfortunate side effect of being a Ranger out in the field.

He closed his eyes and swallowed the bile building in his throat. He could only imagine what his crew was feeling right now. With all the excitement of the last twenty-four hours, the last thing he was sure they wanted was the feeling of being punched in the gut with a sledgehammer. But he had the same mindframe for them as he did with himself. They knew what they were signing up for.

Captain Bellenor regained his composure, then continued to read over the reports. One of his four engine stacks had been damaged moderately in the skirmish, but nothing too serious. There appeared to be a breach on one of the back armor plates where fragments from a rocket damaged the gravity producer. It was just as he guessed. Gravity wasn't necessary to get them back to port, but having his crew floating around, potentially getting injured was a headache he would've liked to avoid. He breathed a quiet sigh of relief that his engineers managed to stop the problem before they lost the artificial gravity completely. He pulled off a sticky note from the booklet next to his pens to write himself a note.

Ask payroll for small bonus for engineers.

The doorbell on his door across the office buzzed.

"Come!" The Captain shouted.

The door slid open revealing the slender frame of his communications officer, Lieutenant Mikaya. Parts of his uniform hung loosely from his tiny build, but Bellenor didn't find it much use telling the young man that he needed to up his caloric intake. After all, did a Ranger working in comms really need to be that big? The way he saw it was as long as he could pass his monthly physical fitness exam, then he didn't rightly care what his crew looked like. Everyone's body adapted to the role they served on the ship.

"Pardon my intrusion, Captain," the young man said, his voice lighter than the feather of an Orange Hawk from his native Guanyin Prime.

"What do you have for me, son?"

"We have successfully dropped out of wormspace. We analyzed the drone we intercepted, and it appears to be programmed to the Ranger responder Theseus of the Kronos System."

Captain Bellenor looked up from his paperwork sharply. His eyes were wider than the thick frames that sat on the edge of Mikaya's nose. "You said the Theseus?"

"Yes Captain, and that's not all. When we dropped out we immediately picked up on her SOS beacon. Whatever is happening, that Ranger is in hot water. Seems it was a good call to drop by and lend a hand, sir."

"That's Locilette of Kronos, a Ranger I had the honor to serve with many times before. He's a wonderful gentleman, and one hell of a Ranger," Captain Belenor said, immediately rising from his chair. "Walk with me, Lieutenant."

Bellenor led the young officer out of his corner and turned sharply down the left corridor. Mikaya rarely had the opportunity to be in the Captain's presence, so he added a prideful pep in his step as he tried to keep pace with the Harriet's senior officer. A duo of security personnel were walking by, then stopped to stand at attention as the Captain strode by. As soon as they were clear, the men resumed their patrol of the officer's deck.

The young Lieutenant could feel the power that the Captain radiated like the heat from a star. Men stopped in their tracks just to acknowledge him as he carried on with his day to day duties. It was an aura that he strove to have himself one day, as well as the responsibility of commanding his own vessel in the Ranger Order. Having a role model like Captain Bellenor in his life allowed him to not only learn from one of the best professionally, but personally as well. He grew to appreciate the Captain's ability to lead with not only his logical, tactical mind, but his emotions.

It seemed to be almost directly opposed to the advice he'd received before of avoiding such things, but Bellemor had proven that wrong on many occasions. The Captain certainly did things his own way, using the Ranger's Handbook as more of a guide than the word of the almighty ones. The way he interpreted how the Captain operated was as long as he was operating in the current laws of the Arkaan Empire, then it was good enough for him. It was an honor to serve with him, both as a leader and a man.

"How long ago was the SOS beacon activated?" Captain Bellenor inquired.

Hearing the Captain speak made Mikaya quicken his pace to keep up. "Approximately an hour ago, Captain. Based on the report, it seems that it was activated remotely somehow."

"I need a little more than *somehow*, son."

Lieutenant Mikaya ran a number of scenarios through his head as they walked. The only way that the Theseus's SOS beacon could've been activated remotely was either by hacking or some kind of back door system. Officially there were no such authorized back door systems allowed on official Ranger responders, but with this Ranger having purchased his own he might have installed one. If this Ranger served with the Captain, then Mikaya could only assume that he was just as experienced with the rules and regulations of a Ranger responder. The idea of installing an unauthorized back door system seemed unlikely.

The Ranger must have some sort of device able to communicate with a third party to access the ship. He wondered if a standardized PDA could have such features, but even with his state of the art model, he couldn't do that. No, it had to be something else. Perhaps he found a way to access his ship's remote feature via the console that remotely locked him out in the first place. The questions kept swirling in his head like a typhoon. Things have been pretty dull in this sector until the pirates attacked, and now this? Mikaya liked to feel useful on the Harriet, so getting a chance to flex his expertise was like a caged animal finally being freed to roam.

"I'll get with my staff and see what I can come up with, Captain," Mikaya said, though he could tell the Captain wasn't satisfied with that answer.

He shot a quick glance to the trailing Lieutenant. "Have it on my desk in twenty minutes."

"Aye, sir."

The massive, ornately decorated doors slid open to the bridge. "Captain on the bridge!" The security officer alerted.

The bridge was flooded with an intense light that showed every speck on the ship's white floor. Every officer on the bridge, including some enlisted personnel passing through, stopped in their tracks to acknowledge the commanding officer. The Captain gave his officer staff a respectful nod, and immediately they returned to their work. Mikaya broke away from the Captain to return to his communications station just off to the side of the Captain's raised seat.

"Captain, here are the reports from the missing Yanagi you requested," his executive officer, Commander Vellenis said, extending his PDA with the missing ship's transcript.

He nodded. "Thank you, Commander. How long until we reach the Theseus's distress signal?"

"We should be arriving at the last known location in the next hour or so. From what we can tell, it's a pretty weak signal, leading us to believe that the Theseus is inside something. There's a high probability that she's sitting in the Yanagi's hangar."

"That would make the most sense. I'd be surprised if Locilette would risk a space walk."

"I agree, Captain," Commander Vellenis said. "Ranger Locilette is a smart guy, however, if it was just a derelict call, I doubt he would've gone through as much trouble as he did."

Captain Bellenor raised an eyebrow. "What are you suggesting?"

"I'm saying that derelicts that size don't become derelicts just by engine failure."

The Captain nodded in agreeance of his XO's assessment. It was far more likely that the Yanagi was attacked by a rogue tribe of Zorvathix that happened upon it in space. Normally, they were a relatively peaceful spacefaring race that were more than content on minding their own business, but if their slumber was interrupted while traversing the endless void, they were quick to aggression. Bellenor always thought they were like children being woken from their nap a little too early that then spirals down into a full-on meltdown. Only, in the case of the Zorvathix, their meltdowns could swarm a ship with thousands of crawling insectal beings that could chew through the hull of even the most advanced cruisers. He could only assume that Locilette would've seen evidence of that before boarding the vessel.

The screen flashed on as Bellenor read over the various digital documents on Commander Vellenis's PDA. He attempted to hide his eye roll as the Josakk Merchants Guild's name came up as its owner. The Yanagi seemed to be bound on a routine haul that, according to the records, she had done several times before. What could've been different about this one? He scrolled through the report after report of the ship's last known check in and cargo inspection. There had been several attempts over the past year of shady organizations transporting weapons and other black market items on ships masquerading as merchant vessels. Perhaps a rival gang or other pirate clan got to her before her destination?

His thoughts began to drift to Locilette stumbling upon a group of pirates as they looted the stalled vessel in space. He knew he could handle himself and was as good as any Ranger with a Plasma Arc Pistol, but numbers game mattered. Especially while in the cramped halls of a merchant ship. However, he was fairly certain that someone with as much experience as Locilette would activate his Secura-Droid to aid him if he thought things were going to get a little heated. Of course he would, why wouldn't he? An idea flashed through his mind as he looked up to his second in command still standing by him.

"Can the Secura-Droid programmed to the Theseus be able to communicate with the ship remotely?" Captain Bellenor asked.

"I'm not sure. Lieutenant Fluegar?" he said, turning towards engineering.

The fair skinned, older Lieutenant turned to him from being bent down going over various diagnostics of the ship's damaged systems. Multiple monitors flashed bits of information, but could wait to hear the commander's request.

"Yes, Commander?" she asked, clasping her hands behind her back.

"Is it possible for a Secura-Droid to communicate with a ship that has been hacked?"

She took a moment to think. "Well, yes, but not directly."

The Commander opened his hands. "Care to elaborate a bit further, Lieutenant?"

"So, there would need to be a third party device that would already be connected to the ship prior to being locked out. Think of it like having a straw in a cup, then sliding a lid on top of it. Even though the liquid inside is now inaccessible, the straw you had in it before still allows you to drink from it."

"Third party device as in, say, a drone?" Captain Bellenor asked.

"Well, yes Captain, I believe that would work."

The Captain nodded. "Thank you, Lieutenant. When we get into range, let's start trying to hail them on all channels. I want to at least try to establish communication with Ranger Locilette, or whoever the hell else thought it wise to endanger one of our brothers. Commander, send us back into general quarters. I need everyone on high alert until we know what we're sailing into."

"Aye, Captain." Commander Vellenis said, grabbing the corded phone from his small console on his chair. The ship's speakers clicked to life as he brought it to his mouth. "Attention all staff and personnel. General quarters, general quarters, all hands man your stations."

Commander Vellenis hooked the phone back into the dock, then took his seat next to the Captain. The lights on the bridge dimmed to a low red as they did through the entire ship after a general quarters had been called. After a few moments they returned to normal, except for a bright neon light above the Captain that always remained the color of the current threat level facing the Harriet. The officer staff scrambled around the bridge trying to find their seats. Captain Bellenor strapped in and waited for his crew to do the same.

He glanced over at Commander Vellenis's monitor, which had each department glowing green when they've signaled they were ready. One by one, in quick succession, they all flashed, followed by the Commander giving him a thumbs up as a final confirmation. The Harriet was ready to go back into a potentially hostile situation. Bellenor wasn't a praying man, but he said a few words for this to be just be a simple backup request.

"Helmsman, full throttle towards the Theseus's distress beacon on your navigation monitor. Impulse power is allowed."

"Aye, Captain."

The Harriet's engines roared to life as she rocketed through the stars toward the lost Ranger's position.

Chapter Fourteen

Phillip's screams echoed through the barren halls of the Yanagi. Each cry for help was only met with a chorus of machinery or the steady hum of the ship's life support system. The sound of his dragging set a standard tone for the noise of the feet pounding alongside him as they escorted him to the destination that would more than likely be his last. One of the men swatted him on the back of the head as he stumbled to the ground, halting their progress. The tears streamed from his tired eyes and he wished they would just get it over with, but once again, they picked him up to continue on.

He struggled against the men that bound his hands. His breath was heavy with the labor of having to walk with his arms held high behind his back. A blend of sweat and blood trickled down his worn face as he fought with all his might just to keep himself from toppling over, but that would more than likely result in another beating. He looked as if he had taken a number or two of those since he got separated from Locilette and Brinks, but if his prediction of his fate was true, it didn't really matter. He was destined to hang from a rope anyway. Maybe that was always destined to be his fate with the Ranger only delaying the inevitable.

The further they went, the stranger things appeared to become. Adorned on the walls were painted portraits of horrific manifestations of what the Yanagi had become. One showed the crudely drawn ship ascending into a bright light, then followed by the image of a man standing in the light with his arms spread wide. Hundreds of stick men stood around him, almost as if being welcomed into some special place. It was almost as if they were being welcomed home.

Phillip managed to lift his tired eyes to the opposite wall, which had what appeared to be a fiery ball floating around the head of a smiling man. A long trail of flames stretched from the ball, wrapping itself around the man's head several times before resting off his right side. Tears were drawn on his face, but the sight of the man's smile made it seem as if he were crying tears of joy. It almost felt as if the drawing was crying for Philip as it witnessed his agony, but smiling as it knew his struggle was almost at its end.

The heraldry of the Josakk Merchant Guild was painted over with the dried blood of those who had come before him. A large red circle with a triangle on top covered the usual large guild emblem. Within the triangle sat a cross with vertical waves moving from left to right. What did it mean? What could it possibly represent? It was too hard to tell, and there was no more energy to be put into thoughts like that.

He tried to listen to the monotone sound of the air flowing through the vents above him. It was the only sense of calm that he clung onto now. The moment he closed his eyes, he tripped on something that sent him falling face first onto the hard dirty floor. The odd taste of dust and copper filled his mouth as he turned his head to the side to spit a stream of blood. The masked man that stood to his side glared down at his boot, which now had the stain of Phillip's blood streaking across its laces. In a fit of anger, the masked men began to violently kick him over and over before he was pulled off by the other two escorts.

"Hey, hey! Too damn rough! Remember what we're doing here!" One of them shouted at his aggressive partner.

"I'm doing as the Enlightened commands!" He declared, pulling himself free to deliver a violent kick to Phillip's ribs. "I'd remember what his words were, if I were you. Do you want to be left alone here in this sad universe while the party ventures onto the higher plane?"

The other two looked at each other, then shook their heads in silence. "That's what I thought. WE act our part, right?"

"Right."

"Right, now get this lousy fucker up before I lose my cool again," he said, nudging the side of Phillip's head with the toe of his stained boot.

Phillip struggled to push himself off the floor. His arms shook violently before giving out beneath him, sending him falling back to the floor. The impact was enough to knock the wind out of his beaten body, but if he didn't force himself up then, would he even make it to his own execution before these thugs beat the remaining life out of him? It didn't matter how he was going to die anyway. He was just a dirty play thing for someone who got off on control and murder.

At some strange level, he appeared to accept his fate. He looked as if the world around him was already starting to fade away as his thoughts of survival turned into thoughts of freedom. The scene that his face painted made it seem that there was only one real way to be free from this. There was only one way he could finally escape the dark halls of the Yanagi. It was his time, and he was ready. Ready now more than he would ever be.

"Let's just get this over with. Please." Phillip managed to squeak out.

Two of the masked men scoffed as they hooked their arms through his, and hoisted him up to his feet. He wobbled for a second as the feeling of lightheadedness looked to pass over him. They tugged him down the hall, but this time he didn't struggle. This time he calmly walked along, following wherever they led him.

Ahead of them was a door permanently open that led into a large cross section of corridors. During the initial take over, the door was forced open with its gears forever jammed to prevent the fleeing unfaithful from finding any sanctuary. Scrapes and dents were like echoes from the past that left a reminder of the struggle those unfortunate people went through to attempt to seal off this part of the ship. Whatever happened to them was a story known only to their murderers and the Pantheon now.

As they walked past, Phillip felt his limb being tugged back by the man hooked into his right arm. His hand squeezed his arm so tightly that he couldn't help but grimace. He couldn't place what the sound was that was coming from behind him, but he didn't dare turn in fear of receiving another beating. Was he choking on something? He thought. That would be quite the ironic way to go, considering what his destiny had prescribed himself.

Phillip glanced over his shoulder to see blood fountaining out of the man's neck. A long, sharpened piece of metal stuck halfway within his neck at an angle allowed the enormous amounts of blood to follow its guide down. The man's face was stuck in a frozen state of surprise, but his eyes managed to lock onto Phillip's. He appeared as if he was seeking help. Help from the death that wasn't promised to him. A death where his master wouldn't be there to greet him at the gates. He attempted to say something, but the only thing that came out was a gurgling mess of spatted blood.

"What the fuck!" the man on Phillip's left arm screamed as he looked back at his fellow party member.

He pushed Phillip into the wall, but just as he caught his footing, he turned to see a large metal arm swinging down another bladed piece of metal. It sliced through his shoulder halfway down to his chest, only allowing the man to sneak out a cry of terror before he faded away. The body collapsed to the floor, leaving a large copper being standing over the corpse victoriously.

The other man tried to run, but another man jumped from the shadows and wrapped his arm around his neck. He ripped off the mask and tossed it to the side, revealing the emblem carved into his forehead. He squeezed as hard as he could until his body went limp in his hold and the life faded from his eyes. Even after he was sure he was dead, he continued to hold tightly, just to be certain. After another few moments, he pushed the dead weight and used the wall to pull himself to his feet.

Phillip couldn't believe what he had just witnessed. It was Locilette! This would make it twice that the Ranger had spared him from hanging from the end of a rope. Not to mention doing it while being outnumbered. There was more to this Ranger than he had given him credit for. Not only was he a survivalist, he was one hell of a killer. Maybe even second only to the Enlightened himself.

Locilette bent over, placing his hands on his knees. He huffed to catch his breath as Brinks rummaged through the newly-anointed mess of bodies lying around them. The Ranger shook his head in disgust as he kicked the arm of the one he had taken out of his way. He didn't want this sight to become a habit for himself, but there was no way he could just lay down and let these people get away with this. Nothing was going to stop him from getting home.

"You okay?" Locilette huffed.

Phillip nodded quickly. "Yeah, I'm- I'll be okay. Thank you so much. You saved my life again. There's no way I can repay you for that."

"Don't worry about it, that's why I'm here. I need your help, though."

"Of course! Anything!"

"Can you tell me if we're anywhere near the bridge?" Locilette asked, wiping the sweat from his tired face. "I have a feeling we're quickly running out of time here."

"Yeah, as a matter of fact, it's around the corridor up ahead to the right. These bastards were taking me somewhere up there though, so I'm not really sure what is in store for us."

Locilette sighed with annoyance. "We're just going to have to take our chances. Brinks, all set?"

"Yes, sir. Though I do advise caution. We must be hyper-aware, as every scenario I have run concluded in this being the hub for hostile activity. We should tread carefully."

"Agreed." Locilette nodded. "Let's get this over with."

Locilette moved off to the corridor cross section with Brinks close behind. Phillip took one last look over the bodies that littered the floor around him and shook his head. He quickly jogged with as much power as his exhausted legs would allow to catch up to his saviors. When it came to protection against the Yanagi cult of the Enlightened, being as close to these two was probably his best chance of survival if such a scenario ever existed. And it didn't.

A single beaming light illuminated the four-way intersection. Directly in front of him appeared to be some sort of restroom with the doors hanging halfway off its hinges. It was a single stalled unisex restroom that was primarily for the officer staff. The little light that managed to find its way inside revealed a canopy of toilet paper that had been strung along the damaged, low-hanging lights. Several messages were written on the walls in black markers with obscene enough material that gave Locilette the hint of most of their contents at a glance.

His time here on the Yanagi had thrown his thoughts upside-down more than once, but this seemed to add another. In times of trouble, people tended to hoard precious materials like food, water, and toiletries. The scene before him was nothing short of chaos at its purest form. Surely they didn't expect to find a hidden stash somewhere on this ship. It wasn't as if there would be some kind of supply run to generously gift them the basic amenities for a sanitary life way out here in the void of space.

As he surveyed the other doors, he couldn't help but wonder if the turned crew weren't expecting to stay too long after the overthrow of the officers. That was the only rational reason he could think of, besides them simply not caring, but he knew deep down they must've cared for their well-being at some primal level. Unless this *Enlightened* truly convinced every single one of them that they were destined for salvation, then wasting resources didn't make much sense.

"What's that way?" Locilette asked, pointing to the big door to their left.

"It's the secondary entrance to the observation deck." Philip explained. "It was a meeting place for the officer staff, but now is used by the Enlightened to preach his sermons to his fucked up flock."

"Best be avoided then. I'm assuming this way leads to the bridge?"

"Yeah, through this door and up the flight of stairs. Normally you'd need a code to get in, but his thugs fixed that issue a long time ago."

"Alright then. Let's-"

Locilette stopped as the thundering boots and the sound of rattling chains echoed back from where they came from. He placed a finger over his lips and waved Brinks and Phillip into the restroom. Phillip ran for the stall while the Ranger and his bot placed their backs against the wall lining the door. Glass and other things he didn't have the time to recognize crunched under his feet. He peeked around the corner just in time to see a group of metallic masked men escorting dozens of people into the observation room. The chains that bound their hands together clanged and rattled with every step. Something felt different this time.

"Something's wrong." Locilette announced after they passed.

"May I inquire, sir?" Brinks asked, his eye lights dimmed to conceal their position.

"I'm not sure exactly, but they just ran by the remains of their fellow cultists. Does that seem like a brotherhood to you?"

"I would imagine not, sir."

Locilette shook his head in the dark as he pulled his head back around. "No, this is different. Something is about to happen, and I don't think we want to be here when it does. Let's get moving."

Locilette checked one last time to make sure it was clear. When satisfied with that, he led the other two back into the cross section. He carefully pushed the door to the stair aside and one by one they slipped through. He glanced back to check on Phillip, who was staring through the window of the observation deck for a moment, then as soon as he caught Locilette's gaze, he rushed to the door to join them.

"What did you see?" Locilette whispered.

"Trust me, Ranger, you don't want to know."

Locilette was more than satisfied with that answer. He looked up the dark staircase that led to a single door at the top. Above the door was a dimly lit neon sign that had *Bridge* encased in a glowing crimson. He could tell even in the dark that the door's lock was engaged while it was open, preventing it from fully closing. When the party stormed the bridge, the officers must have attempted to seal the door, but their failure led to Locilette's present situation.

He couldn't help but wonder who's fault it could be to misidentify the threat that was brewing in these dark halls. Normally there would be a quartermaster that would have his or her ears glued to the happenings of the crew. Beyond crew discipline, they were responsible for sniffing out dissent and mutinous behavior. Could the quartermaster have been in on the plot to take the ship? He resisted the urge to pull out his PDA to jot down his thoughts and questions. There wasn't time for such things anymore. The evidence he had was far more than sufficient to spell out exactly what happened here, the only place his focus needed to lie was getting off the Yanagi to deliver it.

The door was heavier than Locilette was anticipating. It made sense since it was the only way to and from the bridge. Security was the main concern, but look at the good it did them. He motioned for Brinks to give him a hand, and together they pulled the heavy slab of metal. The tracks it rolled on creaked as it moved a few feet. It was more than enough for them to get what they needed and get out without making too much noise.

The bridge was in a complete state of decay. Consoles had been smashed into heaps of electronics and glass and ribbons of blood-soaked shirts tied at the sleeves hung from the ceiling. What he could only assume was the engineering console, by the looks of it, was still occasionally shooting sparks in the air. The metal wall that sat behind it was black from the constant barrage of electrical discharge.

The large view port window at the front of the bridge had numerous cracks that seemed to expand since their initial beating. These people were taking one hell of a risk when they decided to do something as stupid as that, Locilette thought. He couldn't tell if those strikes were initially made, or was from the result of the mayhem that must have occurred. Things happen during the heat of battle, especially when one side is a crazed violent mob.

Locilette was so into studying the poor state of the bridge that he just noticed the smell assaulting his nose. He knew that smell all too well, especially now. He searched around but he couldn't identify anything that could be the source. His eyes carefully rose up the walls, then behind them where the captain's mezzanine was to oversee the bridge operations from an elevated point. He sighed deeply and closed his eyes. He found the source of the horrendous smell that now seemed to surround him as he moved deeper into the bridge.

Hanging from the rails of the mezzanine were twelve bodies with various forms of wires and cables wrapped snug around their necks. Their faces were blackish purple and bloated from entering the beginning stages of rot. Dried blood and a disturbing blend of other bodily liquids stained their dirty uniforms. One on the left side swung slightly as the breeze from the nearby vent blew over it turned into a horrific decomposing pendulum.

"The officers," Phillip said grimly. "The chubby one there in the center is- was Captain Qureshi."

Locilette looked up at the men in disbelief. "What the hell happened here, Phillip?"

"I was on the bridge when they came. We watched them on the cameras as they slaughtered the security all the way up to the door here. Something happened to the locks where it couldn't let us close the door, and the rest is history."

"They do not appear to have been deceased for too long, sir." Brinks observed with a brief scan of the corpses. "If they in fact were murdered during the time of the crew uprising, then they would be quite further along in the biological process of decomposition."

"The fuckers held us in a storage closet for weeks and weeks, and I don't even know how long. Every now and then they'd take one out to do who knows what to them. All I know is when they would be taken, they did not come back the same person. I don't know what they did to them, but I have a feeling I was going to find out if you hadn't saved me from..." Phillip struggled to find the words. "From never seeing a happy face ever again."

Locilette placed a hand on his shoulder. "Phillip, I know you've seen and been through some truly awful things, but I need you to keep it together for me. We're almost out of this, okay?"

Phillip nodded, then looked back at the corpses above them. Locilette could only imagine what this poor man was thinking. He gave his shoulder a caring squeeze, then turned to start his search through the bridge. He raked his eyes around the stations, but nothing seemed too promising. Most of the consoles around him were either damaged beyond use, or offline from the roaming power outages affecting the Yanagi. On closer inspection, he could identify some of the power cables removed from their housing to be used on the unfortunate men than hung above them. This dark place was beyond any nightmare he could conjure.

He kicked a few toppled monitors on the floor out of his way to move past what would've been the Captain's chair, but was at some point set ablaze to act as a bonfire. Pieces of burnt clothing and papers were scattered around it, indicating that these savages must have been attempting to keep it going for as long as possible, but eventually gave up. The Captain may have met a gruesome fate, but at least he wasn't strapped to this seat to burn like Zesper was. Hopefully she and the Captain find peace at the dining table of the Pantheon.

A loose console fell to the ground as Locilette bumped into it on his way by. He turned quickly to try and catch it, but was a fraction of a second too late. He closed his eyes, fearing the worst as it fell, but exhaled with relief as it landed on a smashed chair lying on its side. The last thing he needed was to alert these people of their presence, especially since there was only one way in or out of the bridge.

He wiped the sweat from his face with his sleeve, but a blinking orange light caught his attention. It was a monitor that was situated behind the console he knocked over, the screen was black from being in sleep mode for probably as long as the bridge was taken. He ran his hand along the edge of it until his fingers found the power button on the bottom right side. He glanced back to see Brinks and Phillip still looking around, then pressed it.

The screen came to life after a few seconds, revealing a gift from the Pantheon themselves. It was the console for the communications department.

A wave of uncontrollable joy ran through him like a shot of morphine. A screen that was labeled *Unread Messages* had hundreds of missed communications destined for the Yanagi. He used the arrow keys on the dirty keyboard to scroll over to it, then tapped *select* to bring up an ever expanding list that rolled downward on the screen. Locilette quickly read through the subject lines of the middle pages. There were hundreds of messages asking about when the crew was coming home, or where they currently were on their journey. It was heartbreaking to read the worry within the words of the crew's family that they'll never see again.

One in particular caught his eyes as he was scrolling to the newest page. It was a sister looking for help with their shared rent for their apartment on the Hera 4 Orbital City. Her words painted a picture that showed her desperation as the debts they shared seemed to be swallowing her whole. What started out as a plea for money turned into a spiteful assumption that he had abandoned her with not only her own debts, but his as well. The message concluded with a request to never reach out to her again, because he was now dead to her and their family. What she probably never considered was that her brother was more than likely among the lost souls here on the Yanagi.

How many more messages were like this? People thinking that their loved ones were abandoning them in search of adventure or wasting their earnings away on whores and booze. Locilette wanted to pull away from the screen to send out a distress beacon, but the thought of leaving these poor people in the dark didn't sit right with him. If he would die on this ship, he would want his wife and children to know what happened to him. He would want his story to be told, and not be just another victim of the Yanagi killer. He selected all the personal messages from the crew's family, and began typing a mass response.

Hello,

My name is Locilette, Ranger of the Fifth Degree. I have responded to a call of a derelict vessel the Yanagi, which your relative or associate crewed. I regret to inform you that the events that have transpired on this ship are beyond what anyone could imagine. I won't spell out the details, but I want you to know that the ones you have lost will be avenged as I bring the people responsible for the tragedy here to justice. I will make sure that every single crew member's family is notified by the proper authorities to allow the story here to be told in its entirety. As this is still an active investigation, I can not say too much, but what I can tell you is that I won't stop until everyone responsible for the horrors here is rotting in the farthest prison in the most remote parts of Arkaan space. Please, don't hold anger for the ones you've lost here. May the Pantheon invite them to the table, and their blessings calm your broken hearts.

By the King's will,

Locilette, Ranger

He pressed send, and breathed out a sigh of relief. He knew that there were no words that could bring closure to the people, but he knew his actions were going to at least ease the burden of loss. He hoped that if his family were in a similar position that some wayward traveler or Ranger would contact his wife. The thought of his wife and boy sitting around for months on end believing he abandoned them was a fate worse than death.

"Sir, I have located the navigation console. It appears to be one of the only stations unaffected by hostilities." Brinks announced, observing the ship's charted course.

Locilette turned to see Phillip looking out of the front view port window, then turned his attention to his bot. "Interesting, where are we headed?"

"It appears there is a security wall installed on the navigation controls. I will try to by-pass now."

"Whoever put that in place didn't want anyone to know where they were going." Locilette stroked his chin as he pondered potential motives. "Why would you not tell your followers where you intended to take them?"

"Because you wouldn't want your people to know what their fate really was," Phillip said, his face planted to the window.

Locilette found himself slightly confused by his response. He stared at the man, wondering if he would follow it up with something a bit more insightful, but he continued to keep his sight out into the void of space. The tint from the window washed him in an orange glow by the light of the nearby star. He seemed to stare at it with a sense of longing, almost as if it were a home he knew he would ever see again. Locilette couldn't blame the man for his strangeness. He was sure he only got a part of the story of the horrors he had to endure, and he was fine with just letting it go.

His thoughts were interrupted by the loud beeping coming from the console behind him. He spun around, thinking he was sitting on the keyboard, but his mouth dropped open when he saw an incoming hail. He scrambled to find the correct prompt to accept the request, then tapped it several times. An audio wave popped on screen as a flat line, then started bouncing in the wave of an older man's voice.

"Yanagi, this is Captain Bellenor of the Ranger Cruiser Harriet. Whom am I speaking with?"

A smile washed over his face by that title and name. He almost couldn't believe that help was actually coming. There were times that he almost doubted it as another one of the Enlightened's schemes and games, but the familiar voice he heard was like music to his ears. It *was* real, and he was about to make damn sure every single member of his party would get the appropriate justice they deserved. And he prayed it was going to be as fierce as the hands of the Pantheon.

"Captain Bellenor, this is Ranger Locilette of the Theseus. It's more incredible to hear your voice than you could ever possibly imagine." Locilette spoke into the microphone.

"By every light in the cosmos, I'd never thought we'd ever find each other during an assignment again! What the hell is going on over there? We picked up your drone by simple chance with your

request. My staff informed me that your ship's SOS beacon had been activated. What am I sailing into here?"

"I don't have much time here, but the Yanagi has been taken over by a group of armed fanatics. They appear to follow a centralized leader that committed some serious heinous acts during his tenure here. I've personally witnessed some of the most disturbing things of my career since stepping foot on this hell ship. I'm not leaving until I bring those responsible to justice."

"We're here to help, old friend. Tell me what support you need, and you have it."

Locilette nodded as a plan formulated in his mind. "Okay, I'm going to need a boarding party, as well as guns trained on the vessel itself. It's on a course to somewhere currently unknown, but I have my Secura-Droid breaking the security they have on the navigations."

"Guns trained on the Yanagi? Do you suspect it's going to cut and run?"

"It's a very good possibility. If it tries to access a wormhole gate, we could find ourselves in Therid territory, where we'll have a range of other problems besides these psychos eluding justice."

"Very well," the Captain said. "I'll start prepping a boarding party and lead them aboard myself. Be safe, Locilette. We'll see you shortly."

"You're saving more than just my life, Bellenor. I have a ship full of civilians held captive in need of medical attention."

"We'll get them the care they need. Just hang tight, and we'll come up with a strategy on how to apprehend your perpetrators as well as medivac our injured civies. Captain Bellenor, out."

The channel closed, allowing Locilette to breathe. It felt as if the weight of the world had been lifted off his shoulders for the first time since he stepped foot off the safety of the Theseus. However, the moment was only destined to be short lived.

"Sir, I have by-passed the console's security. The Yanagi has been charted to follow a self-destructive course into the closest star. In ten minutes, the ship is scheduled to fire its impulse engines."

Locilette's heart sank to the floor. "Fucking Pantheon, no! How much time do we have?"

"It would seem we enter the star's corona in four hours at our current velocity, but when the impulse engine activates, we should arrive in twenty minutes."

That was his plan all along. The Enlightened wasn't trying to build a cult of fanatic followers. No, he created a suicide cult. His fear turned to frustration as he turned to punch one of the dead consoles nearby. The impact of his fist echoed around the bridge. His fist stung, but he ignored it. How was he going to capture the Enlightened and secure the civilians before they all met a fiery end?

There had to be a way, there just had to. He came so far and saw too many horrors to have it all burn away. No, he refused to let them get off so easily. Death was an escape for them just as much as it would be to travel in wormspace out of Arkaan judicial authority.

Locilette ran over to one of the starboard side view ports and could see the light shimmering off the hull of the Harriet in the far distance. He thought that if the Harriet could incapacitate the Yanagi's engines before they fired the impulse, she'd be dead in the water. He turned back to hail the Ranger Cruiser again, but just as he went to move, shouts came from the stairs leading to the bridge. Without a thought, Locilette jumped over the debris to get his message out, but dozens of armed men came rushing in, their weapons held high. His fingertips grazed the keyboard, but one of the men thrusted his shoulder into his chest, sending him flying though the bridge a short distance.

Before he could get to his feet to put up a fight, a massive fist collided with his face. Again and again and again and again and again and again and again.

Chapter Fifteen

"Please, please don't hurt me! You can have the Ranger, just let me go! I promise I'll be good. I promise!" Phillip cried as they tied his hands behind his back.

Locilette's face still stung from the horrible beating he just endured on the bridge. He managed to cover up to block most of the strikes, but enough got through to knock him senseless for a few moments. He still struggled to see straight, his left eye throbbed as his blurry vision stabilized. He blinked several times, then saw blood drip down onto the floor beneath him.

He knew he must have a pretty nasty cut above his eye, but as his senses started to return to him, he began to have other, more serious thoughts. He tried to move his arms, but he would feel the electrical wire tied tightly around his wrists. He didn't want to struggle too hard to bring extra attention to himself, because he knew exactly where he was even without looking up. Phillip's pleas solidified his assumptions, even as the loud smack across the crying man's face pierced his ears.

For a moment he allowed the intrusive thought of his life ending to cross his mind. *No*, he thought, he could have thoughts like that when he's on the bad end of a swinging rope. As long as he was breathing, he still had a chance to get out of this, but he would have to think quickly. He tried to quickly run through his options, but there certainly weren't many. Every time they would strike Phillip's broken body, the cheers of people would ring out around him. It sounded like dozens of people, but it could just be the acoustics in the room. He would do a quick head count as soon as he took his chance to look up. That was going to be one of the few assets he had left at this point.

"Now, let's see what we could do with the soulless one!" A man's voice laughed loudly to the delight of the crowd around him.

Locilette' closed his eyes tight, fully expecting to meet his end, but all he heard was the crunching of metal coming from somewhere behind him. It had to be Brinks! Was he still online, or did they beat the digital life out of him? If he could confirm his Secura-Droid was still at least partially functional, maybe he could muster some kind of slight chance of survival. Even then it seemed unlikely, but he would be damned if he just sat here and became another number on the final death tally. His time was up, it was now or never.

His head shot up quickly, taking in his surroundings. They were in the observation hall he had seen earlier. Massive windows lined the forward-facing part of the room at the tip of the Yanagi. This, like similar rooms on merchant vessels, acted as a lounge of sorts for a ship's crew on long voyages. It was here where the craziness of interstellar travel could be toned down, allowing the hard-working men and women to enjoy a quiet moment with the stars. It was a beautiful concept, one that Locilette had thought about installing on his own ship at some point in the future.

The lights were dimmed, if not completely turned off. The orange light of the nearby star flooded the room with a blanket of golden red, not allowing a single bit of dust to be hidden. The tint on the windows did its best to ease the star's intensity, but they weren't designed to block out the light from a red dwarf star so close to the ship. Locilette caught the sight of shutters rolled out above each of the windows, but these people welcomed the sight of the approaching light. This was what they were promised.

His eyes darted to every small detail he could manage to take in as his head slowly rotated around the room. He prayed there would only be dozens of people, but he was sorely mistaken by the ear piercing combinations of sounds. His heart sank as he was sure there were at the very least a hundred people gathered here to take witness of their ascension. What would normally be a rather large room seemed much smaller as the bodies crammed around the see their new victims become the last to be slaughtered before taking the plunge into the fiery blaze of the approaching red dwarf.

In some strange way, he saw the peace that could be brought to people who find themselves lost here in the cosmos. Of course, it was a common tactic among these cultists to offer a sense of belonging to people like that, but to finally have a purpose in their otherwise misguided lives seemed somewhat peaceful. In no way would convincing a group of lost souls to commit mass suicide ever be considered okay, but Locilette could at the very least sympathize with their longing for a home. A longing that was taken advantage of by a mad man; by a horrific wolf in sheep's clothing to lead the flock to his dinner table. Every flock needed a guard dog, and Locilette was more than capable of fighting off the pack.

The sound of metal on metal again crunched to the delight of the screaming people. Each one of them were now maskless, exposing the cult's emblem forever etched into their foreheads. Locilette shot a glance back to see a man whacking a metal pipe across Brinks's head. Several dents dotted all over its still body, but the blue lights that normally shone brightly were gone. Only black screens remained in their place. For the first time, Locilette felt completely alone here. That was a fate he considered worse than death.

"Hey!" someone yelled, his voice was loud enough to carry over the booming sound of the mob. "Look who decided to join the party!"

Locilette looked over to see a large, burly man strolling over to him from the crowd. He twirled a bladed piece of metal in his hand. It was a sight that Locilette was too familiar with now. His boots were stained with dry blood from someone he had probably served with on this ship for years. He stopped just short of where Locilette sat on his knees and knelt down, placing the tip of the blade under his chin.

"Are you afraid of dying, boy?" He asked.

Locilette refused to answer, only meeting his gaze with his own piercing look. His yellow eyes bore deep into his.

There was something different about this man. Something that disturbed him with a wave of unsettling ease the longer he stared into his eyes. He felt unnatural, as if he knew something that hadn't been revealed to him yet was sitting before his very eyes. This was the Enlightened. This was him. The aura of death radiated from his flesh like the flares whipping off the surface of the unsteady star that they were destined for.

"What have you done?" Locilette managed to say with a broken voice. His eye contact never wavering for a moment.

He cocked his head. "What have I done, Ranger?"

"The blood that's on your hands is enough to fill a river. Why did you turn these people against each other? What did you have to gain from the madness you caused!?"

"I'm sorry," he said with a crooked smile. "These wonderful people are the driving force of our ascension, not me! I am merely the hammer striking the anvil for our everlasting life beyond the stars!"

"You're a fucking monster is what you are!" Locilette spat.

"Me? I'm the monster? Last time I checked, you're the one who let a woman fry like a burger on a hot summer's day."

Locilette couldn't help but grit his teeth. Never in his life had he wanted to simply end someone's life, but there was always an exception. This was one of those times.

"You psychopath! I'm going to breathe a sigh of relief as the King's Judge sentences you and your cult of homicidal maniacs to brutal death!"

"Oh, death isn't the end for us, my friend. We shall sit at the table of the new lord amongst the Pantheon!" The man shouted as a rallying cry. The mob returned his call with a rousing cheer.

"You're a joke. No, you're a complete narcissist. Who goes around calling themselves *the Enlightened*, but needed to be broken out of a brig cell like a common criminal? That's all you are, just another nutcase who thinks they are destined to sit in the immortal chairs of the Pantheon. Your story isn't new. You're just another case study." Locilette thundered through gritted teeth.

The entire room grew silent. It was as if someone pressed a mute button that immediately forced all noise to cease. The hairs on his arms began to stand on end as he could feel the eyes of each of the cultists stare into him from all sides. Locilette felt the drips of sweat start to run down his face. He wasn't sure if it was his nerves beginning to crack or the temperature rising from the star growing larger in the window behind the mob. He didn't bother to look around at them, he knew their joy had been replaced by anger towards him. He was about to die, but he almost felt a relief that he was able to let that out before his final breaths were stolen from him.

"You think *I* am the merciful Enlightened one?" The man asked, his face becoming void of all emotion. "No, no, no. I am but a mere apostle to our savior."

Locilette for once felt an alien feeling a confusion fluster within him. "What are you talking about? If you're not him, then who is?"

"I'm glad you asked! Ladies and gentlemen of the Yanagi, I give you your messiah! The one who will usher us into the next phase of our eternal lives!"

The crowd erupted in an ear shattering cheer. Locilette's head whipped around, trying to find the man, but nobody appeared to take the chance to step forward. The mob's cheers then became complimented by a rousing applause as the sounds of clapping hands echoed from all around him. It was like a heartfelt standing ovation after a beautiful closing of a musical forever retiring from production. The people around him began to cry, like the ensemble that held the production together like glue, or the production team filming their last scene. Then, Locilette's heart fell to the floor. Phillip smiled at the crowd and took a stand.

He bowed to the roaring applause. He wiped away a rogue tear that streamed down his cheek, then began to return the applause back to his people. No thoughts were in Locilette's head. No feeling other than pure shock ran through him as his eyes were as wide as the ever-approaching star in the window. This couldn't be. Was this a joke? This had to be another game or riddle crafted by the real Enlightened to mess with him, even as his inevitable death loomed only moments away.

Phillip bowed again and waved to the mob around him. He grabbed a rag from someone in the crowd, and wiped the blood from his face, but there was no cut to be seen around it. He tossed it to someone else, who after catching it, took a deep sniff of it before passing out onto the hard floor. Some of the men pulled a couple of chairs together, and helped him up to be elevated above the mob, who now crowded around him. He waved his arms down to calm their cheers, then shook the hand of the burly apostle who stood just off to the side. The man's tough face was wet with tears as he grasped the hand of his messiah.

"My people," he said, but was immediately cut off by more cries and cheers. He smiled as he waved to calm them down again.

"My people, thank you. It was because of *all* of you that we were able to pull this off. Together we were able to take this ship as our home and rid it from the pests that would hold us back from achieving our shared dream. This ship, this Yanagi, will be our vessel as we cruise into the beyond to dine with the Pantheon before they accept me into their fold. Just as when the ancient Arkaans ascended into the heavens to join the cosmic parenthood, I will lead you there as well to become my most holy retinue!" He preached to his people. "When we enter the red light of the gateway star, our sins will be burned away, allowing us to finally be able to walk amongst the holy beings of the Pantheon. The guardians will be there on the other side to welcome us in with open arms!"

The crowd cheered as he raised an arm towards the window behind him. The red dwarf star almost filled the window completely as they grew closer. The powerful shaders strained to block out most of the intense light, but allowed the unstable plasma whips to be seen rolling off from it. The fear that filled Locilette at its approach was a calming sight to the people around him.

"And this also couldn't have been achieved without our wonderful guest star, who admirably played the part of the fearless Ranger, Locilette," he said, opening his arms to him. The crowd turned to him and clapped for his part in their story.

Locilette's face hadn't changed since the moment Phillip stood up. The disturbed look of horrified surprise seemed to be pasted to his face indefinitely. Tears began to run from the corners of his eyes as they burned from not blinking for several minutes. The hot air around him dried his open mouth, but nothing could break him from the void that plagued his mind. All eyes were on him.

Every person in that room seemed to become shadows as the star allowed only their black silhouettes against the blinding light. There was no more clapping, there were no more cheers, the only sound was coming from the vents as it moaned to keep the Yanagi's interior cool from the excruciating heat. Locilette felt like he couldn't breathe. His mind swirled with a vortex of mixed emotions that left his thoughts in a state of delirium. He was clearly seeing it, but something within him simply refused to believe it.

Phillip couldn't be the Enlightened, he just couldn't be. A stabbing feeling of betrayal swept through him like a blade, but not at Phillip. He felt like he betrayed himself. How could he not see that monster that was under his wing? All the hard years of experience and study to identify people like him, and he was blinded by a ruse of someone in distress. Locilette felt disgusted with himself. He wondered if maybe he did deserve the fate that was about to be handed to him. Maybe this in fact was destiny the Pantheon prescribed to him. Dying in the roaring inferno of a star in a pool of humility that had long eluded him over his career.

"Phillip, how could you do this?" Locilette asked.

"Easily," he said, opening his hands. "Easily for a being such as myself, I should say."

"I don't understand…"

He smiled. "Most rarely do, Locilette. Now, I know this may be a bit of a shock to you, but you should feel honored to be a part of the story that'll move the masses. I've even decided to give you a place at my table in the dining hall of the Pantheon!"

"No, no, no. I fucking saved your life, man. Twice!"

"All because of the incredible performances of my great people!" He called out. The mob around him reignited into a roar of cheers as they congratulated themselves. Locilette could feel his face getting hot. He was played like a fool. Phillip made him out to be the jester in the final act of his homicidal matinee.

"Why, Phillip. Why me?" Locilette sighed, shaking his head.

"Oh, Phillip?" He said with a shrug. "Just a stage name."

"I'd say I'm surprised, but I'm not sure that's even possible at this point."

He smiled as the followers around him raised their hands to him to take in his eternal power. He in turn raised his with a smile, lightly grazing their palms with the tips of his fingers. Each person shuddered and moaned as his skin touched theirs. Locilette felt disturbed just watching something like this happen. His skin crawled as the sounds of their orgasmic moans filled the room, like the chants of a temple.

"My name is Arnold Dekciw!" He called out to the heavens. "All will rejoice in my name!"

The moans from the crowd turned into sobs at the mere sound of his name. They clammered to him just to touch him one last time before they followed him in death. A smile stayed glued on his face as he closed his eyes to the hands running over him. Most of the people in the back tugged and pulled like savages at the clothes of their brothers and sisters at the front, just to get their chance to touch his radiant skin.

"My lord, my god, please accept me into your happily ever after!" A woman shouted between sobs of joy.

"My sister, you will dine with me and the others of the cosmic Pantheon for all eternity!" Arnold responded, but directed the message to the rest of the people around him.

The heat beating on Locilette's face burned his eyes. The heat that now surrounded him felt like he was sitting in front of a broiling stove. He shook his head to regain himself. His senses all at once seemed to return to him as the shock and awe began to slowly dissipate. He looked up to see the crowd adore their false god, but the disturbing sight now seemed to dip into his advantage. No one seemed to even be paying attention to him anymore. They've all accepted their deaths, so what use was it to make sure he was contained?

He struggled at the cables that bound his hands. He looked back to see exactly how they were tied to maybe find a way to untie it when he saw the metal body of Brinks from the corner of his eye. The bot was leaning against the wall, its body dented with exposed wires sticking out of its back. Both of its arms were lying by its side, one hand seemed to be torn from its right arm, leaving it in a state of mangled wires and metal.

Locilette never thought his heart would break for something as lifeless as a Secura-Droid. He felt a strange comradery with Brinks since it was the only other thing to witness the horrors that he had. Brinks wasn't capable of placing emotions with the things they've seen, but Locilette knew that the bot could process how disturbing and wrong such things were. Brinks was more real to him now than any other Ranger out patrolling the cosmos. The sight of the bot's broken body void of power brought tears to his already burning eyes. Locilette was going to die here, completely alone, and nobody would know the things he, or Brinks, had to go through.

"Brinks," he whispered. "Brinks, come on. Please wake up."

He scooted himself closer to the bot, each movement sending a wave of pain shooting up his side. The metal around where his hand was torn away looked to be sharp enough to slice through the cables if he could position himself right. He twisted his aching body to try and reach out his bound arms behind him, but it was no use. The metal just wasn't sharp enough to slice through the military grade cables used in the Yanagi's electronics. He relaxed and sat down to watch the star take him. This was it.

"If only you could power up one last time to see this, Brinks. I'd love to explain the ironic beauty of this. I know you probably wouldn't ever understand, but I know you'd try." Locilette sighed.

Locilette admired the orangish red glow that surrounded him. What was once fear now felt like a blanket of comfort that would ease him into an eternal slumber. The heat was so intense now. His clothes were completely covered in sweat, but it didn't seem to bother him anymore. His body relaxed as he leaned against the wall next to his fallen comrade. The only thing he could ask for was to say goodbye personally to his family, and to take off his boots. He could feel the moisture build up from his scorching feet as his body tried to bring them relief. It was so uncomfortable, like bathing his feet in warm, swampy water. All he wanted was to be as comfortable as possible.

"Powering up complete, sir." A voice came from next to him.

At first he didn't even register what it said. His eyes were entranced by the light that blazed through the overwhelmed shaders. As soon as it came to him to look over, he was met with a single blue light staring at him. Its twin seemed to be forever black as the damage sustained around it was too much to overcome for the electronics within.

"Brinks?" He asked, his mind refusing to believe what his eyes were delivering him. "BRINKS!"

The bot's eye blinked green for a moment. "Sir, the internal temperature of the Yanagi is quite severe. I would advise we exfiltrate immediately, or you could potentially see damage to your organic body tissue."

"Yeah, I know, but I think we're at the end of the road here. Just a spitball guess here, but it seems like we're caught in the star's gravitational pull. Even if the Pantheon gifted us access to the ship's impulse, I doubt there would be enough power to use it."

"Negative, sir. I downloaded the Yanagi's schematics as we investigated the bridge, and I identified a Captain's emergency escape hatch that would allow us to escape near the hangar. This would allow us to reach the Theseus with little time to spare."

He shrugged. "It doesn't matter, Brinks. We're too close to the star."

"Sir, if I may-"

"Brinks!" Locilette interrupted. "We're done. Let's just have some peace before we take that walk beyond."

Brinks's gears moaned as it used the wall behind it to climb to its feet. The bot ran a quick series of equations, then grabbed one of the blades dropped by one of the worshippers still adoring their messiah. Brinks began to slice away at the cables, but Locilette shrugged it off.

"Sir, please advise, we must hurry before it is too late."

Locilette shot the bot a look of disdain. "Brinks, sit down. I don't want to be frantically escaping an inevitable death in my final moments. Let me have my peace, please. Don't make me power you off again."

"*Locilette!*" The bot raised its voice to the level that made him snap his head in surprise. The digital sound of his name snapped him out of his trance-like state. He wasn't even sure Secura-Droids were allowed to acknowledge such private things about their owners, but the sound of his name being spoken sent a skin-crawling sense of urgency rushing through his blood.

"If we make it to the Theseus now, it should have enough power to meet the escape velocity of the star. However, we must exfiltrate *now*. With haste, sir."

The uncomfortable mixture of tears and sweat burned his eyes, but he refused to blink as he met the bot's gaze. "We can make it out? Are you sure?"

"Sir, the time for explanation is little to none. We must leave now."

Lociette's eyes seemed to be glued open wide. Could they really get off this horrible ship? It seemed like the acceptance of death overwhelmed him to the point where the concept of escaping just seemed like something that was completely unobtainable. He felt it at such a deep level that he was going to die here. It felt as if it was meant to happen. Perhaps Arnold had infiltrated his mind too, just like the rest of these poor souls.

Locilette couldn't help but scoff at that man's brilliance. Not only was he good enough to take over the hearts and minds of innocents, he was able to break the mind of someone as highly trained as himself. He shook his head in disappointment with himself. Arnold was like nothing he'd ever seen before. He was a true master of the mind that could rival some of the best politicians throughout Arkaa's extensive history.

If Arnold was a case study in a research book, Locilette might even think to admire him for his almost supernatural ability. However, seeing it first-hand was on another level. Never would he think of the people from the pages of those books existing in the flesh, let alone him coming face to face with one. It only seemed fitting that this one, along with his homicidal apostles, perished by the cleansing fire of this star. And Locilette refused to be a part of it.

"Cut me loose." Locieltte commanded. "Let's get the hell off this ship."

Brinks sliced the cables until Locilette felt the pressure give away. He jumped to his feet and already saw Brinks limping to the door. Sparks shot from the bot's knee, not allowing it to bend properly. With each step, the gears grinded and chewed at the surrounding metal of its leg. The bot ignored it. Brinks stiffened its leg to avoid causing more damage, but it didn't appear to stop the electronics spitting sparks in protest.

Locilette bolted for the door. Something within made him stop just before crossing through the threshold to safety. It beckoned to him, yearning for him to turn one last time. He gave into the feeling, turning slowly to meet the golden eyes of Arnold staring back at him. The others were all facing the light of the red dwarf star, their hands firmly locked together as they took in their final moments together. Arnold too held the hands of apostles, but his smile wasn't directed to the transition to his prescribed afterlife. His joy was for Locilette. Joy of knowing that Locilette would be coming with him.

With a wink and a smile he said, "See you real soon."

Chapter Sixteen

As soon as Locilette turned the corner, the lights above him started to blink. They did that several times before eventually turning off for the last time. The sound of the life support system ceased, sending a new wave of urgency through him. The Yanagi seemed set on killing him one way or another. Whether it was being consumed by the unimaginable heat from the star they were falling into, or being suffocated to death in her dark corridors. He refused to accept either of those as his fate.

Locilette couldn't see a thing. There were no external windows on the way to the bridge leaving the two wandering in the dark. He felt his way around by following the walls with his hand, but they were too hot to the touch now to hold for very long. He knew he was running out of time. The heat was just going to make him breathe heavier the longer they went on, so wasting any time now was nothing short of a death wish.

A thought crossed his mind about Brinks. Could its metal body survive the hardships of space? Certainly not a star, but if the bot could somehow be launched clear of the star, could it get away with the stories of the lost souls that perished here, including himself? A back up plan for the back up plan, he thought. As badly as he wanted to get off this cursed ship, he was also a realist.

The sound of the hull creaking under the intensity of the star was exerting on the Yanagi's interior. They both stopped fearing the worst as the ghostly wails of the ship crying out echoes through the halls. The ship began to rumble slightly as the wails grew louder and louder and louder. What felt like sticking his face in front of an open oven now felt like standing behind a starship's engine exhaust as it powered up. He felt like tearing his clothes away to find just a slight bit of relief, but he knew that no relief would come. The Yanagi was broiling him alive.

Brink's light flickered on from its only functional eye, but flickered off again as they got moving. The bot resorted to banging itself on the side of the head, finally allowing the light to flash on. The corridor seemed to be blanketed in a thick veil of fog from what little humidity in the Yanagi's artificial atmosphere being heated to steam. Locilette grabbed the back armor plate that protruded from Brink's dented back to help guide him though. Every shuffling step he made filled his mind with hallucinations of the trapped souls of the Yanagi reaching out from the steam to keep him here. He closed his eyes tight, and shook the pouring sweat from his face.

"Sir, Captain Bellenor of the Ranger Cruiser Harriet is hailing the Theseus. It would appear the Yanagi losing power broke the encryption that forced my link to be severed. I have restored communications with your ship, sir. Would you like me to patch it through?"

"Our ship." Locilette corrected, struggling to speak. "Yeah, put him through, but don't stop moving. We have to get out of here *fast.*"

"Captain Bellenor, you are patched through to Ranger Locilette. Go ahead, sir." Brinks announced. There was a brief moment of static before the familiar sound of Bellenor's voice came through.

"*Locilette, what the hell is happening over there!*" The Captain asked, his voice breaking up slightly into bursts of static. "*If you don't get off it now, you're going to be fried with the rest of the Yanagi!*"

"Acknowledged. Something unforeseen happened, we're trying to exfil now, though we're quite literally in the dark here."

Another wave of static came through. "*I've ordered my boarding party to halt operations. It's too dangerous to extract you, and I can't put my men and women on the line of danger more so than they already are. I'm so sorry Locilette, but help isn' t coming.*"

Bellenor's words hit him like a shot to the gut. The thing that perplexed him most was that it was something he already knew, and couldn't expect any less. It hurt nonetheless. Maybe it was just someone else acknowledging the extremely dire situation he was in that made things seem real. Locilette couldn't help but let the rush of emotion wash over him.

"Bellenor," he said, trying to steady his voice. "If I can't make it off this ship, I want you to tell Marla and the boys that I love them so much. They are the greatest thing to ever happen to me, and I'll be watching over them standing at the sides of the Pantheon. Please, tell Marla that it's okay to seek happiness. I'll die happy on this day knowing the rest of her life will be full of joy and security. Promise me, Bellenor."

A brief moment passed with dead air. Locilette stumbled on a body that didn't seem to be there prior, but if he was being honest with himself, he had no clue where he was. His faith rested fully in Brinks to get them back to the bridge, but he didn't even have the energy to protest even if he thought they were going the wrong way.

"*Your message has been saved. I'll make sure it is delivered to her personally. It's been an honor, Locilette,*" the Captain said. "*I've ordered every crew member aboard my ship to deliver you final salutes. You've served Arkaa and the King well. Rest Ranger, and I await to serve next to you again among the Pantheon.*"

"The honor was mine, Captain Bellenor. Brinks, end comms."

The channels closed with a fit of static, but faded away as Brinks ended the transmission. The sense of peace returned to him. Something felt good about knowing his family would receive a final goodbye spoken from his own lips. His heart ached for his boys. He never wanted to be a father that would miss the ball games or the academic achievements they would one day gain, but he knew this was different. He wasn't abandoning his boys. Death in the line of duty was the only honorable way he could ever imagine of leaving his boys without a father.

"Sir, watch your step. We are ascending the stairs to the bridge now." Brinks announced, stopping just shy of the first step.

As soon as Locilette found the first step, he kept pace with the bot as they climbed the flight to the top. The blinding steam seemed to have avoided rising too high here as it was lighter in the bridge than below. He was confident that he could make it on his own power now, so he tapped Brinks's back and stepped over some of the debris scattered around them.

Brinks stopped and pointed up. "Quickly, sir. The Captain's Quarters are up the stairs near the back of the mezzanine."

Locilette's eyes darted up to see the bodies of the officers swinging wildly as the ship's rumblings got more intense. They were bathed in the orange light of the star that filled the rest of the bridge with an excruciating heat. Locilette tried to avert his eyes, but he almost couldn't contain his curiosity to look at one of the officers near the middle. His face was horribly beaten, and showed several penetration markings all around his thick neck. The cable secured tightly around it turned the surrounding area purple and blue.

He was meant to be a message. It was quite obvious that he was murdered long before he was strung up here with the rest of the Yanagi's officer staff by the wounds in his neck. Locilette could only imagine those psychoes stashing his body in some dark closet somewhere until they found the rest of them, then strung them all up together as some sort of celebration. There was some kind of comfort in knowing that the souls of these men were about to be set free by the cleansing fire of the burning star. He muttered a quick prayer that peace would finally reach them.

Brinks led Locilette only by a couple of feet as he reached the top of the spiraling stairs. Tables and chairs were scattered around the mezzanine, some with the mugs of morning coffee staining the floor from where it fell on that tragic day. A leather couch was pushed against the railing where the Party hoisted the bodies over to drop them to the end of their ropes. Arnold Dekciw's emblem was carved into the black middle cushion with the clean cuts of a razor sharp blade.

Brinks pulled at one side of the door, making it grind on its tracks. Locilette was sure the sign above the door read something to do with it being the captain's quarters, but it seemed to be smashed in, leaving nothing but a shell of shattered glass. He pressed his body into the crack of the door and pushed it with all the strength he had left to make a gap big enough for Brinks to fit through.

The light from Brinks's eye darted around what was left of the office. Reports and invoices seemed to cover every inch of the carpeted floor. A large bookshelf lined the right side wall, but every single book that had once sat neatly upon its shelves was stacked in a corner and burned. The large wooden desk was toppled on its side, each one of the drawers pulled out and smashed against the nearby walls. Two large banners of the Josakk Merchant Guild hung on the back walls, but were painted over with the calling card of the cult's icon.

It took a moment for him to notice, but the familiar rotting smell of death came across his nose. He glanced in the corner to his left where a decomposing corpse of a man sat slumped over against the wall. Parts of his blonde hair had begun to fall out as the body left the bloating phase of the death process. Without even a single thought more, Locilette knew exactly who this man was. This was Phillip. The *real* Phillip who's name was tainted to become a sick character to be played.

The sound of the desk scraping against the floor broke Locilette from his thoughts. He glanced back at the body one last time, then went back to the bot struggling to move it. He wondered how the desk could be scraping anything on a carpeted floor, but with the two of them pulling at the solid wood frame, they were able to prove Brinks's assessment correct. A piece of the carpet was folded back from the desk running across it to reveal a small metal hatch fixed into the floor.

Brinks tugged at the carpet, ripping it back enough with its one hand for them to gain access to it. A handle remained sunken in the center of the hatch with a keypad lining it. Locilette's heart sank. There was no way they could hack it without power, and even if they did, they didn't have the time to figure it out. He could feel the panic rise within his stomach. Just before he felt himself give up, Brinks twisted the handle and lifted the heavy hatch. It landed to the side with a loud thud against the rolled back carpet.

"How..." Locilette stuttered. "How is that possible?"

"Not much time to explain, sir. When the electricity is offline, all safety hatches automatically disengage their locks for emergencies."

Locilette shot up and grabbed the bot by the shoulders. "You're the most amazing being in the cosmos, Brinks. Let's get the hell out of here."

"Your praise is not necessary. This hatch will deliver us to the cargo hold. After you, sir."

He dropped down and dangled his legs into the shaft that dropped down far below. Even the light from Brinks wasn't enough to penetrate the deep dark of the escape hatch. If this shaft went from the bridge to the cargo hold by the hangar, then that would mean it followed the entire vertical length of the ship. His foot eventually found the foot holding of the ladder and he carefully lowered himself to begin his descent.

Locilette could feel the metal wall close in around him. The heat that ran throughout the shaft was just as unbearable as the rest of the ship. He felt himself grow a bit lightheaded as he shook his head to regain himself. He thought of how it would be just his luck to see light at the end of the tunnel of this whole ordeal just to be taken out by a heat stroke as he made his escape. The Pantheon certainly worked in mysterious ways.

Brinks lowered itself down, gripping the edge of the ladder with one hand. Locilette looked up to see the soles he made on the bot's feet start to peel away from the abuse they've sustained. He couldn't help but feel mildly impressed that they've lasted this long through the hardships they endured. When they made it off this ship together, he would make sure Brinks got a full repair to return back to active duty, as well as some well-needed upgrades. Noise reducing foot pads was at the top of that list, as was proven more than useful here.

Their descent down felt like it took an eternity in the sweltering shaft. Every so often, Locilette would feel a spell of faintness begin to swell over him, but after a quick moment of rest he was able to continue. Brinks, the ever faithful companion, was there to push each step of the way down, sometimes even forcing his metal body downward to make Locilette keep moving. A few times he felt the frustration build in him, but his gut reminded him that Brinks's urgency was more than appropriate, it was a matter of life or death. As Locilette lowered his foot again for the next step, he felt flatness beneath him.

"Hey, I think I found the hatch!" Locilette called up.

"Affirmative, sir. It is designed to be a break-away door, so if you will, please stomp on it with sufficient strength to gain access."

He did as the bot recommended and began to kick at the metal hatch. It didn't budge. He tried harder, bringing his knee up to his chest, then driving his leg down with a powerful thud against the thin metal. Why wasn't it breaking? He could feel the exhaustion deep in his bones, but he still had enough to break through this. He was sure of it.

He dismounted the ladder, and stood on the hatch with both feet planted firmly. Over and over he began to jump up and down, the scorching heat now feeling as if it had taken a few notches up. The walls around him burned his hands as he tried to gain more leverage to jump higher, but he could only keep his hands there for a matter of milliseconds. He had one final idea. Locilette remounted the ladder and climbed up a few steps, then released himself to fall down on the hatch door. With a loud crack, it gave away under him.

Locilette found himself in a free fall. He spiraled down along with chunks of metal from the broken hatch. He caught Brinks's bright eye as the bot watched its owner fall twenty feet from the ceiling. Locilette was surprised that not a single thought ran through his head. Not a single one. Perhaps it was the unreal life draining heat, or maybe it was just the pure exhaustion that ran through him. He just watched Brinks's eye get farther away as he descended into the darkness below until he crashed below.

The impact of the fall knocked the air from his lungs. He gasped for breath, but the life support system being offline didn't allow him much relief. His body ached all over, but he found himself lucky enough to be able to move. Brinks jumped down from the hatch and landed on his feet. Its shocks absorbed most of the fall, but it's knee buckled anyway.

"Sir, are you injured?" Brinks asked, looking him over.

Locilette sat up and reached his hand out. "Yeah, I'm good. Let's get out of here."

The bot grasped his hand and helped him to his feet. With the faint light, he looked back to see that the corpse he found when he first stepped foot on the Yanagi was there to catch his fall. It felt as if she was there to make sure he didn't join the haunted souls of the Yanagi crew.

He knew that fall would've been the end of him if he met the solid metal floor he now stood on. Her story may be over, but her body in death saved him to keep on living. He mouthed *thank you,* then jogged as best he could to catch up to Brinks.

Brinks led the way through the small corridor, and with a quick push of the door, the hangar bay laid ahead. The only glimmer of light came from the Thesus's computer monitors shining through the windows like a beacon in the darkness. The beam of light from Brinks's eyes swept over it quickly to make sure there weren't any of Arnold's men waiting in an ambush. Being satisfied that the perimeter was secured, the bot's eye flashed green, then a moment later the side door unlatched before it slowly lowered to the hangar floor. The sound of the steps coming down almost made Locilette cry in a fit of joy, but he knew he didn't have a single moment to waste on even that.

He struggled to climb the steps. His legs burned with the pain of exhaustion and the sweat that poured from every inch of his skin now stopped. The heat that once felt like it was boiling him alive now seemed less intense as Brinks pushed him from behind up the steps. An overwhelming wave of cool air rushed over him as he stepped onto the Theseus. The sound of the small ship's life support system hummed loudly as it worked to keep its interior livable.

He tapped the button on the side of the exit door and the cabin light above him intensified. The ship was a complete disaster. Reports from previous calls he responded to were scattered all over the cabin floor, some balled up and tossed in the corner, creating a small pyramid. Smashed equipment dotted around the ship with the monitor behind the seats catching the worst of it. There was a massive hole smashed in its screen by some kind of blunt object, but the lights within tried to illuminate the display anyway. It sparked loudly before fading away to black along with most of the other monitors.

His cabinet storage units were raided with every bit of his food appeared to have been devoured on sight. Packages of dried food completely bare of even a single crumb were tossed about without a care. The jars his wife canned herself before he departed on his current assignment stained the walls with the juices of the rations that were kept within. Locilette recoiled a bit at the disgusting sight of tongue licks lining the wall where one of the cans of sauce was broken. Even his emergency supply of hardtack was broken into, leaving only bits and pieces around the ship's cabin like a rodent scurrying to find safety from a looming predator.

Locilette quickly made his way to the cockpit and swiveled the seat around. Arnold's crest was sliced in the cushion of his seats, just like the couch on the Yanagi's bridge. That could be replaced. The food can be rebought and re-canned. The ship's displays can be repaired, but none of that would be possible unless he could get off this forsaken ship. It was time to leave.

He took his seat as he had done for years and strapped himself in. One by one he flipped the switches to bring power to the Theseus's control panel, but like the monitors, some of the flight instruments were smashed. His eyes raked over the damaged ones, trying to decipher if he could reliably pilot the ship without some of them. He shook that insane thought from his head. It didn't matter if he could fly it safely or not, because there simply wasn't a choice. The Theseus had to get him off the Yanagi either in one piece, or well enough away so they could get help.

The ship's power supply flashed on a small screen to the right of the flight controls. A red light flashed in the corner, alerting him that the ship was functioning on reserve power, and by the looks of it, the battery cells were almost completely drained. At this rate, there was going to be no way he would have enough power to hit the escape velocity of the star. He didn't like it, but he knew what had to be done.

He spun the chair to the right, and brought up the Theseus's power allocation screen. He scrolled down with the broken arrow key and selected the life support system. With a few confirmations, and an emergency prompt, he disabled the only thing protecting him from the inferno. The loud humming soon faded away, and the only thing he could hear was the creaking of the Yanagi around him. He gave the rest of the ship's power to the engine, then held the ignition button bringing the Theseus roaring to life.

"Sir, may I inquire as to why you disabled the life support system?" Brinks asked.

"We're going to be lucky if we have enough power for impulse engines as it is. I need every drop of power this bird can muster to clear us of this damn ball of fire."

The bot cocked its battered head. "If I may, sir, if you do not have the air to make the travel to safety, is it not pointless to escape the gravitational pull of the star?"

"We don't have to make it far," Locilette said, observing the little information he could decipher from the smashed screens and instruments. "We just need to make it far enough for the Harriet to pick us up."

"That is quite the unwise option, sir."

He glanced over his shoulder at the bot. "It's our only option."

Green lights began to pop across the ship's status screen. He pushed the throttle slightly to listen to the roar of the engine coming from the still opened side door. She sounded perfect. He was surprised that Arnold's thugs hadn't thought to disable it in case he ever found a way to escape. Maybe they never thought they would actually get to this point on their journey that's been spanning months now. He wondered if some of them didn't actually want to see this thing to the end, and figured the Theseus could be used to escape. Maybe those people who had those thoughts were dead now. Murdered along with anyone else who wanted to get away from Arnold's horrible schemes.

The console to his left beeped loudly as the engine's launch thrusters were at 100%. "Brinks, you need to get the bay door open and hurry back. We're already out of time!" Locilette commanded, his hand hovering over the launch button.

"At once, sir," Brinks said, turning and dashing out the door.

Locilette reached his hand behind his seat, feeling for the power switch for the massive radio system. His fingers followed the familiar power cable which ran right up to it, then as soon as the metal switch met his finger tips, he flipped it. He didn't have much faith that it was going to even work, but he had to still try. He breathed out a long sigh of relief as the sound of static began bouncing through the cockpit's speakers. The Pantheon was truly watching over him. He reached over and pulled the headset off the floor, and slid it over his ears, pulling the microphone down to his mouth.

"Ranger Cruiser Harriet, this is Ranger Locilette of the Theseus, please acknowledge." He transmitted.

There was no response. The sound of the creaking hull of the Yanagi and static filled the air around him. Was the star interfering with the radio broadcast? Even if it was, the Harriet should've at least picked up something from this distance.

"Ranger Cruiser Harriet," he tried again, "this is an SOS from Ranger Locilette of the Theseus. I am going to attempt to make an emergency exfil, but I don't think I'll have enough power to break the gravitational tug of the star. Please provide immediate assistance."

He let go of the button with only the crackling of static returning his please. Could the Harriet actually have left him here to plunge to his death in the star? How could Bellenor do that to him? He wasn't just some grunt dying in the line of duty, they were friends. They were brothers in defense of his Majesty's law. Locilette felt such a mixture of rage and panic seep into his stomach. He tried to calm his breathing, but it was too much. This was all too much. He balled up his fist tightly and punched the flight panels over and over until his hand went numb.

The sound of electronics moving snapped him out of his rage momentarily. He turned to the side door of the Theseus closing. His eyes quickly darted to the monitor which flashed *remote close in progress* on the badly-beaten screen in a bold red font. The door came to a close, then sealed tightly to keep the cabin pressurized. Locilette couldn't understand what exactly was happening, but then the hangar bay doors slowly started to open. The pure blinding light of the star assaulted the hangar, forcing the Theseus to quickly shade the view ports.

Crates and debris from inside the hangar were shot out into the vacuum of space as the doors slid apart. The Thesues's magnetic landing pads were holding firm, but alerts began to pop on screen that her energy reserves were being drained by the strain of holding the ship in place. Locilette lifted himself out of his seat to peer over the nose of the ship to see Brinks staring up at him, its hand held tightly on a yellow lever. Quickly, he switched the channel on the radio to the ship's internal comms, which ran through Brinks as well.

"Brinks!" Locilette yelled into the microphone. "Get your ass in here now!"

"Negative, sir. The Yanagi's lack of power will not allow the hangar doors to open. It must be opened manually and held in place or they will immediately close."

Locilette's mouth dropped open. "No, what are you saying, Brinks?"

"Sir, you are out of time. You must leave now or meet the fate of the Yanagi. Please, sir, it's now or never. I will hold the door open, but you must exfil with all haste! Now, sir!"

Locilette slumped back into his seat. He felt his throat tighten as he searched for words to say, but nothing came. This wasn't just a machine. This wasn't a robot just existing to provide light security. Brinks was a battle brother if he ever had one. The things he and that bot had been through on this hell-bound vessel forged a bond stronger than the steel that formed Brinks's body. He would grieve Brinks in time, but the bot was right. If he didn't want to join Arnold's suicidal descent into the eternal burning star, it was now or never.

"Ranger Brinks, it's been an absolute honor to serve by your side," he said.

"The honor was mine, Ranger Locilette."

Brinks's words echoed through the speakers of the cockpit. Without a moment's hesitation more, Locilette tapped the launch button, disengaging the magnetic landing pads. The ship jolted up, then he banked the flight stick to the port side to allow the vacuum to drag the Theseus out of the Yanagi. The blue light of Brinks's eyes flashed green for just a split moment before the large vessel continued on into the final stop on its journey.

The flight stick shook violently in his hands. He whipped it to the right to straighten it out and face away from the star, then grasped the throttle tightly and pushed it with all his might. The sound of the engine working overtime roared through the cabin as the engine room door blew open. He didn't dare turn to see what was happening, he just kept his eyes on the throttle screen, watching as the energy gauge climbed higher and higher. The green bar slowly crept to the top of the screen and changed to a glowing turquoise to show the Theseus had entered maximum impulse power.

Locilette looked over his shoulder to one of the viewports. The star didn't seem to be moving away from him even at this speed, which made him wonder how close he actually was to it. A whip of plasma flew by the window, extending out wide from the star's unstable surface. He threw himself back in his seat, his eyes wide at the unbelievable miracle of how the flare missed his ship. The all too familiar feeling of uncertainty crept in the pit of his stomach. Again, he glanced at the viewport behind him, knowing full well that he should be at some distance now at maximum impulse, but he cried out in horror as it still remained, preventing him from taking leave of its powerful embrace.

His stomach churned in knots. The Theseus was giving it everything she had, but it was struggling to meet the escape velocity needed to break the star's gravitational hold on it. He couldn't understand how this could even be possible. His ship had escaped much larger stars before, how could it not pull away from one as small as a red dwarf? Something was wrong.

He leaned forward and tapped the screen displaying the status of the ship's systems. The throttle bar to the right flickered, changing to a different number than it initially showed moments earlier. Locilette's heart sank as it sat well below the power output needed to achieve escape velocity. He quickly adjusted the power allocation to shut off everything nonessential to deliver more power to the engines, but that was it. There was nothing else he could divert. Every single bit of power the Theseus could muster was already being poured into the engines, and it just wasn't enough.

The screens around the flight controls began to flash red with alerts all across the ship. The energy allocation monitor flashed with a black battery with a blinking lightning bolt in the center of it. He tapped the sides of the monitors, praying that it was the same issue as before, but nothing changed. Suddenly, the screens went black, and the sound of the Theseus's engine sputtered before finally dying with a long hiss. In an instant, the cockpit was quiet.

"No!" Locilette screamed, slamming his finger on the ignition over and over. "No! No! Come on, please!"

Nothing happened. The Thesesus was completely dead, delivering him back to the same fate he just escaped from. He sat there in his seat, his eyes fixed on the flight instruments as if it would miraculously flicker back to life at any given moment. It didn't, and he knew it was never going to again.

Locilette couldn't rationalize why this was happening to him. He was a good man, he knew it. He put his life on the line every single day to protect those under his care. He worked day in and day out to provide the best life he could for his family. Everything he did, he did it in service to the betterment of somebody else. He couldn't understand why it had to be him of all people. Why was he in the area for the derelict call? Why couldn't he just have worked a desk job, or even work in logistics at some merchant guild? Why didn't he just give up being a Ranger to stay home with his wife and kids? Why was he going to die alone?

The endless questions swirled in his head, infuriating him. In a fit of rage, he ripped off his safety belt and began slamming himself into every monitor surrounding the fight controls. He stomped on the radio system with every ounce of strength he could manifest. Pieces of hardware cracked away with every hit. He turned to the blank camera monitor, drew back his fist, and shattered the thick glass, leaving his hand a bloodied mess. He slowly pulled his hand away, revealing shards of glass protruding deeply into his skin. Crimson blood streamed down his open palm onto the floor, pooling around his feet.

He watched as it fell from his hand. It reminded him of the facet that sat on top of the sink in he and Marla's bathroom just off the master bedroom. Every once and a while it would become loose, preventing it from shutting off all the way. It was a simple fix, but Marla would always ask for him to fix it, even though she was more than capable. He wished she could ask him that now. He would fix that facet a million times over if it meant just being with her again. Just to hold her one last time.

The Theseus began to violently shake, snapping him out of his trance. The walls around him began to creak and moan at the star battering the ship's hull. He could feel his feet lift up with the motions letting him know that his magnetic soles were nearing the end of their battery life. He couldn't help but smirk at the other worldly unfortunate circumstances of that. Like the Yanagi, the Theseus, and now his stupid boots, all those systems failed him when he needed them the most.

A photo of his family came sliding out from the back hall and found an unsteady resting place amongst the shattered pieces of the radio system. Without hesitation, he scrambled to pick it up before it disappeared behind the flight consoles. He held tightly to the flight chair to steady himself as he leaned over and the ship around him felt like the quaking of a planet's crust. He straightened himself as he struggled to get himself strapped in, but not for safety reasons. He just wanted to be sure when the time came he would die with the dignity of not being jostled to death bouncing off the cabin's walls. No, if he was meant to burn, then he wanted to meet that head-on.

He struggled to look down at the photo, but he knew this was going to be the last time he would see his family's faces. His eyes floated down to the sight of Marla and their boys looking up at him. Their smiles were the biggest he'd ever seen before. The joy on their faces made him feel as if the universe didn't matter. Nothing mattered in the universe but them, and he would die with that thought firmly in his mind.

He placed the picture on his chest, the closest thing that will be by his heart. He leaned the flight chair back slightly to get as comfortable as he could. He could feel his skin begin the burn from the intense heat building in the cabin. The Theseus couldn't hold out much longer, but he began to wonder if he would be dead by the time his ship even burned away. There was a loud thud from on top of the ship, making him believe he had his answer.

He breathed as slow and steady as he could, the hot air filling his lungs stinging sharply. The Theseus began to shake more intensely now. He closed his eyes for a moment, and a flash of home came before his eyes. He could feel the wind whip through the trees and kiss his arms. The clouds above provide him with the perfect shade for a day out of the lake. Maybe this was his heaven that awaited him on the other side of the Pantheon's gates.

He opened his eyes just to see if he was still alive as the sight of a massive rectangular shape passed over the top of his ship out from the star. Locilette wasn't quite sure what he was looking at. His only thought was how could an asteroid be able to come this close to a red dwarf star and be intact? The length of the object kept going and going until the bright purple light radiated from the back. Locilette had to sit up and squint just to make sure his mind wasn't playing tricks on him. It's an engine stack! He thought.

As the vessel drifted farther away, Locilette could see the long wire of a tow cable coming from the back of it to the top of his ship. In a matter of seconds, the cable tightened, pulling the Theseus with a strong tug. The dark space that was out of the front view port whipped from side to side as the tow cable sent him into a spiral. Every few seconds, the spin would reveal the star looming farther and farther away. He didn't know what to do. He didn't know how to feel.

The ship rotated again to show the side of the vessel towing him, now banking to the starboard side. The banner of Arkaa adorned her side as it passed in front. In immaculate gold lettering read *The Harriet*, letting the entire universe know who she was. Her opposite side was black with the scorching of the star that she rescued him from. She was an angel, she was *his* angel that pulled him out of the clutches of death as it tightened its nasty grip around his throat.

The tow cable began to glow blue, and moments later the Theseus's systems slowly started to buzz to life. Locilette leaned back in his chair as the sound of the life support system kicked on, sending a wave of cool air rushing through the cabin. He held the photo of his family tight to his chest and let the emotions take hold of him. He wept like he had never done before.

He was going home.

Kronos Prime

Thirteen standard Arkaan months later...

The rays of the binary suns of Kronos kissed her light amber skin, almost appearing to radiate off of it. Her hair flowed just above her shoulders with every passing breeze. She liked it cut short during Kronos Prime's summer months to make life outside a bit more bearable, and the easy access to tan her neck never hurt either. That was the way she always was, since she played in the vast fields around her childhood home, and she never intended on changing. Two boys brushed past her as they ran about the market square looking for the strange gadgets the sellers found out in the galaxy.

"Boys, do be careful!" She called out, waving at them.

They both laughed as they disappeared into the crowd. She shook her head and giggled at their boundless energy. They may be rambunctious, but they were good boys. When raising two boys mainly by herself a lot of the time, she was just thankful that they were respectful enough. In her opinion, goodness followed respect, and that was just what she instilled in them. It also didn't hurt that she had the father card she could play when they got really rowdy. She squeezed his hand tight with that thought.

Life without her husband was hard. She loved that he was out protecting their little part of the galaxy, but it sure was nice having him home. However, something seemed to weigh heavy on him since he came back from his last assignment. Something happened out there that she knew better than to ask him about. As bad as she wanted to know of all the ugly things that plagued the cosmos, something deep down told her that she would regret it if she was privy to such information.

Marla ran her other hand up his arm and squeezed it tightly to remind him that she was there. It wasn't because she ever feared of him becoming absent-minded of her presence, but she wanted him to always know that she was there for him, and all the troubles that came with being a part of the Order of Rangers. Troubles that would probably break any weaker man.

Locilette looked down at his wife and a smile crested his lips. He always seemed to be so put together, so joyful about life despite her knowing otherwise. His ability to mask the fight that was happening within him was something truly admirable. Not once did he ever find a desire to bring what happened out there home on Kronos Prime. This was his sanctuary away from all of that, and she would do everything in her power to make sure it stayed that way for him.

"Jasper, Maxon," Locilette sighed as the pair brought back some strange devices. "What did I tell you both about just grabbing things off tables?"

"Father, look! It's like some kinda water gun!" Maxon said, displaying it up to his father.

Locilette hated to take the joy out of the boy's eyes, but this was quite the exception. "Son, that's a body waste spray conductor."

"A what?"

"As in, that's what cleans your butt on long space voyages when you can't waste storage space for toilet paper."

Jasper burst out in a fit of laughter as Maxon threw it from his hands with a look of pure disgust. Locilette joined in with the boys as he scooped it off the stone ground and began to chase him around with it. Marla, who wasn't one for such humor, couldn't resist a smile. Seeing them all together again was a true blessing. One that she had prayed many nights for. The boys eventually got the best of him, running off into the many merchant stalls to find more treasures.

"Don't bring back any more bathroom stuff!" Locilette called out. A group of elderly people turned to give him a scowl, but it didn't seem to bother him. Nothing really did anymore.

He returned to his wife's side as she took her place around his arm. They strolled together through the bustling market, occasionally stopping to view some exotic fruit or interesting things found on other worlds far away from their own. What her eyes were really on the hunt for was a new desk for her personal study. Marla had inherited the one she currently used from her sister after she graduated from university, but the years were starting to show on it. After being repainted over three dozen times in the span of a few years, she couldn't even remember what the original color was.

Under the cover of a large tent sat the stalls where merchants and craftsmen could set up the various larger pieces they had for sale. It was abnormally giant, like a warehouse made of waterproof cloth. The elements could be quite rough on furniture left outside overnight, especially on a planet with such unpredictable weather as

Kronos Prime. Without warning, the trickling of a summer rain could come pouring down, sending these small-time sellers into a frenzy to protect their merchandise. That sort of thing had to be taken into account if you wanted to be a traveling merchant in the Kronos System.

The entrance of the tent was opened wide, allowing Marla to take a quick glance in as they walked past. A beautiful, redwood antique desk sat just off the right side, making her stop in her tracks. The woodwork was immaculately designed in the style of the antique Arkaan Homeworld. Her heart pounded at the thought of it nestled between her two massive bookshelves flashed in her mind. The stacks of books and letters awaiting to be sent to her closest friends scattered upon its aged wood. It would be the absolute perfect missing piece to her puzzle; she had to have it.

"I'm going to run in here for a quick look at that desk. Do you think we can fit it in the Trotter carriage?"

Locilette gave it a quick glance. "Oh, I'm sure we could figure something out if it can't fit."

"Okay, because, I'm not going to lie," she said, smiling, "I *really* want it."

"If you're that passionate about it, then it's yours. If it can't fit in the carriage, then we'll pay a little extra for the merchant to hold it for a day so I can pull the Theseus down here to load it up."

Marla grabbed both sides of his face and kissed him, then ran off to appraise her newly discovered treasure. He just stood there as she jogged to the tent, joy radiating from her with every step that brought her closer to it. He didn't care what it was she wanted. If it allowed him to see her look like that, then he'd give her one of the moons if he could. *Thankfully for his bank account it was only a desk*, he thought.

He continued on to the section with a large sign that pointed the way to the machinery parts. Various parts and odds and ends were scattered about on long lines of tables. The Kronos stars beat down just a little bit heavier in this part, thanks to the lack of overhead shade. Locilette couldn't help but chuckle a bit at the thought of a section meant for engineers and builders who didn't have anyone of those to build them one. It was either that or these small-time merchants didn't want to band together to fork over the funds to build such a thing. Something told him that it was most likely the latter.

His eyes floated over the seemingly endless amounts of miscellaneous goods, some in pristine condition while others showed signs of years of wear and tear. A large chunk of the tables were dedicated to spare starship parts that didn't appear to be up to Ranger code. Life support parts had rust climbing on the sides, engine parts were stained black from the blast of fiery explosions, and even whole console systems bundled together with string dotted around him. No, he thought, these were definitely for civilian use, and from the looks of them, he prayed people would only use these in an emergency.

He was by no means against building custom starships from the scraps of others. Frankly, he'd seen some rather nice looking ones who would go on to sail the stars for over twenty years. He understood where people couldn't find a living on a planet or orbital city, they could find it out in the void above. If throwing scraps together to make a small sloop ship meant transporting goods to feed your family, then by the Pantheon they had any right to in his book. If it passed safety standards before test flights then that would be good enough for him.

At the end of the second row of tables had a neon sign that read *Weapons and Arms.* Locilette was surprised at the brightness of it to be able to outshine the stars in broad daylight. He shrugged as he reckoned that it did its job. It got his attention.

As he walked up, an older bearded man was tuning a radio to the yearly address from the Duchess of the Kronos System. Her voice scratched with static until the man found a good enough frequency to patch it through. Locilette never cared too much about politics beyond the Count's office here on Kronos Prime. However, the Count was probably there, so he figured maybe he should care just a little bit more.

Every Count in the system would be there, each one representing the habitual planets within the Kronos System. They were the highest position that the everyday Arkaan could elect until the King's death. The democratically elected monarch was a great idea in theory, but only could be performed once a lifetime if the people were lucky. Dukes and Duchesses of star systems were appointed by the crown to balance out the powers of the King and people. Marla was deeply into the local politics of Kronos Prime, so he might as well call himself an expert now from the late night explanations of the happenings in the Count's court while he was away on assignment. He smiled at that thought. He was happy to be home.

Weapons of various models laid in a straight line on the two tables pushed together. A white sheet covered the table to make every part of the weapons pop out to the eyes of browsers who would walk by. He couldn't help but feel impressed by the amount of weapons this man had acquired. Mostly were the cheaply made magma shot pistols, but he had several of the larger musket variants and even a couple of plasma arcs rifles lying behind the tables just out of reach. Based on recent experiences, he considered maybe even picking up a few of the pistols just in case.

He turned and froze at what his eyes landed upon across the market. He couldn't believe what he was looking at, his eyes slightly burned until he was forced to blink. He hurried across the stone ground, almost bumping into a group of Kronos Militiamen before standing face to face with it. An 89-01G Class B Secura-Droid stood tall on a rack, its eyes black, having been deactivated. The bright light reflected off its silver plating.

"Excuse me, sir? Where did you get this unit?" Locilette asked, prying his eyes off it for a moment.

"Hm, shit, lemme think for a moment," the man said, scratching his messy black hair. Black grease marks stained his face as he pulled away from a repair to answer his question. "I believe I may have bought it off some feller out of the Themis System. Got quite the licking off of it, if I do say."

"Is it still for sale?"

The merchant shrugged. "Sorry, mister. Some feller paid for it about an hour ago. Just waiting for him to come back and pick it up."

"Damn. How much did he pay for it?"

"It was for sale for 4,200 Astrids, but I gave him a deal cause he said he was buying it to protect his small Pantheon temple on some frontier planet way out yonder."

Locilette frowned. "I'll pay double for it. I will go to the bank right now and pay 8,400 Astrids if you sell it to me right now."

"Whoa, mister, you must be passionate about these old hunks of junk." The man's eyes struggled to shrink back from being so surprised by the number offered. He thought for a moment, then said, "I'd be a fool to at least not try to get out of that deal. Give me a few minutes to try and talk to the man."

The merchant walked off, wiping the sweat from his wide forehead. Locilette's eyes were fixed on the hollow ones of the bot. He glanced back to see if the merchant was still trying to reach the man, then pulled out his PDA. He extended the cable from the top, then plugged it in the chest port that was exposed on the opened plating. He scrolled down to a large file and smashed the upload button.

A few minutes passed as Locilette anxiously waited. The bar on the screen slowly inched over until it fully filled with a green light. The screen changed to a prompt asking if he would like to activate the 89-01G Class B. With a press of confirmation, the bot's eyes flashed into a bright, neon blue. Its head slowly raised to meet the gaze of the Ranger standing before him.

"Good day, sir. At last update, we were in an emergency exfiltration aboard the merchant vessel Yanagi. Is everything well now, sir?"

Locilette fought the water forming in his eyes. "Yeah, buddy. All is well."

The Merchant came walking back with some paperwork in his hands. "Well, good news for all of us. I got a hold of that feller and he said he'll take a full refund, which will allow me to sell it to you for that cost. The only thing he wanted was for me to sketch out something and give it to you which was weird as shit, but whatever."

Confused, Locilette grabbed the torn piece of paper out of the man's hand. He certainly wasn't in any kind of mood for some invitation to some new sect of Panteon worship no matter how religious he had gotten since the Yanagi incident. However, if it had some contact information on it, he could at least send the man a thank you for his kindness to void the sale. He unfolded the paper and looked down. His heart sank as he dropped it to the stone ground below, his body began to tremble.

The gut wrenching crest of Arnold Dekciw stared back up at him from the paper at his feet.

John McCool

John McCool comes from a humble beginning in a small town in Mississippi. He fell in love with writing at a very young age, oftentimes writing stories during class rather than paying attention. He now resides in Rossville, Illinois, where most of his time is spent attending to the day-to-day operations of a local coffee company, which is like a second home to him. When not writing or sipping coffee, John loves spending time with his wife and kids, who give him the inspiration to pursue all of his dreams.

Follow for all things dark & mysterious

https://johnmccoolauthor
.com/